MISSION OF Merit

BEVERLEY HOPWOOD

MISSION OF MERIT
Copyright © 2023 by Beverley Hopwood

Author Photo by Katie McManus

Scripture quotations taken from the Holy Bible, King James Version, which is in the public domain.

This is a work of fiction. Although all of the main characters are based on real people, a few are entirely created through the imagination of the author. Notable characters may have been used in fictitious meetings with the main characters.

ISBN: 978-1-4866-2460-7
eBook ISBN: 978-1-4866-2461-4

Word Alive Press
119 De Baets Street Winnipeg, MB R2J 3R9
www.wordalivepress.ca

WORD ALIVE
—P R E S S—

Cataloguing in Publication information can be obtained from Library and Archives Canada.

Acknowledgements

First, to our Lord and Saviour, without whom there would be no story.

Second, to my stepfather's family, who "saved everything," allowing me the opportunity to discover material for this book, and to their ancestors, who went forth in His name.

A heartfelt thank you to my writing partners, Sara Davison and Helen Smrcek, who have offered advice and edits throughout the writing process and to my long-time friend of Chinese heritage, Marlene Han for reading the manuscript with a sensitive ear. To my husband Peter, who allows me the solitude needed to research and write.

To the wonderful staff of the Braun Book Awards and Word Alive Press, for their helpful advice and excellent guidance for a techie dinosaur.

To the reader: may this book challenge you to carry on searching into the depths and be blessed.

FOREWORD

Although this account of Mary Sibley's life is fictionalized, the background and historical setting is based on extensive research by the author. While sorting the contents of my parents' attic, I found two hand-carved bamboo paintbrush pots, instigating a conversation with my stepfather, Dr. John Sibley Kitching. As he described his cousin Mary's arrival at the parsonage after the sudden death of her mother in China, tears came to his eyes.

The story of his missionary aunt and uncle intrigued me for years before I began writing it. Three years of research and background reading allowed me to become immersed in the culture of China and historical events as I wrote and rewrote the novel. Biographies, articles, and news reports of Christians and Canadians in China all had an impact.

Keeping as close to facts as possible, I wanted to develop Mary's ancestry and life story, realizing that the threads drawn through the century between 1880 and 1980 are but a few in a vast worldwide tapestry. It can only begin to answer the question of Christian missionaries' success in China. How had a young teen managed to get by while being separated from her parents until the next sabbatical, six years into the future? What was Mary's view of the Western world's attempt to Christianize the Chinese?

This story is unique because it is a rare attempt to examine missionary work in a very different culture and time through a work of fiction. By including the work of all denominations, the novel attempts to tie the human race together in its search for that hope which Christians can share through the knowledge and life of Jesus Christ.

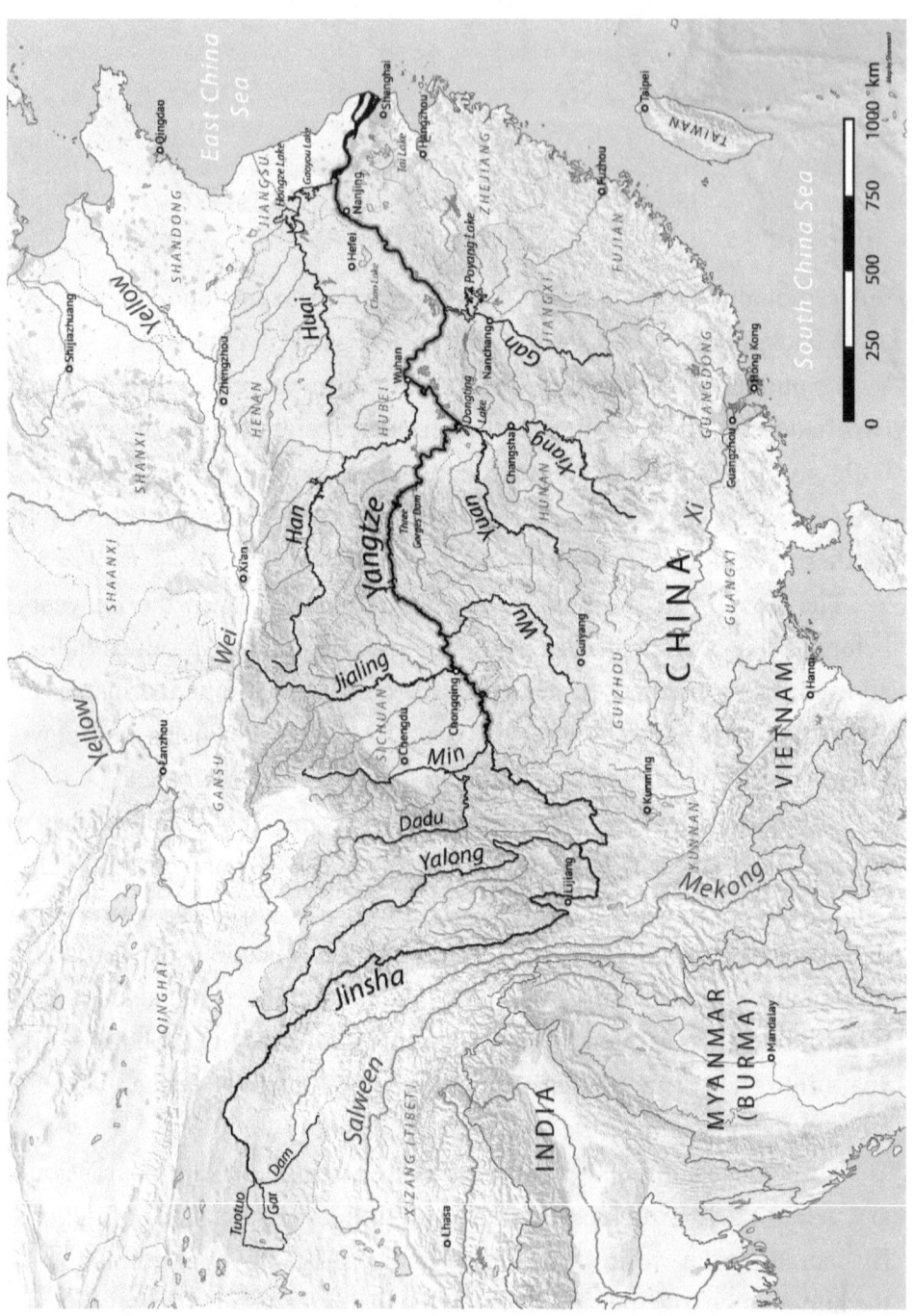

Map taken from https://commons.wikimedia.org/wiki/File:Yangtze_river_map.png

FAMILY TREE

Siblings of William Edward Sibley
Mary Ann Sibley= Rev. John W. Kitching
Margaret A Sibley= Thomas PB Blackwell
Florence E Sibley= John Cairns
Rev. John C Sibley= Mary Shaw
Helen Sibley
Ethel I Sibley= James B Smith
Eunice M Sibley=Morley Paul

Siblings of Mary Edith Harrison
Ellie Knox Harrison
Edmund William Harrison= Alice Claire
Beatrice K Harrison= Thomas Reed

Siblings of Rev. John Wesley Kitching
Mary Ann Kitching= John Moffat.
Rev George Robinson Kitching= Annie Lemmon
Elizabeth Jane Kitching= Rev Henry Caldwell
Ida Hannah Kitching= Christopher Moffat
Emily Watson Kitching= Charles Harris McCulloch
William Robert Kitching= R. Anna
Franklin Percy Kitching= Ella Johnston Richardson
Elias Easterbrook Kitching= Mary

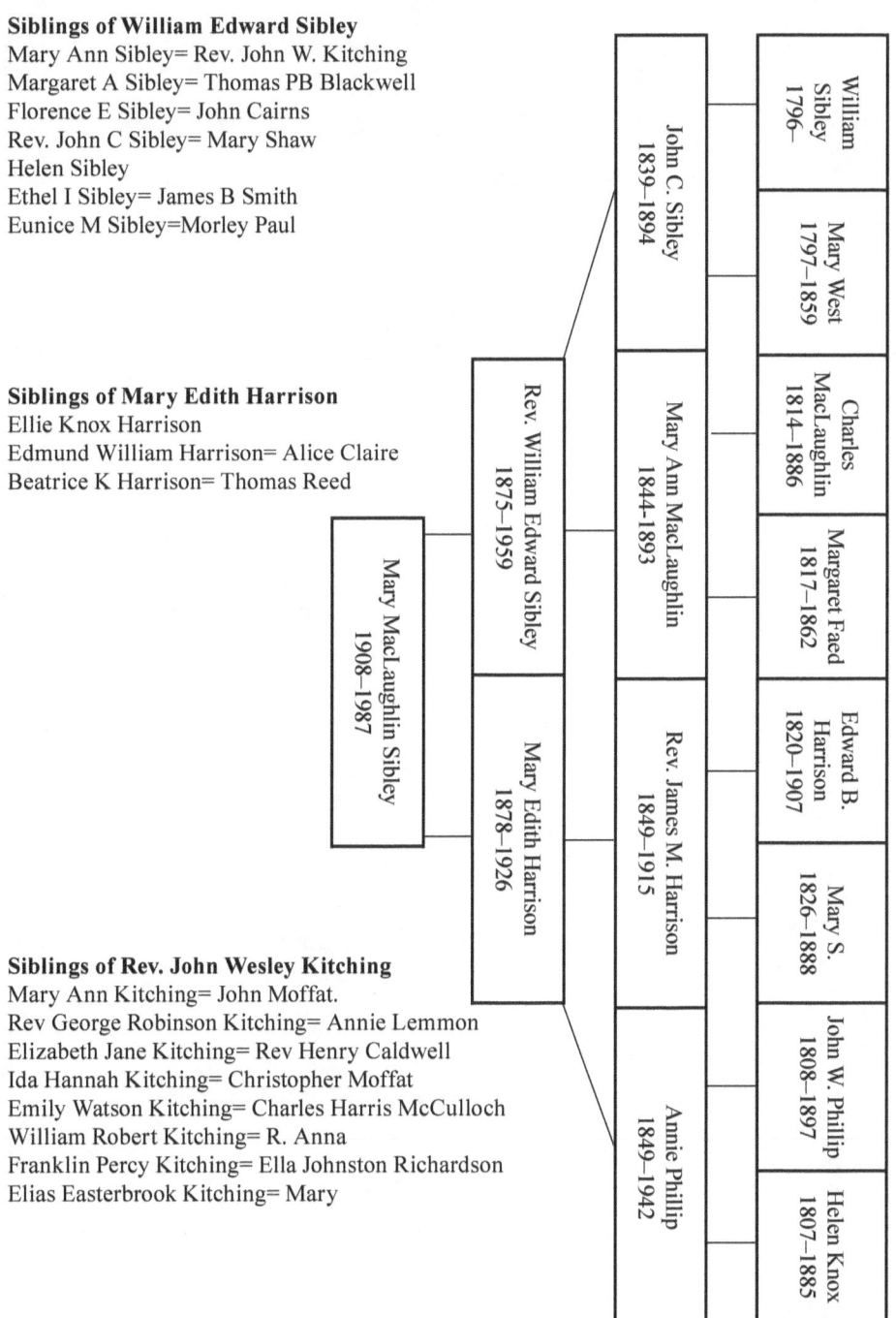

One

1945

KINGSTON, ONTARIO, CANADA

Mary flipped over the paper, hands trembling. Perspiration smudged the list of names. Of the many places she had tried calling so far, Miss Wilder's home remained the only possibility left. She refused to think about the alternative to securing this lodging.

From the other end of Nelson Street, a tall woman carrying a suitcase and canvas rucksack hurried in Mary's direction. Instinctively, Mary quickened her steps, glancing at the house numbers as she passed 225 and 227. The other woman sped up as well, now almost running.

They reached the steps of number 229 at the same instant. The determined look of the dark-haired, athletic woman equalled Mary's resolve.

After pausing only an instant, they both turned and dashed up the steps. Mary was at a disadvantage, as the buzzer was farther from her than the other woman. She wouldn't let this set her back, though, and gripped her suitcase more tightly. She would speak up. It was imperative that she get lodging with school starting in only a week.

A heavyset, grey-haired woman pulled open the front wooden door, scrutinizing them through the screen.

"I've only one room left."

"I'll take it," Mary said, but two voices had spoken at the same time. She looked sideways at her competitor, who squinted at her.

"You said on the telephone the first to arrive would get the room," the other woman said, drawing her shoulders back in a challenge. "We've arrived at the same time, so you'll have to make a choice between us."

The landlady contemplated, the screen still a barrier. "What are your occupations?"

Mary spoke up first. "I'm in the Household Economics Department at the Kingston Collegiate and Vocational School."

The dark-haired woman grinned. "I'm head of the Women's Physical Education Department at the university."

Mary quickly recovered from her surprise. Was this woman really a teacher, a department head at Queen's University? Her physique, tall and muscular, and her age, late thirties, were about the same as her own, though Mary considered herself gaunt. She assumed the persuasive woman would demand preferential treatment; instead the woman gave a little shrug and grinned in friendly rivalry.

Mary accepted the challenge and returned the grin. A sporting competition. After sizing each other up, they turned to face the landlady again.

The woman's forehead wrinkled, one hand gripping the door jamb, the other clamped around the door itself. "I don't rent it out much, but there's a dormer room in the attic. It gets pretty cold in the winter."

"I'll take it," the university professor said. She pointed in Mary's direction with her folded and marked up newspaper. "And she can have the regular room."

The landlady pushed open the screen door. "My name's Miss Charlotte Wilder, and you both better come in and read the rules of the house. I run a Christian boarding home and there won't be any smoking or drinking of alcoholic beverages on the premises." She held the door as they brushed by her.

Both women set their suitcases in the long, dark hallway and followed Miss Wilder into a comfortable sitting room, where she handed Mary a piece of cardboard with a list printed on it titled *Household Rules*. After skimming it quickly, Mary nodded.

"There's nothing here I would disagree with," she said, handing it to the dark-haired woman. "I'm quite happy to be in a Christian home, Miss Wilder. I like routine, and you'll find my activities are quiet. My name is Mary Sibley."

Miss Wilder gave a crisp nod.

The dark-haired woman said, "I certainly will agree to everything, but I may need to have a cold breakfast some mornings. The volleyball, basketball, and tennis teams meet very early." She handed the list of rules back to Miss Wilder. "I'm Miss Marion Claire Ross, but I go by Claire."

She stretched her hand toward Mary, who returned the firm grip, and then Claire extended it toward Miss Wilder.

"Oh. A handshaker."

Even Mary could see the reluctance of Miss Wilder to shake as she held out a pale, limp hand for a brief touch. A few blinks of her eyes and Miss Wilder appeared to relax, satisfied with the situation.

A woman in a full apron, her hair in matronly swirls, poked her head around the door frame. "New boarders, I presume?"

"Nita, this is Miss Mary Sibley, who will take the empty room on the second floor. And this," Miss Wilder pointed a gnarly finger at the woman Mary had raced to the door, "is Miss Claire Ross. She'll be taking the dormer in the attic." Miss Wilder scrutinized Claire. "You'll be expected to empty your own chamber pot."

Claire smiled. "I grew up using an outhouse, Miss Wilder. That's no problem."

Either Claire feared being turned down or she was exceedingly accommodating. Mary hoped it was the latter. She didn't care for any sort of bickering. In the classroom, she clamped down on that kind of behaviour immediately.

"Mrs. Anita McClelland has been with us for the entire war while her husband serves in the Forces," said Miss Wilder. "We call her Nita and she looks after the cleaning and laundry and helps me in the kitchen. My sister Emma is not a well person. We share the bedroom on the main floor so she doesn't have to climb stairs. We also have Miss Mable Langevin, Nita's sister, a dietitian at the hospital. She and Nita have the other two rooms on the second floor; you will all share the upstairs bathroom facilities."

*

Nita carried the bowls of vegetables, pork stew, potatoes, and a sauce to the table. After Mable said grace, the six women and David, the six-year-old son of Nita, politely passed the food around. Mary knew she couldn't stomach the lumpy white substance. The similarity in colour to a thick soup she had been forced to eat as a child was enough for her to pass it along without serving herself any.

"I'm very grateful to have a roof over my head in Kingston this year, Miss Wilder." Mary tried making eye contact with Charlotte, but the woman focused on her plate. "I'm sure we'll all get along famously."

Claire jumped in quickly. "I'm sure we will."

"Where were you living last, Miss Sibley?" Mable asked.

"Please call me Mary. Princess Street at the east end. The landlady's two sons and a daughter-in-law are expected back shortly. They're being demobilized September 1."

"Oh, yes. My Leonard is returning to Canada the minute they can get transport for the soldiers. We're so excited, aren't we, David?" Nita gave a little nod of encouragement to her son, but he only opened his eyes wide.

Has he even met his father? The boy is so keen to please his mother, but he doesn't understand her excitement. Mary carried on chewing small bites of the stew.

Mable, her auburn hair coiled up at the back in a victory roll and swept into two prominent curls at the front, listened attentively to the others, then asked, "And you, Miss Ross? Where were you lodging before this?"

"Please, my colleagues and friends call me Claire." She brushed her long, wavy locks behind an ear and spooned a generous portion of stew onto her china plate. "My brothers called me Clarion, like the trumpet." She laughed. "I had an apartment in the back of a house owned by the university, but after the plaster ceiling caved in I decided it was time for a change. I believe they're tearing it down soon and building a new student residence."

Claire tucked into her food with gusto.

Mary had seen Miss Emma Wilder look askance at Claire's wide-legged trousers as she entered the room, but the buttercup-yellow blouse was a decidedly feminine pairing. She admired the natural confidence with which Claire carried herself. Mary straightened her own back.

The women fell into a pattern that would continue through the next nine months. After dinner, they helped clear the dining room and take dishes to the kitchen. The two Wilder sisters washed, dried, and returned everything to its designated place. Nita read to David on the couch while Mable knitted socks and Claire read the newspaper or consulted student score charts.

Mary preferred a little time on her own at a desk in her room to prepare lessons, but she would return to the dining room for an evening cup of tea and chatting. Mary, Claire, and Mable, all in their thirties, engaged in lively conversations about growing up and their challenges in attaining higher education.

"I almost feel guilty," Mary said, "admitting I had a scholarship large enough to get a four-year degree and do the master's program at Toronto without having to work at part-time jobs to supplement my tuition."

"Makes a difference, being an only child or having four siblings," Claire replied.

"A lonely child, did you say?" Mary raised an eyebrow.

Claire and Mable glanced at each other and laughed. "You're right, Mary," Claire said. "An only child can be a lonely child. After my dad died, it was hard for Mom to give the five of us children much attention. It was all she could do to work and keep everybody organized, although Kate and Maggie did much of the cooking. We all helped when my brothers and I weren't playing some sport out in the street."

Mary nodded in approval. "I believe sports are a great stabilizer in young peoples' lives. That and music."

"And having grandparents, an aunt and three siblings under the same small roof never allowed one much quiet thinking time," Mable said, reaching over to give her sister Nita's arm a playful squeeze.

Mary nodded again. "I enjoyed coming back to Canada and visiting with aunts, uncles, and lots of cousins. My Aunt Mary Ann and Uncle John became my Canadian parents."

Mable looked at her closely. "Where were you born, if not Canada? Your English is perfect."

Heat rose in Mary's cheeks. "I was born in Chengtu, Szechwan, China."

Two

1945

KINGSTON

"Were your parents missionaries then?" Claire asked. "Is that why you were born in China?"

Mary nodded. Often people asked about her early life and expected her to sum it up in five minutes. There were too many details which were likely so different from these other women's experiences that she really didn't know where to begin.

She allowed her pent-up breath to escape. "It's a lengthy story."

"Then you must begin earlier tomorrow night," Claire said. "No, Monday evening. There's a basketball tournament this weekend. Will you tell us, Mary? It's fascinating to meet someone born in such an exotic location."

"Oh, if you wish to hear. But you'll stop me if you're bored? And the basketball tournament? Is it open to the public?"

"Certainly, yes. Spectators are welcome. Why don't you come, and you too, Mable?"

Mable scrunched her nose. "I'm not very keen on sports."

But Mary leaned forward and said, "I was on the women's team at the University of Toronto. I'd love to go. What time?"

And so began long conversations about conditions in Canada since the war, education, the Christian Church, sports, and Mary's childhood in Chengtu, forging lifelong friendships.

＊

Emma Wilder retired to her bed following supper on Monday, but the other five gathered with cups of tea and after-dinner biscuits.

Mary smoothed her straight skirt down over her knees and sipped her hot drink. "My mother, Edith, remembered the heat being so intense that she was perspiring before rising from her bed in the early morning. Will Sibley, my father, was going to a meeting with the mission board to visit the new building site in Luchow. He'd wanted to check on the progress of the surrounding West China mission developments and knew my mother was in no condition to accompany him. She was expecting me at the time…"

1908
CHENGTU, SZECHWAN, CHINA

Edith leaned up on an elbow, her abdomen bulging under the thin sheet. "Can you be sure to return tomorrow, Will? I don't know how much longer this baby will wait. It could be any time."

"I will make every effort to, my dear. Just try to hold off, will you?"

She smiled at his wistful request, knowing how important the meeting at the university was to Will. The American Baptists and Methodists, the Episcopalians, and Quaker Friends from Great Britain and Ireland were uniting their efforts with the Canadian Methodists at West China University, and the campus had been enlarged to sixty acres.

Will's eyes and voice radiate with excitement at the prospect, she thought.

She only wanted to remain in bed this morning. His kiss on her forehead was endearing, but then he hurried off to get into the rickshaw awaiting him.

✳

Light cramping awakened Edith during the next night, and in the morning she sent Mrs. Yi to fetch one of the midwives from the hospital, just to be sure. She threw back the covers, planning on using the outhouse, but water gushed down her legs and soaked her long nightgown. Then contractions began in earnest.

Edith leaned against the dresser for a few moments of reprieve. She bowed her head, tears dripping down her cheeks. She felt so alone. If only Will were here.

Her abdomen clenched and Edith gripped the dresser top, wanting to scream with the pain.

"Here, here, Miss Sibley. I have some herb paste. We will put this on your belly." Mrs. Yi came into the room with a bowl containing a horrid-smelling greenish substance.

Edith immediately vomited into the tin washbasin on the dresser. "Please, Mrs. Yi, take that away." The odour was disgusting. What was that? "Where is the nurse?"

Another strong contraction gripped Edith and she dropped to the floor on hands and knees, struggling to draw in breaths until it subsided.

I might make it through this. Another contraction hit. *Oh, God, help me.*

A stiffly starched nursing sister appeared at the door in her grey and white uniform.

"We won't be needing that, thank you," the nurse said, turning Mrs. Yi around to head back out the door with her bowl. "I'll take it from here, thank you. Mrs. Yi, we *will* need a kettle of boiling water please. And a fresh nightgown." She touched Edith's arm. "Let's get you cleaned up, shall we?"

Edith stared at the inflexible linen of the nurse's cap. How did it keep stoically firm in this humidity? She allowed the nurse to help her out of her wet gown.

Another contraction gripped her and she leaned on the dresser again, gasping, beyond caring that she stood naked. Edith sucked in a deep breath and clamped her teeth to keep from screaming.

"All right, Mrs. Sibley, slip this gown on and climb back into bed. I've put some clean padding down, so don't worry about the sheets. Breathe deeply. No point in trying to do any pushing yet."

Hours passed and there was no sign of Will. The contractions intensified. *I can't believe they're so violent. How will I carry on?*

"Basin, the basin."

Edith vomited again. Why was this happening? Other missionary wives had survived childbirth without their husbands.

Good heavens, my own mother gave birth in a small prairie town without assistance or nearby hospital. My father was familiar only with calving, so would he have been—

Edith gasped. Another contraction. She gripped the nurse's arm.

"Things are moving along now, Edith. Keep breathing." The nurse glanced up from where she had been concentrating on counting diapers. "This is all normal. The next time you feel a contraction, you can start pushing."

How will I have the energy? It had been hours and hours.

Suddenly, Edith tensed with the strain of a powerful spasm. She summoned every bit of strength she had left and bore down as the nurse moved to the foot of the bed. A gush of warmth spilled out as the baby swished from her body. She laughed in relief.

"Very good, Edith. It's been a long haul for you, but the main work of labour is over. Mrs. Yi, you've washed your hands and brought a clean towel?"

Edith could hardly feel a thing now, the pain having numbed her sufficiently into exhaustion. She lifted her head, trying for a look. "The baby. Is the baby okay?"

Mrs. Yi stood with dark brows pinched together, lips thin.

"You have a perfect little girl, Mrs. Sibley. I'm just going to wash her off and then you can see her." A shrill cry from the newborn protested the arrangement.

Edith flopped back. Had Mrs. Yi been hoping for a boy, or was she just unhappy that her herbal paste had not been required? Or maybe it was the cloth thrown over the small statue of some local god she had tried to slip in with the tea tray early this morning. Edith had been too preoccupied to have it removed, but the nursing sister must have seen to it.

"Thank you, Mrs. Yi, for your help. I'm very happy to have a daughter."

Mrs. Yi seemed to relax her shoulders a little.

"Could we have a fresh cup of tea, please?" The nursing sister tucked in fresh sheets around Edith and the newborn, beaming with the results of the birth.

Will came to the door of their bedroom. He slowly opened it an inch, and then wider. Edith lay with eyes closed, a gentle smile on her lips. A baby wiggled its small body, cradled in Edith's arm.

"Mary or Edward?" Will spoke in a whisper.

Edith half-opened her eyes as she lifted her face toward her husband. "Mary."

Will knelt beside the bed. "You're fine, are you?" He clasped Edith's arm and raised the back of her hand to his cheek. "I'm so sorry I wasn't here." When she didn't respond, he waited a moment. Had she drifted off to sleep?

His wife smiled. "You can hold her if you like."

She lifted the baby a little, and with that Will felt the joy of being a new father, awed by an unaccustomed responsibility in the form of a tiny, precious, fragile life. He carefully held his daughter for a long while.

Three

1945

KINGSTON

Mary finished her cool tea and reached for a biscuit. "Mother must have been very nervous. I remember how many children had to be buried. Some women delivered stillborn babies. Other babies died after a month or so without proper nutrition—or from disease."

Nita perked up. "It's improved so much with better medicines and vaccinations."

"But back in 1908, there was a high infant mortality rate in all the big cites of the world. We studied the statistics in nutrition." Mable's silver teaspoon clinked on her saucer.

"I completely agree," Mary said. "Poverty and overcrowding have much to do with it. The infant mortality rate is lowering every decade, but it was high in Africa and Asia in those days. Very high."

Claire picked up the last crumbs on her plate. "What made your father and mother go to China? I thought it was dangerous around the turn of the century."

"Oh, it was dangerous." Mary circled over the embossed design on the teacup handle with her thumb. "Many Chinese hated foreigners and blamed them for whatever went wrong in the country. I was horrified to learn that 189 missionaries and their children had been killed in 1900 during the Boxer Rebellion. Still, my parents and thousands of others like them chose to go anyway. Renting buildings for use as a school, hospital, or church took months of negotiations, but local people came a few at a time to help. Some would listen and watch the kindness of Christian nurses or missionaries and want to follow Jesus's teachings.

"However, when there was a famine and the missionaries tried to feed those in their schools and churches with what little they had, they were accused of favouring only the converted Chinese. Then we all became targets. It was as dangerous to be a Chinese Christian as it was to be a foreigner. Missionaries, nurses, doctors, and teachers were lumped in with the Western opium traders and targeted. We children were called names and suffered attacks if left unattended. But there were loyal Chinese who risked everything and stood by us when rebels or bandits struck.

"Until that time, I easily made friends with some of the Chinese orphans while we hoed the gardens. Speaking Mandarin came naturally to us missionary kids, as our parents spoke it to all the Chinese. I practiced writing on my own simply because I enjoyed the artform.

"If we went out, which wasn't often, we were back before dark. Attacks appeared to be random. The teachers at the children's mission school in Chengtu were nervous. I believe they knew more about the dangers than they let on. Sometimes rumours filtered down to us— groups of four or five soldiers on horseback riding through town at dusk or twilight searched for unwitting recruits. Often a few hungry people gathered at the back gate, and usually they left with packages hidden in their garments. It wasn't that the missions had huge stocks of food. If there were shortages in the community, there were shortages at the missions. We learned what it felt like to be hungry.

"Some nights, the other girls and I gathered in the dark at the window of our second-floor dormitory. From there we could watch swinging lines of lanterns winding along the paths in the hillside. We were warned about the young women of the Shining Red Lantern Society.

They practiced their martial arts at night, a threat to any foreigner on the road in the evenings. Isolated groups of Boxers continued to exist, regardless of it being illegal. The Red Lantern Society was the young female component of the Boxers, all of them meeting in secret, dangerous to Christians, and seeking opportunities to destroy our buildings and houses. Our young imaginations were often stimulated by a sense of intrigue and the excitement of it all. Real danger didn't cross our minds.

"Anyway, despite all this, by the early 1920s the city of Chengtu had a boys' school, the Union Bible Training School, and the West China University with a medical faculty and hospital. The number of outlying mission stations in Szechwan's towns increased."

Nita nodded. "It must have been so gratifying to have those successes."

Mary tipped her head thoughtfully. *Yes and no.* "It was very dangerous, but progress was being made gradually. Not only among the Canadian missions, but American, British, Dutch, Scandinavian—all denominations. In times of trouble, differences in theology had to be ignored to save lives. All the while, Chinese people trained as ministers, teachers, nurses, doctors, even dentists.

"At the end of their second furlough to Canada, my parents left me at boarding school in Toronto. I was fourteen when they returned to Chengtu. We had known for years ahead that it was bound to happen, but it didn't really prepare us for the pain of separation."

Claire frowned. "I can understand your parents wanting to keep you in a safe place, but that must have been excruciatingly hurtful."

Mary swallowed hard. "Things seemed to have settled after the main Boxer Rebellion in 1901 when foreign countries pressured the Chinese government and Empress to impose protocols, but on June 8, 1926, I was called to the school office…"

1926
Toronto, Ontario, Canada

Mary tapped timidly on the wooden door of the office. A throat cleared on the other side.

"Come in." Miss Black, the headmistress, sat behind her broad wooden desk, straightening stacks of papers and then shifting a folded telegram from one side of the green blotting paper in front of her to the other. "Please, Mary. Sit down."

Mary sat in the wingback burgundy chair, placed at an angle to face the desk and window.

A muscle below the headmistress's left eye twitched. "Mary. I have some very unfortunate news." She paused, unfolding and refolding an oblong piece of paper. She frowned and took a deep breath. "Your father has sent a telegram and asked me to inform you of your mother's death."

Mary jerked upright, staring at Miss Black in alarm. *What happened? When? Mother's thousands of miles away. I'll never see her again.* The overstuffed padding swallowed Mary as she shrank back into it.

Miss Black patted down her starched collar at the neckline, her gaze flitting from desk to chair. "She was killed in the street by an angry Chinese peasant."

As the headmistress conveyed this horrible news, the bile rose in Mary's throat and her eyes burned.

"I'm sure she didn't suffer, dear." Miss Black put a fist to her lips and cleared her throat. "Your father asks that you go to your aunt and uncle's home in Hornby."

Could she even stand? Mary rose on shaky legs, bumping into the chair. The headmistress's cheek continued to twitch and her focus darted about the room, never meeting Mary's eyes directly.

"Would you like to stay a few minutes and collect yourself? I can ask the secretary to find Florence to be with you."

Mary mechanically shook her head and then turned to escape from the office in a stupor. Her palm pressed against the pale, olive-green wall in the hallway as she placed one foot in front of the other. She broke into a run up the stairs, grabbing the banister when she tripped. She regained her balance and swiped at tears before careening toward her dormitory room, where she threw herself across her bed. She didn't care if everyone heard her. She couldn't help but sob loudly as she gasped for air.

Oh, Mother, Mother. Why you?

1945

KINGSTON

Mary focussed on the dark red and blue pattern in the carpet of the Wilders' sitting room. "It broke my heart. Mother died the first of June, and I didn't hear until the eighth."

She frowned at the memory, rubbing her temples, then glanced up to see Claire and Mable exchange looks of dismay.

"I'm so sorry, Mary. What a tragic thing to happen." Claire pressed a handkerchief into Mary's hand.

Mary appreciated her new friends' attempts to comfort her. She didn't often allow the painful memory to surface.

Four

1926

Junghsien, Szechwan, China

The burial of his wife had been a hurried affair, partly because of the nervous unrest Westerners were experiencing, given the unsettled political situation with Chen and Li's newly formed Communist Party in competition with Sun Yat-sen's Nationalist Party, and partly because of the heat and quick decay of the human body.

Chinese workers within the compound kept their heads down and eyes averted as Will approached them. His colleagues shook hands silently at the graveside ceremony, their heads lowered in heartfelt dismay. Will stood numbly. Hollow thudding and clunking of earth and rubble echoed through the rough box hastily constructed for Edith's interment. The effort to keep himself from collapsing had been draining.

Will Sibley sent telegrams to his brother-in-law John Kitching, as well as his daughter's headmistress. Though not immediate or swift, it was the fastest way, and he hoped the kindest, for Mary to find out about the death of her mother. The British consul had been informed. The newspapers would make a big deal of this event as soon as they found out.

He would write to Mary, sparing her the gruesome details of his wife's decapitated head being kicked into the gutter. He couldn't get the image out of his mind, though he hadn't been with her. Perhaps if he had been...

He needed a distraction. "Ma Ling. Can you bring me the latest magazines from the hall cabinet, please?"

Will nodded to acknowledge the housekeeper's presence when she shuffled into his study with a handful of them. Her plain black high-collared cotton dress hung as far as her ankles, tight around her middle, buttons down the side. Thinning hair had been piled on top of her head, but wisps escaped, framing her weathered face.

With her free hand, she used a hankie to wipe her eyes. "Just dust, Mr. Will. The air is thick."

True enough. The winds down the hills and across the Chengtu Basin were dry, and summer grit covered every surface.

Will viewed the sad figure beside him, magazines outstretched. Would she want to stay, continuing to work at the house now that Edith was gone?

"Do you wish to continue here, Ma Ling?"

Her eyes widened with alarm at the thought of leaving. "I will stay. You stay, I stay. You need help, don't you?"

Warmed by her words, Will shifted his burning eyes to the stack of papers. "Yes. Thank you."

"Okay. I'll make supper." She toddled out of the room, her size three feet in worn house slippers.

Will took out his hankie and wiped his eyes. *How will I continue, Lord? My flesh and blood are so far away. Is it your will, God, for me to remain in this place?* His hands trembled as he picked up what would be the last copy of the Methodist *Christian Guardian* and set it beside the first edition of *The New Outlook*, the recently formed United Church's publication. The others would also welcome the distraction of new magazines.

Stanley and Agnus Annis had become friends with him—and Edith. Her death grieved them. Many others lamented too, of course, but the entire mission staff at Junghsien had been a godsend for him.

Pushing aside thoughts of writing letters to extended family, he flipped through the *Guardian*, landing on headlines. He was pleased Shao Wen Roh was to visit Canada, and yes, the local Chinese should have more say in the types of buildings constructed as churches. They would soon have to be self-supporting. Cuts to the missions' budgets had been in the works since March when three denominations had formed the United Church of Canada.

Missionaries' expenses increased annually. Theft, arson, and intentional sabotage of deliveries added to costs. They rarely received fifty percent of the value of their personal losses while on the field. And the disappearance of much-needed supplies such as books, paper, Bibles, and medicine during transport over thousands of miles across the country discouraged everyone.

Building and rebuilding had been going on since the West China Mission had started in 1890. Waste and more waste. Yet it was the only way to demonstrate the depth and breadth of their commitment to building the church, and there *were* more second-generation Christians among the local Chinese than ever before.

Oh, Edith. You made the ultimate sacrifice and I'm still here. Am I making any difference at all? Elbows on the desk, he propped his head up, grasping handfuls of his thick, pewter-grey hair.

1945

KINGSTON

Some food remained scarce long after the war. Thankfully, Mary had always enjoyed the challenge of making nutritious meals with limited ingredients. She'd taught Nita how to prepare rice, first washing to rinse the mouse droppings and starch away, then measuring the water up to the first joint of the thumb and then cook. Rice pudding had been the only form of the grain most of this household had ever eaten, but Mary bought little packages of Chinese spices and Szechwan chili oil from a local Asian shop to make delicious changes.

"I didn't know rice should be washed first," Nita said. "I often wondered what those black bits were. I really appreciate you helping me in the kitchen, Mary. I feel much more confident I'll be able to run my own household one day and entertain with interesting meals. I only wish Leonard could get to Kingston sooner than May."

"Of course you do, but he is alive and the war is over, thank God. So many men didn't make it back." Mary thought of Claire's fiancé, who'd been killed in the first air raid on London, England—a wound Claire kept hidden.

Work at the university occupied most of Claire's time and energy, although she golfed at the Cataraqui Golf and Country Club and volunteered with various organizations like the professional and business-women's chapter of Zonta. Mary found it peculiar that Claire, who was such an athlete, would be interested in promoting women in business. Perhaps it was the suffragette side of her, as she definitely encouraged young women to get involved in establishing their place among athletes and politicians. Could Claire's involvement in Zonta be seen as pushing back to maintain the gains made while men were at war?

Almost all of Mary's cousins had married and produced offspring, but her role model was Aunt Helen Sibley, a full-time teacher. Mary had never regretted her decision to stay single. She sometimes wished her father and his second wife, Vida, had stayed in Canada after they married, but she'd also understood the draw of China for them. Taking Christ to the masses was her father's life mission.

She remembered sitting on the floor at his knee on one rare occasion in Penghsien.

"Father, tell me about the time you helped Li Wang so he could be a preacher..."

Five

1911

PENGHSIEN, SZECHWAN, CHINA

The final construction of a mission school and church had been in the works for more than a year at Penghsein, a large city north of Chengtu. Will couldn't help but smile each time he viewed the structure of their new posting. It would be completed prior to Mary and Edith's arrival. The two-story school was surrounded by the second-floor balcony and an extended tiled roof supported by brick pillars. Of the dozen large buildings in the heavily populated town centre of Penghsien, he felt the newly finished church was the most attractive. The modest slope of the roofline swooped to corner eaves in the traditional dougong gable roof structure.

Tradespeople lived in modest brick houses on the main road above the street level shops. Larger buildings swallowed the narrow Confucius shrine at the end of an alleyway. Farmers' huts dotted the surrounding fields where rice, corn, wheat, and vegetables grew. Outlying hills were mined for tin and coal and everyone added to the energy of the city streets going about their daily activity.

At last, Will had begun to understand the local dialect; subtly delicate twists in interpretation still popped up, causing disruption or alarm. He tried preserving a serious, impassive guise when this happened, but his was no match for the stoic expressions of the Chinese.

"Ling Yan." Will bowed. "Have you brought your children to the mission school yet?"

The wiry gardener turned his face away. "Soon, Mr. Sibley."

That might mean he was giving it more thought, but more likely he was waiting to see how the others fared. After locking the gate to the compound, Yan hurried off in the opposite direction, carrying his rake, his loose-fitting dark pants tied at the ankles.

Will hoped there might be a day school soon, but the present challenge of keeping diseases out of the boarding school was enough. There were no medicines available for bacterial infections, and it would mean having to clean all the students of lice every day, necessary to keep typhus away. As well, the danger of picking up other diseases from the primitive sewage conditions was still too great to chance spreading them in a school.

Sometimes I wish I had the skills of an engineer.

Will watched as men carried water from the town supply in buckets hanging on the two ends of a pole. He winced at the layers of scar tissue lining their bare shoulders. Sewage was carried the same way, sometimes with lids. They trudged to the fields with this fertilizer.

"Cook your vegetables. Peel your fruit." These warnings had been drummed into them at the training centre in Shanghai. Most of that great city had sewers and a clean water supply, but the rest of Asia did not. Village wells that were hundreds of years old, if not a thousand, depended on local rainfall each season. Rice grew in areas where natural floodwaters from rivers allowed the creation of paddies.

Girls found abandoned filled the orphanages and several Chinese women were employed as housemothers to help feed, bathe, and clothe these children. Infant care classes also helped instruct new mothers.

Christ's words came to mind every time Will doubted. *Suffer little children, and forbid them not, to come unto me: for of such is the kingdom of heaven.*[1] Oh, how insignificant his work preaching to a handful of converted adults seemed at times. Yesterday on the church step he had found yet another infant girl, too weak to cry. He had hurried to the women's clinic with the limp, ragged bundle, praying he was in time.

Will entered the compound's residence for high-school-aged boys, prepared to teach a scriptural study on Luke. Dr. Hart's printing presses produced small tracts highlighting Bible verses. He distributed these to the students, hoping to attract the parents' attention as well when they took them home. The Chinese respected anything written.

Thank the Lord more translations are being completed and all the missions are getting printed pamphlets to hand out.

"Chin Lo, you're standing," he said. "Would you lead us in the Lord's Prayer, please?"

Will pulled a gentle smile as Chin Lo opened his mouth in protest, quelling the boy's resistance. Chin Lo's heavily padded vest had been neatly mended. He wore it over a clean shirt. His hair had been trimmed straight across his forehead, making him appear younger than his fourteen years.

When the young man finished, Will asked him to sit down.

"Gentlemen. Do you know why I am in China?"

The boys exchanged furtive glances. A slim lad raised his hand.

"Yes, Sun?"

"Because you want us to become good servants to Westerners and get rich."

Will swallowed, a sick feeling in his stomach. *Haven't I taught them anything?* "No. That is not correct. I'm glad I asked the question. Why am I in China?"

"To teach us how to read and write?"

"To show us how to keep disease away?"

"To 'lead us not into temptation'?"

"Yes, all those things, but I'm here because I love God. I'm here because God sent his Son to show us how we should all love one another. I care about each of you and love you the way Jesus loves each of us."

Usually, he couldn't tell what they were thinking, but the tall lad Wang started to sniff. Was he crying? Emotional reactions were rare.

"Please get your notebooks out and write an essay explaining how you can show your friends and neighbours love. I'm talking about love beyond your family. Two hundred characters, please."

He stepped over to Li Wang. Rather than draw attention to the real tears running down the boy's face, he patted his shoulder and moved on along the row of tables and chairs. What might the boy be suffering?

When the bell clanged for the end of class, Wang came up to Will's desk with his head bowed, smoothing his pantlegs.

"Yes, Wang. Did you wish to ask something of me?"

Wang nodded. "I… I'm sorry. My older brother is coming to take me away to the south to join an army. He says it's Father's wish. He thinks the army will make us powerful and wealthy." He lifted his head, his gaze meeting Will's. "I don't want to go. I want to love Jesus and show others his love. I want to be a minister like you, not fight and kill."

Will sat motionless. A convert. Someone who wanted to do Christ's work, but would the family's demands overpower the young man's desire? "Do you really wish to serve, Wang?"

"Yes, I am sure." The lad drew his shoulders back as he straightened to his full height.

Will sat thinking for a minute. How could he handle this without causing dissention? Tensions ran high between Chinese Nationalists and the foreigners. He'd have to speak to Macklin or one of the others to make the decision on how to help Li Wang. "Follow me."

Will hadn't wanted to let the young man out of his sight, but by custom, as the teacher, he should go first. As they passed a cluster of boys, Will was sure he heard "white foreign devil" under someone's breath. These boys hadn't quite grasped Christ's love for them yet.

Will tapped on the headmaster's door.

"Come right in."

"Sir, I have a problem to discuss with you. And Dr. Smith, you can help too." Will ushered Li Wang into the room and led him to a seat. "This young man would like to give his life to Jesus and become a minister. The problem is that his brother is coming to take him south to join the rebels, and he doesn't want to go into the military."

Will patted Wang's shoulder and nodded encouragement. He would need all of their support.

* * *

Will lay awake, alert to the sounds of the night. At first, he might have attributed the scuffling outside the compound wall to an animal, but as it rose up the wall it became apparent it was human.

Edith stirred. "Is Mary all right?"

"She's fine, Edith. Stay in bed. I think it's our expected visitors." He slipped on his long black outer gown, buttoning it as he stepped into his sandals. He closed the door quietly behind him. There was no way to bolt it.

He hurried down the steps and around the corner of the residence. He could see Drs. Smith and Macklin with lanterns. Two others followed, heading toward three young men who had their backs to the wall, squatting in semi-crouched positions.

Will swallowed and cleared his throat. "Good evening, gentlemen. Which of you is Li Wang's brother?" He shuddered as a knife blade flashed in the light of the lantern.

The three in black cotton pants and long dark shirts remained silent as the others with lanterns joined Will. An incongruous whiff of jasmine floated across the courtyard. Everyone stood locked to the earth.

Dr. Smith spoke. "You honour us with your presence, sirs." Smith bowed. "What brings you here over the garden wall?"

The one with the knife stepped forward, dropping his hands into the folds of his loose pantlegs. "Where is Li Wang? I am his brother, and I'm here to take him home. It is our father's wish."

Smith smiled. "Of course. Your father would be happy to see Wang, but the Nationals would also be happy to see him, or is it a warlord?"

The young man's expression didn't change. Only a slight pulling back of his shoulders gave any sign he had heard.

"It is most unfortunate for you that Li Wang does not want to leave," Smith said. "He wishes to stay."

"I am the elder brother. You cannot hold him back. He must come with me."

"We will bring Li Wang to speak to you, and perhaps he will convince you that he has a great desire to stay." Smith turned to one of the porters. "Please bring Li Wang."

The porter disappeared into the darkness; the boys and men remained statue-like, facing each other. No one prepared to back down.

Will stood frozen in position, listening to the night sounds. In the distance, the resonance of a Chinese police patrol beating their hollow wooden tubes grew louder, the dull thudding a warning to thieves to be on the lookout. A few dogs barked. A baby cried from within the residence. Clouds hid the new moon or any stars, and only the wavering glow of the paraffin lanterns gave light.

Now, three figures bordered by two lanterns made their way to the assembled group of stationary souls.

"Brother, you are here." Li Wang stepped toward the wary young man in the middle of the three, who appeared poised to launch themselves at the missionaries if threatened.

Will viewed the two groups, spearheaded by the brothers. *Thank goodness Li is as tall as his brother. Please be with us now, Lord.*

"I have made my choice, Sung. I wish to follow Jesus and lead others to become followers. It is the only way to give value to our lives."

"You show disrespect for our father," Sung snapped.

"He could come himself to take me home. Your way of a soldier is not for me."

Sung stepped forward. "You will not make me lose face, younger brother."

However, Wang was prepared and pulled a bag from his sleeve. He held it out, a purple square of fabric gathered and tied to hold coins. Will was pleased with the amount they had collected from all the staff, adding to what Wang himself had offered.

"You will need provisions along the way," Wang said. "It's a great distance. This will help."

Sung wavered. "You will displease our father."

"You chose to stay on the land you will inherit. Father chose me to get an education. That was his decision."

Will held his breath. Wang pushed the bag against his brother's outstretched hand. Sung snatched it, then bounced it in the palm of his hand. He glanced at one of his companions, who snapped a curt nod. Sung tossed the bag to him and spit on the ground between him and Smith.

Smith beckoned with his hand. "We'll let you out the compound door." He clomped toward the locked escape route.

As Wang walked toward the gate alongside Sung, presumably to say goodbye, Will was struck with a deep, sinking weight. He quickly caught up and came alongside Sung, prepared to pull him away from Wang should he draw the knife.

Wang stopped within three yards of the gate and bowed deeply, turning away abruptly from his brother and friends, toward the safety of the interior residence. Will, cognizant of Sung's weapon, strode to the gate opposite Smith and opened it wide, clutching the wooden timbers while the three would-be kidnappers exited. The hollow pounding of the patrol faded into the background as he and Smith closed the gates and slung the wooden latches across. They stepped back toward the lanterns of the inner compound.

Six

1945

KINGSTON

The heat of a Friday night in early October had Mary suggesting they sit on the front veranda and steps. "You can leave the door open, Nita, and listen for David. It's so much fresher out here."

Claire lounged on the steps, her back against the wooden pillar. "Tell us how your parents met, Mary. What made them decide to go to China?"

"You'll stop me if it's too dull, will you?"

"You're never dull, Mary. I find it fascinating," Nita said.

"Well, my father was training at Victoria College at the University of Toronto, and his student placement was out in the western provinces, now Manitoba. I used to ask them about why I was born in China but wasn't Chinese. I couldn't understand being a different race when I was little." Gazing up at the starry night sky, Mary smiled.

"My father, the Reverend William Sibley, describes stepping off the train, swinging his valise onto the dusty platform before him. There were no buildings, no houses, no stores…"

1903
MANITOBA, CANADA

Coming from the booming city of Toronto, it shocked Will to look beyond the steam billowing from the engine and see… nothing. Well, fields, maybe a dirt road, a few trees clustered in the distance, and a small cloud of dust headed his way. He looked up to see the engineer wave and jumped back from the spitting, chugging behemoth beside him. If he was correct, the approaching cloud heralded his supervisor, the Reverend James Harrison.

"Hello!" A young man drew the carriage to a sudden halt in front of him, pulling hard on the reins of two sleek brown horses. "Are you the Reverend William Sibley?"

The lad jumped from the carriage and stepped over to a slightly bewildered, exhausted Will, pumping his hand in greeting.

"I'm William too, the Reverend James Harrison's son." The lad glanced up and down at Will in his wrinkled suit. Will ran his fingers through his thick, dark hair, wishing for a drink of water. "Ooo-eee. Will the girls be happy to meet you! Come on. Throw your bag in. We've got a bit of a drive."

Will tossed his bag up and climbed into the open buggy before this muscular, tousle-headed lad of about twenty years and exuberant nature could take off without him.

"What countryside, eh, William?" he said to the lad. "I never could imagine the wide, open spaces you have here. Everything is so far apart."

"Oh, I hear it's even flatter out in the territories. Lots of good farmland," the younger William replied.

"Is that what you wish to do? Farm? Not follow in your father's footsteps?"

Young William shook his head, now leading the horses in a more subdued canter. "Not got the mind for all that book learning. I love tilling the soil and making things grow."

Will gripped the seat without a moment's rest for the next two hours, wind in his hair. He'd not felt this exhilarated in many years. He'd better remember to comb his mop before being introduced to the family.

How far will my own charges be from the Harrisons' place, and where are the people living who might attend church?

The rolling hills appeared empty of civilization.

＊

On Sunday afternoon, Edith pumped away at the small organ, glad that the Reverend William Sibley would be staying with her parents, at least for his first few months.

Oops. Which verse of the seven are they singing? Pay attention, Edith.

＊

Established with his own circuit of charges two years later, Will agreed to come around for dinner to the Harrison home in Roland, Manitoba. He'd been many times and enjoyed the family, especially since he missed his own so greatly. His oldest sister, Mary Ann, had given birth in May of this year to a son named John, of course, and Sibley in respect of their family name. He'd met the little chap right before leaving for his student placement.

Edith brought up the topic of missionaries coming to visit during their furlough from China. They had made a vivid presentation last month, a couple even more engaging than the first she had heard.

"I was sorry more didn't make an effort to come and see the presentation, but so many are farmers who have animals to look after," she said. "I found it interesting indeed, and exciting, that so many are being led to the Lord. Teaching is all very well, but what do you think of the missionary movement to the Orient, Reverend… William?" Her voice quivered.

Will glanced across the table at Edith, noting her keen attention directed toward him. "There is no end to the work of the church in Asia. I understand there are as many as four hundred million people in China alone, and most of them are farmers living in the countryside. They use manpower rather than machines." He brushed his thick, wavy hair to the side and then picked up his fork to spear the piece of pork he had cut into. "The missions in Chengtu, Szechwan have been rebuilt after the terrible fire and loss of life in the 1895 uprisings, and they are continuously asking for more clergy, nurses, doctors, and teachers to help in the Christian missions. The Boxer Rebellion seems to have been squashed."

"Who are the Boxers?" young William asked.

"The Boxers were a secret organization of Chinese peasants fighting against foreign missionaries. They called themselves the Righteous and Harmonious Fists. They believed if they practiced calisthenics and boxing, they could stop bullets."

William's eyes widened. "And can they?"

Will shook his head. "No. They *are* human. They've killed many foreigners and Christian Chinese, but they've been stopped by laws and retribution payment to several countries. We've all lost people, missions, and schools. That's why there is such a push to rebuild what was lost. They need education and Christian training."

Edith's eyebrows rose on her broad forehead. "You seem to know much about it. Is it safe?"

He nodded, hurrying to chew and swallow in order to continue a topic very close to his heart. "The British have negotiated more control so they can help any foreigners during troubles with the peasants. Their steamers patrol the Yangtze River. And foreigners have stronger legal rights now than some of the Chinese." He frowned. "I hope that doesn't create ill will between missionaries and the people." He stabbed a piece of potato dripping in butter and savoured the fresh flavour as he ate. "The British will soon open a consulate in Szechwan. I'm learning all I can, as my intention is to serve in China someday and maybe not too long off."

"I daresay you would make a good ambassador for Christ anywhere, but we would be sorry to lose you in Manitoba," James said.

It pleased Will to hear the compliment from Edith's father. "Thank you, sir. I appreciate that. There is some talk among my colleagues from the Vic about gathering a group to head out in oh-six. I'm thinking ahead. The newsletters are full of photos and reports of new mission stations in central China. It's very heartening."

※

After this visit, Edith and Will began corresponding. Edith's father had been given an exciting opportunity to establish a new church at Medicine Hat, in the newly formed province of Alberta. James had packed up his wife and three children, his son helping to load everything on board the boxcar so they could begin afresh in their new home. To be truthful, the reverend was far keener than the children. Mrs. Harrison had resigned herself to follow her husband, no matter how barren the country.

Between Manitoba, where Will had his circuit of churches, and Alberta, where Edith now resided with her family, lay the width of Saskatchewan. It made the distance too far to cross for a casual visit, especially since train rides were expensive.

Edith was able to continue her schooling to become a music teacher while Will buried himself among books and papers for many hours of the day. Writing and receiving letters from Edith were the highlights of any week. Sometimes he had to remind himself to get out and take a short walk before supper.

Seven

1906

Will returned to finish his studies in Toronto, trying to squelch any distractions, though Edith would dart into his thoughts every now and again. His brother John now attended theological classes at Victoria College. The two renewed their kinship on campus and planned excursions to visit family.

The steam from an incoming engine hissed from beneath its frame onto the platform. Porters pushed carts and people dragged cases along as they searched for the correct carriage.

"Will. Over here." John waved an arm in the brisk air. "I thought you were going to miss the train. Where is your valise?"

Will grinned and, turning his back to his brother, showed the canvas knapsack he carried slung over one shoulder. "Need practical things to take with me in the fall. This is waterproofed and protects my belongings from insects and mould." He contemplated John's leather suitcase with straps. "We'll have trunks for most of our things."

His brother scrutinized him. "You won't be changing your mind, Will?"

"About being a missionary? Absolutely not. It's been a call since I was young."

"Are you disappointed I'm not going to be a missionary?"

"No, not at all. We need people to minister to the folks in Canada as much as missionaries are needed elsewhere."

The arrival of their locomotive blasting out steam onto the platform at Union Station cut short the discussion.

After stowing their luggage, John carried on the conversation. "Well, I for one am looking forward to seeing Mary Ann and the girls. What's little Ethel like now that she's eighteen and has a three-year-old nephew?"

Will smiled. Their sister deserved to have her own child, having raised their three youngest sisters.

He was relieved it was only a short walk to the large and roomy manse in Tyrell where Mary Ann and her husband John Kitching resided.

"I understand they're doing well," he said. "Helen loves teaching in Mount Forest and hopes to stay there for a while."

John shot a sideways glance at Will as they settled into the wooden third-class seats. "And you? Are you going to remain a bachelor missionary?"

Will pursed his lips. How much should he reveal? "I'm a little concerned about being lonely. We've been so fortunate to have plenty of siblings and aunts and uncles. Uncle John has recommended I get married before leaving."

"And have you thought about it? Who would it be? Not Doris, surely. She's one pushy woman."

Will smiled to himself. "No, not Doris. I'll let you know when I need your permission."

John gave him a playful punch. "Mum's the word then."

They made the most of opportunities to visit with sisters, cousins, aunts, and uncles in Erin and the surrounding Wellington County. Between study and lectures, Will met with friends, all engrossed in travelling as missionaries to the mysterious East. He often joined in the discussions with the "Vic Eight," as some had started calling the group.

Yesterday he had gone to the office of the school's paper, *Acta Victoriana*, to have his photo taken. They showed him the layout of a front page intended for November's edition, when the Vic Eight would ship off to China—among them Charles Jolliffe, H.D. Robertson, C.P. Holmes, Arthur Ozawa, and their wives; Bowles, Morgan, Wallace, and himself remained unmarried, so far. He first had to complete his final examinations to graduate, but having been named part of the group had fortified him, perhaps strengthening the courage of them all. It certainly made the commitment very real.

Sitting in the university's men's lounge with *The Toronto Star*, Will contemplated his future. Between the ornate stone pillars, tall windows reached up the full fifteen feet to the ceiling, making the room bright and cheerful. There were plenty of tables and several groups of comfortable maroon leather tub chairs.

I won't likely find this kind of comfort in China.

What a challenge it would be to dive into a completely new culture! And how would the people receive them... receive him?

"Will. Mind if I join you?"

"Not at all."

Bowles made himself comfortable in the next chair, placing his briefcase on the plush patterned carpet beside him. "So what do you think about the latest news out of China?"

"I'm not sure. I thought Sun Yet-sen had the strongest support and would win over the country with little resistance. That would be such an opening for Christianizing the population. It seems there hasn't been much headway since Westerners started." Will wondered about Sun Yet-sen's political sway.

The tall, confident Jolliffe pulled a chair from the table where he had been reading to join them. Morgan also approached the group of friends and swung another chair to fill a spot opposite Jolliffe. He greeted each with a handshake and cheerful smile.

Will continued. "You know the Brits have a head start. They've established two Anglican Bishops in China and now work in five provinces and eight cities, according to Frank Norris of *Project Canterbury.*"

Jolliffe tapped his pipe to empty it in the red glass ashtray beside him. "They may well have established a few churches, but they don't have a million baptized yet, and to think there are more than two hundred million people in those five provinces alone." He gave a little laugh. "It gives the people a choice as to whether they want high Anglican, Wesleyan Methodist, or Presbyterian. The Papists have been there forever, of course." Jolliffe waggled the pipestem. "We're going to have much bigger challenges where we're to be posted. Szechwan Province is far, far from the coast and the Westernized population."

"The American Disciples of Christ have made a start. They seem to concentrate on education and establishing hospitals," Will responded as Jolliffe crossed his legs, relaxing to fill his pipe. "And we've got missionary doctors from this very college who would have us focus on health, and others the schools."

"I wouldn't broadcast that view," said Bowles. "We don't need dissention when we're trying to raise funds. We have to put up a united front or nothing will get done."

After pouring himself a cup of coffee at the sideboard, Wallace quietly entered the circle. He placed the cup on an end table, then sat bouncing his knee, his lips tightly pursed.

Will scrutinized the frowning face of Wallace before leaning forward and lowering his voice to ask, "Everything all right, Wallace? Not having doubts, are you?"

Wallace glanced around the group. "I am concerned. It's not just trying to learn all those characters, but the language itself. I'm having a devil of a time trying to reproduce some of the sounds. Hebrew and Greek were difficult enough. Languages don't come naturally to me."

Will waved away the cigar smoke drifting his way. "Look at how the Chinese here struggle to learn English. I've been busy studying for the finals and not spent much time on the language itself. Does using the Pinyin system with our alphabet help?"

Wallace shrugged, studying his shoes. "Could for some. Maybe I should be more worried about what the food is like."

Bowles slapped Wallace on the back. "Cheer up, lad. They're giving us at least eighteen months in Shanghai to learn the language. Don't you think we'll pick it up more easily once we're immersed in it than trying to do it here from a book?"

"You're right. I suppose I shouldn't be concerned." Wallace took a sip of his coffee. "The calling is as strong as ever."

Will smiled. "That's the important thing. The rest will fall into place—God being our helper."

"Right you are," Jolliffe agreed. "Although I for one will miss Sunday roast beef dinners. And there might be other concerns. Russia and Japan are eyeing China's borders in Manchuria and Korea to connect mines and industry with the sea using rail lines."

Will kept abreast of all the news from China he could find. "They want access to ports." He folded his paper, preferring to join in the conversation than to try to read while the group was together. "Here's hoping the Nationalists will agree to opening train services and creating work in industries. It would advance our cause tremendously."

"But look at the exploitation of children and other damage the industrial revolution did in European countries a hundred years ago," Morgan countered. "Progress is all well and good, but only if managed properly."

Jolliffe harumphed. "You're right, of course. That's why it's so important to send theologians as well as Christian doctors, nurses, and teachers."

"True." Wallace bobbed his head emphatically. "But the common people are forced to live in such poverty that they need to be cured of disease and fed first. Then they can thrive enough to be open to Christian teachings."

Bowles opened his leather briefcase and pulled out some leaflets to pass around to the group. "These are some copies of the latest being printed in Central Szechwan. We give them hope with the Gospel while we're feeding and healing them. If we convince the local Chinese politicians that healthy, happy workers will benefit everyone, maybe they'll agree to more telegraph lines, at the very least." He flipped the lock of his case over the top and snapped it shut.

"Can we change the buying and selling of children?" asked Wallace. "Can we change the practice of foot-binding? Apparently, many of the women can't even walk."

Will shivered at the brutal concepts.

＊

In late spring, plans were advancing for the Vic Eight's journey to west central China. All worked raising funds, filling in papers of permission, and scheduling passage overseas. The cluster of comfortable chairs in the men's lounge at the university where they met informally had become their own. Others left the area open for them but would cluster around in hopes of hearing their exciting plans. Their photos in the school paper promoted the adventure and many young scholars wanted to assist in gathering funds for the missionaries, filling all with a worthy sense of purpose.

A few met late in the afternoon, the pink and orange rays of late afternoon sun refracting through the uneven panes of glass.

"How are the plans coming for our sendoff with the Young People's Forward Mission?" asked Jolliffe.

"I've spoken to a couple of chaps from the YP and they have a huge volunteer group to help with fundraising, organizing speakers, and printing pamphlets," said Will. "There is so much enthusiasm for foreign missions, I sometimes worry about our own congregations." He shifted in his seat, tapping his fingers on his knee. "I do have an announcement to make along another line."

"Ha!" Bowles pointed his finger at Will. "You're getting married. Did that blonde nurse Doris finally hook you in?"

Will cocked his head, his forehead wrinkled. "Not a nurse and not a blonde, but dark-haired and a music teacher. Her name is Edith. You've never met her, but I've asked her father permission, and she's given me an affirmative answer."

"Are you abandoning your plans for China?" Robertson asked.

Will pushed back his shoulders and grinned at his exceptionally tall classmate. "No. Edith is coming with me. The wedding will take place in July in Medicine Hat where her father is the clergyman. I've an Albertan pulpit supply until November, after which we'll take the train across the mountains and meet you in Victoria."

Robertson said, "That means most of us will be married. Do the women know what they're getting into?"

"Of course they do. They're well educated and do a tremendous amount of reading about the situation in central China." Will let out the breath he only now realized he'd been holding. It was a relief to have shared his marriage plans with his colleagues and not be kidded.

Robertson nodded. "Then congratulations are in order, Will." The tipping of an imaginary cap accompanied his jolly laugh.

"Aha, the Vic Eight meet in Victoria. Strength in numbers," Jolliffe said, pumping his fist in a cheer.

Eight

1945

KINGSTON

Mary could more easily speak of her parents' passionate calling as she approached middle age. Their struggles had strengthened her faith and realization that, once converted, Chinese Christians would work to evangelize others, no matter what war or disaster befell them.

For the second warm night in a row, Claire suggested they sit on the veranda to hear about the Sibley family's journey. The Wilder sisters shared the padded seat of a hammock, gently keeping it in motion. Mable and Nita took the rattan chairs with cups of tea steadied on the laps of their cotton dresses, and Mary and Claire sat opposite each other, leaning on the red brick posts. Voices of exuberant university students walking in the neighbourhood filtered through the heavy foliage of colourful fall maples.

"My parents found the trip exciting and very stimulating," she told the other women. "For my mother, who had only travelled between Manitoba and Medicine Hat, it was the adventure of a lifetime. For Father, it was the culmination of years of study after a call to the ministry…"

1906
CANADA TO CHINA

Will took Edith's hand rather forcefully, for his excitement over the coming journey across the ocean would not contain itself. Although they hadn't stayed overnight in the Banff Springs Hotel, they'd wandered the bare patio overlooking the steep, dusky mountains. Now they were among those mountains, taking one of the world's most spectacular train rides.

Edith looked up at her new husband. "Is it the journey itself or the quest for new converts that excites you most?"

Will clasped her hand to his chest. "To be honest, both. But you, my dear, are the reason for the joy I have at the moment. I understand why the mission board desires men to be married." He sobered in reflection. "There are bound to be difficulties ahead, and we shall need to rely on each other as helpmates in our work."

Edith twisted in her seat to get a full view of the scenery. "But, for now, there is the beauty of these rocky, green mountains, dark and almost overpowering. I'm wondering if avalanches might be blocking some of the passes. I don't want to miss our sailing."

Will squeezed her fingers in an attempt to reassure her. "Avalanches occur later in January and February after a great accumulation of snow, I'm told."

The train porter pushed a rattling trolly along the aisle, stopping at their seat to ask if they would like anything to eat or drink.

"Oh, a cup of tea with milk, please." Edith pointed. "One of those cakes would be nice. Are you getting one, Will?"

"Yes. I'll have the same."

They spent a few minutes in silence, nibbling on their treats. "I've looked forward to this journey for so long, I can hardly believe it's happening," Edith said. "Do they anticipate bad weather on the ocean voyage?"

"The Pacific Ocean is the biggest body of water on earth, so I imagine there will be some. Before that, we'll have a few days to take in the sea air, and Victoria has some impressive buildings, but I think you'll enjoy the beautifully landscaped gardens. The island experiences mild weather and we are unlikely to see much snow, even though it's November."

※

Aboard the *Empress of China* on the twenty-seventh of November, Edith and Will gathered for a hearty evening meal with the others, sharing stories of their trip across Canada. Of the twelve couples around the table on the last evening before sailing, eight were on their honeymoon.

Several Women's Missionary Society workers had joined them. "You know, it's a rule that we can't marry should we meet someone while in China," Miss Best said, glancing around the table.

"Really, Adele? Why not?" Edith was relieved she wouldn't find herself in that situation.

"Well, WMS workers are required to be single. If they marry, they must quit their job and repay the wages they have received up to that point."

"That's difficult. It would make it harder and harder to leave. I suppose you must know that before joining up?"

"Oh, yes," Miss Best said. "And there are still plenty of volunteers. Although I suspect they would have many more if the rules were different."

Jolliffe began relating experiences of the main group's cross-Canada journey. "The old boys gave us extravagant banquets at Winnipeg and Calgary. Of course, we were expected to make little speeches, and this we did with exuberance, heartened by the vigorous support of those gathered. All along the rail line—Kenora, Brandon, and Moose Jaw—

Vic women and men greeted us. The head man in Vancouver said to poor Edward here, 'And now I want to meet Mrs. Wallace.'[2] You should have seen his look, but his response was all the better: 'And so do I.'"

The group laughed, particularly the bachelors. Everyone was in high spirits, exciting prospects ahead of them.

Edith glanced toward Miss Best. She was keeping her head down, focusing on the delicious cake with fruit glaze.

Of all the members of the group, only one was not seasick within a day of being on the open ocean.

"I'd better keep my wife company. Edith's unwell." Will excused himself from the table.

Gripping the rails both for steadiness and to hold himself upright, Will made it to their stateroom, where he and Edith fought the motion of the waves for three days, unable to eat a thing or drink very much.

By Sunday, everyone appeared on deck and, though thinner, most were eating lightly, having learned their lesson after the first night's celebratory meal.

After dining one evening, Jolliffe asked Will to come with him for a stroll around the deck. Despite wearing long overcoats and scarves to bundle up against the squall, they had to take cover in a small enclave to be heard against the wind.

"Sorry to bring you out into this for a talk, Will, but I'm worried."

Will frowned. "Any particular worry? Is the sea voyage concerning you?"

Jolliffe shook his head. "No. It's an article my father sent me from the *Atlantic Monthly* in Boston, called 'The Missionary Enterprise in China.' I really get the feeling that Western, especially American, businessmen have feelings of resentment against the missionaries. The author quotes them as saying…" He cupped two fingers on each hand to indicate a quotation. "'Their persistent and impertinent attempts to force an alien and undesired religion on the Chinese are offensive, a hinderance to peaceful negotiations, etc., etc.'[3] It's in the September issue of this year."

Will's eyes widened. "Really? Who is the author? And does he agree with their sentiments?"

"Chester Holcombe wrote it. I'm not sure if my father sent it to discourage me from going or just to give us a heads-up as to what we might be up against, but the article put up a great defence for missionaries, especially in the western, poorer part of China. He points out that it was the unchristian policies of aggression that brought about the Boxer Rebellion, even though missionaries were targeted."

Will nodded. "Easier targets than a British gunboat or well-armed trading ship, I suppose. In a way it's a relief to know, but it's disheartening to learn about that particular attitude. Do you think it's only the American businessmen? Surely not the Brits. Their churches have been established in the Chinese port cities for decades."

"The Americans are interested in making headway into trade with China. They see other Western nations making profits, so they want in."

"That fact might more likely be the root of resentment by the Chinese." Will pulled his collar up over his ears. He took a deep breath of the brisk sea air. "Thanks for discussing this with me privately. Everyone's spirits are so high right now. We're all excited to finally be on our way with such a strong mission. It would only put a damper on things if we brought up the topic."

Jolliffe pulled his coat closer. "You're right. Time enough to deal with difficulties when we arrive. Let's keep that tucked under our hats for now. Should we go in and join the games? It's darned cold out here."

A tournament of quoits engaged them for the many days it took before reaching Yokohama in Japan. Arthur Ozawa bid his companions farewell there. Calm waters allowed everyone glimpses of Kagoshima and the southern Japanese coast as they sailed toward the East China Sea and their destination.

Edith leaned a little over the railing of the upper deck of the ship. "I'm surprised to see guns on the boats, Will."

"We are not long past the Russo-Japanese war, and nerves are still taut." He gripped Edith's hand, his protective sombreness calming their excitement of arrival.

Eighteen miles up the Whang-poo River, a tributary of the great Yangtze, the ship arrived in the centre of Shanghai. Soon they were settled at Astor House among the "rush and multitudinous noise of a Chinese City," as they reported back to the university newspaper: "It is cold, raw weather. We are almost at Christmas. Yet about us surges a hurrying mass of busy people to whom Christmas means nothing. At times we wonder in despair almost if ever it will be possible to raise the ideals of these people."[4]

Nine

1945
KINGSTON

Seeing that Claire and Nita were waiting for her to continue, Mary took a sip of lemonade and carried on with her story.

"My mother really enjoyed Shanghai. She often talked fondly of her first year there while they were being trained to speak Mandarin and write the Chinese characters. By the time they left for inland China, she realized she was carrying me..."

1907
SHANGHAI, CHINA

Edith and Harriett walked arm and arm up the narrow wooden stairs to the upper hallway where the women resided with their husbands. The main floor consisted of classrooms where groups of missionaries took Mandarin lessons from articulate Chinese scholars, many of whom had travelled abroad and spoke English fluently.

Edith said, "Today's tour has been the most interesting history lesson we've had so far. I had no idea Japan and the Europeans had been so aggressive with China, demanding their own concessions in Shanghai."

"I suppose all the countries want to have a piece of the city. It seems like the centre of businesses from all over the world."

"True. It's very cosmopolitan. The new marble bank doesn't impress me all that much. It's the crowded buildings on the side streets where all the Chinese people shop that are so interesting. I found a delightful selection of brushes and paper in a little store on Fong Pang Road."

Harriett shrugged. "Once we crossed to Ming Kuo Road, I found that part of Shanghai very congested. The noise of swarms of Chinese people talking and the vendors trying to shout above the din made my head ache. I felt uncomfortable with people brushing so close to my skirts—and all the streets are terribly narrow, and the rickshaw pullers, aggressive. It's all so foreign."

Edith raised her eyebrows. "Harriett. This is China, and Shanghai is supposed to be a Chinese city. It's only foreign to us."

Harriett grinned. "So it's all right to have Edward the VII Avenue in the British Settlement, and the French in their section, is it?"

Edith half-smiled. "Well…"

"Oh, Edith. I guess I'm not used to cities." Harriett said nothing for a moment as they turned a corner in the hallway, arms hooked. "Did you see the way Miss Yu looked at me when I asked if there was any danger from the patrons of the opium den? I believe she didn't want to acknowledge its existence."

Edith was a little surprised at her companion's view of the city. "Harriett, it's not the type of place the Chinese would be proud of. Would you be so happy to be asked about the saloon down the road, or the gin parlours back at home?"

Harriett gave her new friend a nod. "Right. Of course. And I'm a clergyman's wife." She threw her hands into the air. "What was I thinking?" Then she giggled. "It's all so new to me. Married to a missionary, and only for two months now. All these changes in culture!

My stomach never stops growling, and then I see things like rats rummaging in bags of rice, or smell urine in the garden, and I think I shall never eat again."

Edith nodded as well once they reached their respective doors. "It's new to me too. Marriage, I mean, and the culture. Will and I have our first-year anniversary in a few weeks. Three months after the wedding ceremony, we said goodbye to my parents and climbed on board the train bound for Vancouver. With my father being a preacher, church has been a way of life for me."

She patted Harriet's arm in parting, then closed the ill-fitting wooden door and watched the thin walls shake. Did earthquakes happen in Shanghai?

Edith removed her hat and gloves and sat down to write a letter to her sister, as she didn't have kitchen duties this evening. The walk all the way along the Bund by the water had been most interesting, but exhausting. She might never get used to the humidity.

Will entered, clearly forgetting how fragile the door was. It quivered noisily.

"Oh, Will. There were some wonderful new buildings along the waterfront. They're finishing the Palace Hotel out of stone, six stories high, and the banks look like something in pictures of London or Edinburgh. Square and sturdy, especially the Russo-Chinese Bank. I didn't realize China had ties with Russia."

Will pressed his lips together. "There are many things we don't know about China, my dear. You may hear the Sassoon and Kadoorie family names attached to big houses and hotels. They're some of the wealthiest Jewish families in the world. Originally, they came from Baghdad and have expanded their empire throughout Asia." He leaned over Edith and placed an arm around her shoulder, glancing at her letters and envelopes spread out on the tiny desk. "Never mind all that. Did Miss Yu take you to purchase the fabric you wanted? I don't suppose we'll need much in the way of clothing for western

China, since the requirement is that we wear traditional outfits to do our work."

"Yes, I've been given specific instructions on how to design garments in the provincial style. I think it can get quite cold, and they don't have trees to burn for fuel. There is no fireplace for heating, only for cooking. Oh, and the Yuyang Gardens are splendid, even after being destroyed again during the Taiping Revolt. And the Temple of the Town God had so many carvings…"

"Edith. I realize everything is exciting and new, but remember that we're going to an area far more isolated than any prairie town."

"But Will, it's all so different. Just the smells, the spices, and all the jangling bells and tinkling chimes, the whistles, the singsong talking… It's so full of life; I want to take it all in while we're here."

Edith gazed into her husband's face, appealing to his kindness toward her. She hoped he would allow her to go with the group of more progressive missionaries' wives on some city tours, providing she had the energy in the heat.

⁂

Will straightened his tie before he tapped on the large wooden door to the Reverend Arthur E. Moule's office. He had heard much about the Church Missionary Society's Anglican bishop and had arranged to meet him prior to their leaving for the western mission.

They enjoyed a hot cup of tea, Will having learned to drink it without milk or sugar.

"Yes, I was the first CMS missionary in Hangchow and became a bishop back in '80." The bishop set his cup down in front of him on the desk. "Trinity College Ningbo is teaching divinity classes for catechists and pastors. We really must have local Chinese clergy to effectively spread the Gospel in China, though. It won't work otherwise."

"What do you think of Westerners wearing the long garments of Chinese scholars? Will we fit in better dressing like them?" Will adjusted himself in the chair opposite the desk. He used both hands to balance the teacup on his knee.

"At the moment, it's law. Here in Shanghai, it's common to see scholars, Europeans, and priests, but you'll see fewer inland and less appreciation for education in general, I imagine. No matter how you dress, you'll stand out. Height, for one thing. You know, between droughts and floods, the average farmer barely subsists in his circumstances. My understanding is that the heat in summer is more pronounced inland than here. Cotton is the best summer fabric. Don't let the tailors talk you into any silk suits. And loose fitting is cooler."

Will flushed. He had been thinking about how smart the silk suits looked and had contemplated getting one made, but the price had stopped him. "Do the tradesmen and grocers tend to overcharge Westerners, sir?"

"Call me Arthur, please. They do in the city. The wealthy Chinese are also charged more, but they haggle for better prices."

"What about the crops? Do they have big poppy fields?" Will studied the distinguished man across from him.

Arthur Moule met his gaze steadily. "You are under the belief that the Chinese supply their own people. I suppose you, like every foreigner, believe that the people want opium brought into the country, that it's an insatiable habit of all Chinese?"

Will dug his finger around his collar, frowning. "I had heard such things, yes."

"For decades the British, Dutch, and Portuguese traders all smuggled opium into the country." Arthur stood and plied the pile of documents on the sideboard. "Here, I have a copy of my publication for the London Society for the Suppression of the Opium Trade. It's a few years old, but still relevant. You can keep this copy, if you promise to read it through and pass it on to others working in the field."

As Will picked up the thin document, he skimmed the introduction.

I. What is the Opium Trade?
II. Has the Church any responsibility in the matter?
III. If so, what is the extent of that responsibility?[5]

"I take it that we do have a responsibility as Christians," Will re-marked.

"Absolutely. Opium use is not a weakness of just the Chinese. Britain has been plagued with opium dens along with gin parlours. Before the British East India Company took over the opium monopoly, the Portuguese imported about two hundred chests of the drug. The trade has grown to eighty thousand chests of opium yearly, despite the Chinese *prohibiting* the imports."

"Does the government get tax from the imports?"

"Not when it's illegal. Smuggling carried on, and in 1834 the Emperor asked the people if they should tax the trade or annihilate it. 'Annihilate it' was the overwhelming answer!"

"Is this when so many chests of opium were seized and destroyed?"

"Yes, and anger started to grow among the traders, causing two opium wars—in 1841 and 1860."

Will patted the drips off his forehead with his already damp handkerchief. "But then Chinese opened ports allowing Christian doctors and missionaries inland up the Yangtze."

Arthur tapped the pile of papers on his untidy desktop. He nodded but shook his finger in the air at an invisible enemy. "The early missionaries arrived on the very ships carrying opium."

Will's shoulders sagged. "They hated us all. I guess if opium users didn't work, their families went hungry. Do they still dislike us that much?"

"You'll learn that the Chinese hide a great deal of emotion. The Westerner can never *read* a Chinese face. On the other side, the

Chinese cannot believe there aren't underlying implications and motives to everything we foreigners say. Even the most sincere, innocent statements will be analyzed. Their language and characters offer alternative meanings. Learn the local dialect well."

Will left the Reverend Arthur Moule's office feeling discouraged in a new way, the challenges of language, food, and crowds not yet having overwhelmed him. How could they make any converts when the people held an underlying hatred of the foreigner? No wonder, at that.

He would read Arthur's paper and ask some of the others to discuss it with him. Were the Chinese right in blaming the Westerners for pushing opium on them? There had to be a desire in China for the product.

Yes, Will argued with himself, *but there's a demand for alcohol in our country too. It's broken many a man and women as well. What can we do?*

Ten

1907

YANGTZE RIVER, CHINA

The group of a dozen missionaries, their wives, doctors, nurses, and teachers gathered at the dock on the bank of the Huangpu River in Shanghai. They stood, surrounding their bundles heaped in the middle. Everything had been securely wrapped with rope, lists had been checked, and now they waited for appropriate transportation. They were at the first stage of heading inland to western China.

Edith would have liked to sit in the shade, had there been any. She'd lost her breakfast to the fish in the dirty brown water and her head now ached. Unsure of how the steamer trip might worsen her nausea, she dared not eat or drink anything further. She had no doubt about her condition, though. She would be delivering a child by mid-March of 1908.

The humid heat sapped her strength and she allowed herself to drop onto the closest bundle and sit.

"Are you all right, Edith? You're looking pale." Her new acquaintance, Ethel Garret, leaned over her in concern, then whispered, "Are you in the family way?"

Edith nodded and tried to force a smile. She was delighted, really, but had hoped to avoid pregnancy before arriving in Chengtu. It would be a gruelling six to eight weeks.

From the prow of the vessel, Will couldn't stop looking side to side, up and down, at every turn of the river, despite knowing Edith would be fighting to hold down her latest meal.

"This is quite the river," he said. "It must overflow its banks during floods. There doesn't seem to be much protection for the fields and mud houses along here."

He had to admit, the smells alone made his own stomach lurch at times. The night soil was regularly removed, but, along with greasy cooking oils, the strong smell of perspiring sailors, and the lack of a breeze, the odours lingered heavily.

Edith kept her grip on his arm as they leaned on the railing. "I suppose we'll get used to the smells, do you think?"

Will nodded. "The experienced bunch say we will. Oh, look at those lovely fields of yellow-flowered plants over there. And look. Water buffalos. Are they pulling carts with solid wooden wheels?"

Edith nodded, but her face had lost its colour.

He patted her arm with his free hand. "Never mind, dear. We'll reach Chinkiang soon. We can stop there while they do their business of trading."

He wondered if any crates of opium were aboard this very vessel, ready to be smuggled into ports along the Yangtze.

1945

KINGSTON

The daylight hours shortened toward the end of October and the household on Nelson Street moved into a steady increase of indoor activities. David's evenings were harder to fill with quiet pursuits and so Mary recommended he join the new Scouting group for younger boys. Cubs depleted some of his boyhood energy. He'd acquired enough reading skills that his mother relented and purchased *Boy's Own*, a magazine for boys with imagination.

Nita's cooking had taken on new vigour with Mary's prompting, and Mable's work at the hospital kept her on her feet for ten hours a day. "The wards are stuffed with returning wounded soldiers. There is such a shortage of nursing staff, I'm sometimes wiping brows while interviewing new inmates about their dietary requirements."

Claire's golfing season had finished in October and the school basketball season was in full swing. "Mary, there's another game at the university gym tomorrow evening. Would you like to go?"

Mary hesitated. "I would love to, but I need time to prepare for a presentation at the Chalmers United Church Women's meeting. They've asked me for a second time, so I guess I didn't offend them too much the last time. Enjoy yourself, though. Root for the team on my behalf, will you?"

✳

On a Saturday afternoon in late November, Nita stopped Mary in the upstairs hall. "We're waiting for the next segment of your story, Mary. Do you have much schoolwork this afternoon? David is off playing at a friend's house."

Mary smiled. David had been getting more active so Nita rarely had time to herself. "I do have two classes of papers to grade, but I'll be down by three in time for tea."

On the stairs, Mary passed Claire, who carried a pair of bricks on her way to the kitchen. Mary frowned. "Is it so terribly cold up in your attic room, Claire?"

"Well, I get most chilled when I have to sit and do paperwork." She nodded to the bricks. "I'll put these by the stove for tonight and then go out for a walk. I'll be ready for tea at three. You're continuing your story, I hope?"

Mary smiled. "I feel like I'm doing a radio program, you girls are so interested. And it'll be nice to have the Wilder sisters join us."

The hall clock was striking three when Mary made her way down to the sitting room. The others assembled in various chairs, layers of sweaters and shawls draped around them.

"Can I help, Nita?" Mary frowned at the peculiar smell coming from the oven. "What are you baking?"

Nita laughed. "Only Claire's bricks for tonight. I've put in extra for each of us as well. It's going to be a frosty one, so I've kept feeding the coal fire since noon. Nothing like the winds off Lake Ontario to put a chill into the bones."

Mary shivered at the thought of other winds, the north winds in winter, whipping down the red-earthed Chengtu Basin over the peasants in their thin clothing. Even though they stitched layer upon layer of fabric to worn padded jackets, their feet were ill-clad. Thankfully, it never got much below freezing there.

"No, I suppose not," she replied to Nita.

Mary picked up the large teapot and Nita followed her to the sitting room with a tray of cups and saucers and a piece of lemon cake from last night.

"Here's your milk, David," Nita said to her son. "Now you be a good boy and play with your trucks in the hall when you're done."

"He really is a well-behaved lad, Nita," Miss Charlotte Wilder said from her favourite needlepoint-covered chair.

"I hope so. His father will be proud of him, I think."

Patting Nita's hand as she sat beside her on the blue jardiniere velvet sofa, Claire said, "The time is passing quickly. You'll have the handsome Leonard home before you know."

Though the large floral design had nearly been erased with wear, the sagging cushions of the sofa offered comfort.

"Yes, and I'll be grateful for it," Nita said. "But let's hear about your family, Mary. It must be really something to have a minister in the family."

"Well, in the previous two generations," Mary began counting on her fingers, mentally naming her Grandfather Harrison, Great-Uncle Thomas MacLauchlan, Uncle Thomas Reed, her father, his brother John Sibley, and her Uncle John Kitching, "there have been six ministers. I often wondered how my father and Uncle John Cynddylan Sibley managed to pay tuition. Both their parents died young."

"They must have had a difficult life," Miss Emma Wilder tsked.

"The siblings were all close, and I think my father's sister, Mary Ann Kitching, had a great deal to do with that. Back in the 1890s, there was a very strong push to send missionaries over to the Orient, especially China. My father enthusiastically described his first call to serve. Out in the centre of a lonely concession on the Guelph Line, Ebenezer Methodist, the Kitching family's church, swelled to overflowing when visiting missionaries came to speak."

Mary smiled off into the distance. The memory of the solid country church of her uncle's family filled her with a delicious contentment. Lights would have beamed from every window and, despite the chilly air, the front door of the red brick structure would have remained wide open as people filed in...

Eleven

1890

NASSAGAWEYA TOWNSHIP, ONTARIO

Young William Edward Sibley watched four-year-old Eunice cling to their eldest sister's hand as they crowded into the pew behind their parents, along with his other four sisters. He and his younger brother, John, had chosen to sit on a side bench with some of their friends. Restless jostling for seating and a view of the missionaries visiting from China created a few minutes of rowdy anticipation—that is, until the Reverend John Hough stepped up onto the wooden platform in his black suit and stiff clergyman's collar.

The reverend introduced the missionary couple. Will focused his attention on the thin man and his wife, noting how their glances flitted round the sanctuary, searching for friendly faces. The crowd stilled and strained to hear every word.

"We wish to share some of our experiences with you here at Ebenezer, as we do in many churches of nearly every denomination across Canada and the United States," said the visiting missionary. "Like most missionaries to Asia, we spend our furlough visiting congregations, sharing the dream of Christianizing millions of Chinese, Indian, and Asian peoples. We passionately desire to stir the hearts of those who have not heard or known about God and the love of Christ.

"Four years ago, Hudson Taylor appealed for one hundred new recruits to go to central China. The goal of the Methodist Church in Canada is to send a contingent of missionaries, doctors, nurses, and teachers to the inland city of Chengtu, situated in the province of Szechwan where Taylor has established an interdenominational mission. Here the China Inland Mission constructs buildings of the most basic materials, chiefly bricks, stone, and wood. Aided by the population of the city, they build structures in the Oriental style of tall roofs with upturned eaves sweeping to a point at the corners.

"Many hundreds of people who have no other means of gainful employment can be paid to build the mission and hopefully learn our Christian ways. Everything is done by hand in Szechwan Province. The carts are pulled by men, and the mixing of mud for bricks is done with hoes in wooden frames and packed down by foot. Beams are raised into place by ropes and manpower. Women carry heavy loads on their backs and labour in the fields. These things are done the way they have been for centuries."

The man wiped perspiration dripping from his brow. "I'm sorry to be sweating so profusely, but illness has weakened me. There's no danger to you. Please allow my wife to continue."

He dropped onto the nearest wooden chair.

His wife, a fine-boned woman, stood tall and erect behind the pulpit. "Do not be deceived into thinking that our Christian missionaries live a life of ease. Yes, there are servants and many willing to serve for a few coins a day just to feed themselves. Without their help, no one can accomplish a thing in the unrelenting heat, nor in the disassociating culture. We teach those willing to listen. We rescue babies and look after orphans." She cleared her throat. "As with many foreigners, we head to Mount Omi, or Cave Mountain, during the hottest weeks where we camp in the most primitive conditions.

"First is the weeklong train ride to the west coast of our land. This is the most comfortable part of the journey, during which we are reminded to appreciate the green, open spaces of our glorious, free country of Canada. Then comes a month-long sea voyage across the largest ocean of the world, the Pacific. The destination is the port city of Shanghai, a conglomeration of Western foreigners, competitive vendors and shopkeepers, rowdy sailors, wealthy Chinese noble families, and opium dealers of all nationalities.

"In this city, Catholics from Ireland, Episcopalians from the United Kingdom, Methodists from Canada, and Presbyterians from the United States and Sweden have begun to build churches and congregations. New, Western-style schools, orphanages, and hospitals are being built so nurses and doctors can take care of a small portion of those who are ill. They plan a university. Often there is conflict with government officials and the superstitious ways of China.

"Leaving Shanghai, we begin the long, inland journey to western China. After nearly two weeks on the Yangtze River in a crowded junk, a flat-bottomed sampan, or British steamer—if there are no mishaps—we land at the mission in Chungking."

The woman pointed to the easel, which held a large sketch of a winding river contained by tall cliffs. Small cottages clung to nooks in the limestone, and a variety of vessels crowded the waterway.

"The denominations have tried to unite in their efforts to form missions and outposts. Chungking is a gateway to the farmlands of central China. Here, established churches and mission stations offer a chance for the travelling missionary to rejuvenate. Preachers and their wives often hold dinners and meetings, delighted to encourage other English-speaking people who will heal, feed, clothe, educate, and give spiritual guidance to the suffering masses. In spring, there is the occasional garden, a haven of greenery and bright colours, in contrast to the grey landscape of fall and winter seen everywhere. Gardens are traditionally planted by peasants only for the food they can produce.

"After a few days' recovery, the journey is continued by human transport. People of all statuses are carried over the roughest, most desolate terrain imaginable in enclosed sedan chairs. This is the Over-land Limited, a human chain carrying square bales of goods as heavy as themselves or the covered chairs slung between bamboo poles with a missionary, doctor, or nurse seated in each."

The woman stepped to the side to periodically change the sketches and continue with her well-rehearsed presentation.

"Be they rich or poor, they know not our Lord, the need is so great. There are so many crowded into small houses, eking out only a basic living… begging for food. At least one child per family is expected to beg daily for a handful of grains of rice or a tiny coin that could mean the difference between surviving and starving…"

Gripping the back of the pew in front of him, Will allowed the exhilaration to build. The visiting missionaries stirred his imagination. The prospect of going forth and Christianizing the masses in Asia filled his mind and heart.

Excited twittering among those gathered broke out in places. If people couldn't go themselves, they would pay so others could. The collection would provide supplies for missionaries, their travel expenses, food, and building supplies.

He listened as Mrs. Smith described how youth groups rallied support in North America and Europe. Many like himself were growing up with the burning desire to take the message of salvation to these struggling people. His eagerness was whipped up by pictures, maps, and talk from the missionaries.

At the conclusion of the evening's presentation, Will, aged fifteen, made a vow to his creator that would become a lifelong ambition: *Lord God, you have shown me the way. I will preach to the heathens in China. I will show them the love of Jesus, tell them of heaven, warn them of hell. I will take the Holy Bible to the unsaved souls.*

Will's oldest sister, Mary Ann, glanced at a young man a few rows ahead of her to the right. She knew him to be John Wesley Kitching, enrolled at the Methodist's Victoria College of Theology.

Outside, after the presentation, Mary Ann smiled as she caught John's eye. He wove his way through the small groups of parishioners, excitedly discussing the evening's presentation.

John snapped a nod in her direction. "Good evening, Miss Sibley." He stretched his torso to meet Mary Ann eye to eye, his narrow-brimmed derby hat remaining in his hand as he spoke. "How is your year at the Model School in Orangeville progressing?"

"Very well, thank you. I have six more weeks, and then I hope to be assigned a school near home for the coming fall." Her cheeks warmed. "And you? Are you returning to Coburg in September?"

"We're going to be the last class at Coburg. Victoria College has agreed to federate with the University of Toronto so some of my time will be spent in Coburg and the remainder at Victoria College. The formal decision will be announced in November."

"Your program is quite long, I understand, and intense." Mary Ann focused on John's starched white collar and black tie.

"Only six more years to go." John brushed the bit of stubble on his chin and drew his eyebrows together. "I look forward to some of the challenges of Greek and Hebrew."

"Not Chinese, then?" Mary Ann drew her top lip over her bottom lip, suppressing a tiny grin.

John frowned. "*That* is beyond me. I don't have an ear for languages. I understand it can take up to five years to learn Mandarin."

Will stepped up to his sister, with their brother, John Cynddylan Sibley, trailing behind.

"Did you ever hear of anything so exciting? To go to China as a missionary and share the Gospel with the millions who know nothing of Jesus." Will's wide eyes shone. "What an adventure. Don't you think it would be wonderful?"

His glance flicked repeatedly to the church door.

John Kitching said, "I'm sure, but no point in expecting to meet the guests. They have to make an early train in the morning, and I don't think the Reverend Smith is too well. They must spend nearly all of their furlough making appeals to congregations and mission societies across the county."

Mary Ann studied John and Will. Though younger by six years, Will was already two inches taller than John.

"Tell him, John, how many years he'll have to study Chinese," Mary Ann said.

"I've heard the missionaries are sent out after two or three years, but learning the local dialects can take another three years. Then there is learning to read and write the thousands of characters. Many work on translating the Bible. There's news of missions in the *Acta Victoriana*, Toronto University's publication, if you're interested."

Will raised his eyebrows. "Could you please keep your old copies for me?"

"Sure, I'll send them on. They may be out of date, but they're still interesting."

"Thanks." Will stepped up into the family carriage, leaving John to talk with Mary Ann.

Others in the congregation clustered around their family buggies, juggling seats and blankets in preparation for the trip home. The stars were bright and the April evening air brisk.

"We'll see you at the Sunday school picnic in June then, will we, John?" Mary Ann's father shook the lad's hand firmly.

"Yes, sir." John nodded.

Mr. Sibley climbed up to grab the whip out of its slot and plopped onto the wooden seat beside his wife. Mary Ann opened her mouth to protest but gave a shrug instead, offered John a small smile, and gathered up her long skirts to reach the footstep and swing into place among her sisters. Her father clicked his tongue to get the horse moving. It was a long drive home to Erin.

John Wesley Kitching was somewhat taken aback when Mary Ann's father cut their conversation short. Only John Corbett Sibley's half-grin had softened the parting, suggesting that John Kitching would be welcome to see Mary Ann in good time. Yes, all in good time.

He nearly groaned aloud. Six more years before ordination. A fine occupation, and one he felt called to, but getting through some of the courses would challenge every part of his intellect.

In the meantime, as the oldest of five boys, he was expected to set a good example by pitching in on the family farm whenever possible. He wondered how many of his brothers would become farmers. His next youngest brother, George, wanted to follow his footsteps in becoming a clergyman. Their father would be pushing for sons Will, Percy, or Elias to carry on as third generation farmers at Corwin, the family homestead, south of the city of Guelph.

John's grandfather was a tough, pioneering man. The illegitimate son of Elizabeth Kitching, he had left the village of Westmoreland, Yorkshire at the turn of the nineteenth century, seeking a better life in Canada. His three half-sisters from his mother's two later marriages had all died from illness between the ages of eighteen and twenty. Still, his stepfather, John Winter, had written at least one letter that survived among his papers. In it, he'd advised that his stepson wear warm clothes and long underwear to keep from getting chilled.

His grandmother, Ann Watson Kitching, had also been born in Yorkshire before emigrating. Their seven surviving children had in-cluded three boys. John's father had taken over the family farm, and now three generations lived in the granite fieldstone homestead.

Twelve

1945

KINGSTON

On a Sunday afternoon several weeks after her last discourse, Mary waited until the other women of the household settled with tea and some crumb cake before continuing.

"My grandfather, the Reverend Harrison, was a pioneer himself, being among the first to establish small Methodist churches in communities in the West. I think my mother got her pioneering spirit from him, but she also had very strong desires to serve in foreign missions. She told me of her first encounter with missionaries…"

1890

WESTERN CANADA

Edith and her sister waited patiently in a modest wooden Methodist building in midwestern Canada for their father's appearance. He entered, holding the choir door open for the thinnest man Edith had ever seen. His cheeks were hollow, but his eyes gleamed.

Edith drew herself to alertness. What was this missionary's story? His long black robe with a high Mandarin collar was fastened down the side. His wore his long hair in a braid. What new things would she hear?

Her father led him to the pulpit facing a nearly full sanctuary. Men, women, and children were still dressed in warm coats after their journeys to the church, bundled in horse-drawn carriages.

The missionary began by quoting Mark 16:15: *"Go ye into all the world, and preach the gospel to every creature."*[6]

The guest gripped the edge of the pulpit. "In 1883, we had our first woman graduate of a Canadian medical school, from Victoria College in Toronto. This person was Dr. Augusta Stowe. In China, the situation for women is very different. Many die in childbirth. When they are as young as thirteen, some are married for a price to high-ranking officials or royalty as a second, third, or fourth wife. They are not educated, and their beauty is often reliant on the size of their feet, which are bound from early childhood. This leads to terribly painful deformity."

He wiped his brow and continued. "They need education... they need our modern understanding of cleanliness and medicine. Drs. Hart, Kilborn, and Stevenson, along with the Reverend Hartwell and their wives, are among the first groups of Canadian Methodist missionaries sent to Szechwan Province in central China. There are nearly one thousand missionaries, but only one in two thousand Chinese are baptized."

The missionary's voice raised a notch. "Many families need food..."

Edith thought of the lean years in her childhood. There had always been something to eat, though, even if just bread and beans. She had been barred from becoming a minister or preacher in Canada, but she could do mission work overseas without impediment. The Women's Missionary Movement accepted single women, so maybe—

Edith focused her attention back on their guest.

His voice dropped, adding a dramatic emphasis. "But mostly they need the love and encouragement that hope in Christ will give them." With that, he brought his message to a conclusion. "And quoting from the Toronto University paper in the missions' column: 'The Master says, "Go! We urge. Come! Come! For the soul of men. Come! For the sake of Christ. Come! For glory of God."'"[7]

The collection plate was filled with coins and even a few dollar bills—generous offerings from a struggling farming community.

⁕

The Reverend James Marcel Harrison made sure each family member used their skills and talents to provide worship services for the farming communities they served. Edith's talent was music and she was fortunate to be able to take lessons. Pumping away at the pedals and fluently performing on the ivories, she had led the singing during services from a young age.

Edith could picture hordes of people in the streets waiting to soak up the Gospel, reaching out for the hand of Jesus, their Lord and Saviour. Her dark eyes sparked with images of spicy foods, Oriental silk gowns, and petite women, their black hair twisted high and decorated with flowers and jewels. Thrilling.

She listened intently to the missionary's talk, and gradually a sense of unease tamped down her excitement. It sounded like hard work and there was no guarantee everyone would want to be saved, even among the thousands upon thousands of poor, louse-riddled, diseased, and starving. There would be conflict with pagan gods, wealthy foreigners dealing in opium, and men who chose to have many wives. There apparently were warlords who held poor farmers ransom to pay for their soldiers or their crops, and homes would be destroyed and their families hunted down and killed. Drought often brought despair. Edith would have to learn more.

1945
KINGSTON

Two weeks before the Christmas break, Mary gathered a collection of gifts and began packing a suitcase.

Claire leaned on the doorframe, watching. "I guess I should think about packing up to head east to the family. My, you're organized."

Mary smiled. "I remember my mother packing two *months* before furlough began. We always had so many gifts and trinkets and could only bring so much with us. It was harder on the return trip to China, knowing there were so many needs. Most returning missionaries paid extra cartage, so they could bring along those items unavailable in China."

"Where will you be going for Christmas?" Claire asked, arms crossed.

"Father and Vida have asked me to go to the parsonage in Ancaster where they're living."

"Is he still working?"

"Oh, yes. Preaching is his life's mission. I can't see him stopping much before seventy-five, unless ill health prevents him."

Mary recalled the many Christmas holidays she had spent staying with her Aunt Mary and Uncle John Kitching, and of course her cousin John. He'd been like a brother, making her laugh and forget the constant nugget of loneliness in her stomach. Once her parents had returned to China, she'd spent many holidays with them, their warmth and welcome helping to overcome her feeling of abandonment.

The Kitchings' home changed location regularly since the Methodist conference moved their ministers often, but the family's furnishings accompanied them. It warmed Mary to see framed family photographs and decorative gifts from her parents displayed prominently.

"Aunt Mary Ann believed I should know all about the family history, and even Uncle John chimed in once in a while, but cousin John... all he did was make me laugh, imitating the old Scottish aunties in perfected turns of phrases and gestures with a thick Scots' accent. Aunt Mary Ann would follow me as I poked around, waiting for my questions..."

Thirteen

1920

CAYUGA, ONTARIO

A large, beautifully framed photo hung in the hallway of the manse in Cayuga.

"When was this picture taken, Aunt Mary?" fifteen-year-old Mary asked during her holiday visit. She pointed to the older of the two boys. "Is this my father?"

Her aunt stepped up beside Mary and placed an arm around her waist. "It is, and he would have been about your age at the time." Aunt Mary Ann sighed. "I suppose you must miss them very much."

Mary turned and hugged her aunt, pulling her wide mouth into a beaming smile. "All of you make me feel so much a part of the family. We were never able to celebrate Christmas or holidays so lavishly in China as we do in Canada."

"I suppose you think we are extravagant here, do you?"

Mary tipped her head in thought. "No. Not really. Of course, there is so much bounty in North America and heaps of food, but it's family that makes my heart satisfied. Not that there weren't celebrations in China, of course."

She recalled the New Year's celebrations, the noisy firecrackers, the shiny fabric in a variety of colours worn by those who could afford it. The others simply enjoyed the sights and sounds of the masses in crowded streets.

Arm snuggly hugging Mary, her aunt explained, "I insisted on a family photo with all my siblings the day of our wedding. Photos were a priority in both the Sibley and Kitching families. Fortunately, we could afford it at the time."

Mary frowned. "Where were your parents, Aunt Mary Ann?"

"Very sadly, my mother died in 1893, but Margaret and I were able to keep the household running adequately with the help of relatives. Then, a year later, our Aunt Mary Hewgil came to our house with the terrible news that our father, your grandfather, had been killed in a carriage accident."

"That must have been terrible for you."

Mary Ann pursed her lips and nodded. "It was. I grew up very quickly, but we had always been a very close family, and my sister Margaret tucked right in helping with the younger ones. Your father was away at Victoria College by then, so the train ride home was an easy distance.

"At least my parents are alive and I know I'll see them again in a few years." Mary patted her aunt's hand.

Her uncle came up behind them to gaze at the photo. "Life often requires painful separations…"

1895

BRUCE AND GREY COUNTIES

The Reverend John Wesley Kitching's first appointment after completing his studies was in Tobermory, the most northern part of the Bruce Peninsula. Far from his fiancée, family, and school, he used the time to study.

The small Methodist church was back in the woods. Unlike St. Edmund's Anglican Church, which overlooked Big Tub Harbour with a spectacular view, this was an ordinary treed lot with a few houses nearby, a block from the meagre town centre and fishing vessels. It was only a year-long assignment, although he had been assured of a position in Grey County afterward.

John's parents had attended the service of his ordination in Tobermory, but his fiancée Mary Ann taught school and hadn't been able to come. A few classmates and their families had also joined in.

On that day, everyone entered with solemnity, the floor-length black taffeta skirts of the women rustling beneath muted speech as people took their places.

Seated on a narrow, wooden pew, John opened the small, leatherbound Holy Bible. From the open door, a light breeze cooled the air at the back of the church. He read the fine cursive writing:

> Presented to John W. Kitching on the Occasion of his
> Ordination to the Ministry of The Methodist Church by
> the Hamilton Conference. Wm Kettlewell, President;
> Saul Sellery, Secretary. Paris, Ont. June 23rd, 1895.

Finally, in the summer of 1896, weeks before his wedding, John was received fully into the Methodist church, having completed his final examinations. He arranged to rent a rather large house in the furniture-making small town of Durham.

Although Queen Street Methodist Church was right in town, his charges were out in the country: Varney and Hampton. Rail transportation ran through Varney and Durham, if he needed it. All had been arranged so Mary Ann's three youngest sisters could be registered at schools in town, the younger two at elementary school and Helen at the Durham High School.

John's Varney charges were busy and growing farm communities, with many opportunities for Mary Ann to assist in the young people's programs and encourage the Women's Missionary Society to be effective.

The Reverend J.W. Kitching arrived in Guelph by train on September 23 and was met by his brother-in-law to be, Will Sibley, for the short ride to the church in Erin where the wedding would take place.

1896
ERIN, ONTARIO

Mary Ann called all her siblings together into their uncle's parlour after the ceremony and luncheon. She had insisted on a photograph remarking the day.

"You stand in the back row, here beside me, Will. My goodness, aren't you tall. And handsome too. Any special girls yet?" Mary Ann jested, knowing Will had no time for girls with his studies.

Trying to keep the mood lighter than she felt, she made a fuss of her three youngest sisters all dressed in white. "You look lovely, my dears."

Florence had not smiled once before or since the ceremony. Too young to marry or be on her own, she was unhappy with the forced separation from her sisters.

"It's fine for you to be happy, Mary Ann," Florence said. "You and John deserve to be happy. And you'll have Helen, Eunice, and Ethel with you in Durham. You don't have to go and live with Uncle Thomas and Aunt Florence. The Reverend Thomas McLachlan." She swirled her tongue around the name, imitating that side of the family's Scottish accent. "All those stories from Great-Uncle Charles about the duel, and Malcolm and Douglas McLachlan on horses."

Florence slouched in her designated chair and crossed her arms with a pout.

"You'll have our brother John with you for another year, and your cousin, baby Gladys, to help look after. Besides, you have more schooling to finish."

There wasn't much choice now that the aging aunts and uncles were unable to keep all the family together.

Mary Ann had waited patiently for today and wouldn't let it spoil the photo. Her black lace collar scratched at the neck, but the effect of its appearance was rather pleasant, rolling up and over itself into two fine points. She adjusted her Grandmother Faed's pearl brooch and ran her fingers over the gold cross on a chain John had given her as a wedding present. He had agreed that the black satin dress with billowing puffed sleeves was very suitable for a clergyman's wife's wedding dress.

She took her place behind her new husband, who sat on a plain wooden chair; the photographer asked them to hold still... and the picture was done.

If only our parents had been here, we might have smiled, even a little.

Reverend John told his wife of less than two years that he was being moved to Oxenden, up the Bruce Peninsula, just outside of Wiarton.

"It's not so far away," he explained. "I mean, as a Methodist minister, I expect to be moved every two years." A regular stage service could transport him south for his Mondays off and return him to a rooming house where he would board weekly. "It will mean you'll have the running of the house with the three girls, but Helen is near graduating."

"Yes, I suppose it's for the best." Mary Ann placed a plate of egg sandwiches on the wooden kitchen table and sat down to join her husband for lunch. "She really does want to attend Model School in Orangeville as I did and become a teacher. She says she's definitely not cut out for nursing, and I insist they all get an education. It was always important in our family and, well, you never know what may happen."

John unfolded his linen serviette to drape across his lap. "Yes, Mary Ann. We never know what may happen, and we have to pray that the Lord will prepare us for whatever hardships befall us." John took his wife's hand in his and stroked it. "We'll have our own little family someday."

Mary Ann nodded, still serious. "Yes, we can hope, but for now we just have to make the best home possible for the girls. Oh," she said, brightening, "I received a letter from Will with news that our brother John is enrolling in the divinity program at Victoria. He decided medicine wasn't for him and that a calling to serve as a clergyman has resonated with him at last. Will is so pleased."

John nodded. "I think Will has been a fine influence on young John."

Fourteen

1945

Kingston

Even the Wilder sisters were anticipating the upcoming Christmas celebrations. The household had agreed that having a special luncheon on Saturday, December 15 would be a good occasion on which to exchange small gifts with each other. Another sister of Emma and Charlotte Wilder would be visiting while the others were away with their own families. There was much to do.

"Mary, can you take the sandwiches into the dining room? I'll bring the tea," Nita directed. "Claire, have you finished the centrepiece and lit the candles yet?"

"We're all set in here, Nita. Dessert plates and forks are on the sideboard," Claire said.

After Charlotte blessed the food, the six women and David ate and talked in comfortable companionship, having now lived together for several months.

Emma said, "Have you booked your train ticket to Toronto for next week, Mary? I'm sure it will be very crowded and busy."

"I have, Miss Wilder, and paid for a first-class seat just to be sure. Claire, have you booked yours?"

"Yes, two weeks ago. Mother insisted she know well ahead of time when I would arrive in Halifax. I'll meet my sister in Montreal and we'll travel together from there."

Nita tried to draw her son into her own anticipation. "We're looking forward to the first Christmas with my in-laws, aren't we, David?"

David tipped his head. "They're my grandparents, right? Will I get any toys, do you think?"

Nita frowned. "David, we mustn't expect anything. I've explained how difficult toys are to find. You *need* winter clothes."

David slumped and munched on his pickle.

Mary hid a grin. They all knew what David would be getting: a hand-knitted toque and scarf from his Aunt Mable, a hand-knitted vest and sweater from the Wilder sisters, and boots ordered from the Eaton's catalogue from Mary and Claire.

After the luncheon was cleared away and everyone sat around the small table, the top of a cedar tree sitting upon it, decorated in tinsel and glass bulbs, they began their exchange of homemade gifts. Only David received a purchased gift besides his boots.

David let out a whoop when he tore off the wrapper of a small model plane. He swooped in and out of the rooms, giddy from all the special sweets. He flew his plane up and down the stairs until finally his mother stopped him.

"David. Please get your outdoor clothes on and go outside. You're making it difficult for Miss Wilder and me in the kitchen. Stay in the back yard."

Nostalgia plagued Mary after the luncheon, and the debris of the gift exchange had been cleared. "The Christmas holiday always kindles memories of staying with my Aunt and Uncle Kitching."

Mable settled with another cup of tea. "Will you tell us more of your story, Mary? It must have been hard for you after the passing of your mother."

"It was, I admit. Aunt Mary Ann never fussed but showed a great deal of understanding and sympathy for me after my mother's death. I felt deep comfort while staying with the family. Perhaps losing her own parents at a young age accounted for my aunt's empathy. And my cousin John's humour always eased moments of tension or brought a laugh.

"It took my father ten months to return to Canada, and I grievously mourned alone until March of 1927 when he finally made his way to Ontario. After the initial shared tears, my father grew less tolerant of displays of sadness, reminding me frequently that we would meet again in heaven."

She had clung to this hope and allowed it to fortify her in every endeavour.

"I try recalling snippets from my childhood, from our few adventures during the holidays to attending the boarding school in Chengtu for missionary children," Mary went on. "A few weeks each year, most missionaries escaped the heat by retreating to Mount Omi, where the rough structures had forced a simple lifestyle. At least we were away from routine and in fresher, cooler air where we could breathe freely. I had friends among the other missionaries' children. Some friendships lasted even through university. A large proportion of 'mish' kids ended up at the Methodist Victoria College at the University of Toronto.

"I sought to connect with my parents as often as possible through the mail. Their replies would arrive in bunches, and sometimes I wondered whether they even received all my letters. Mother tried to reply once a month, usually with a postscript from my father attached, but it never seemed enough to fill the void of not having parents nearby. I took to asking Mother more questions about her personal life…"

1921

JUNGHSIEN

Edith sat at the dark wooden desk with ink and paper to write to her daughter. It seemed a small thing to reply to all her questions. She missed her daughter with an acute sense of loss. She missed her very presence, and it took every bit of her love for the Lord to keep this sadness out of the letters. She wrote,

> You've asked about our very first trip up the Yangtze on our way to the Inland China Mission. It was a strenuous journey, partly because of the constant movement of people and boats, as well as river smells. You remember what that was like, I have no doubt, Mary.
>
> One remarkable thing happened when we reached the city of Chinkiang. The steamer pulled up beside the dock where for several hours traders would be exchanging goods and gathering more supplies for the remainder of the trip upriver...

1907

YANGTZE RIVER, CHINA

Edith leaned on a railing with three of the other wives who remained onboard. The men had chosen to get off and explore, investigating the local American and British missions. A woman in a light-coloured cotton dress with a wide-brimmed hat came tripping down a path and beckoned to the missionaries' wives lined at the portside railing.

"Please, ladies. Come up to my home for tea. I'm Carie Sydenstricker. My husband is the Reverend Andrew Sydenstricker. Won't you come ashore for a cup of tea in my garden?"

"That would be lovely, wouldn't it, ladies?" Gertrude Jolliffe waved them forward.

Then Carie spoke to the captain's assistant, asking in fluent Chinese to sound the horn to give them a twenty-minute warning so the women could return in time to reboard.

Edith looked at Muriel Bowles, Mrs. Robertson, and Charlotte Holmes before following along, as it appeared Gertrude knew Mrs.

Sydenstricker. They accessed the path up the hill from a set of stone steps and, single file, reached the top. They headed farther away from the shore along another path until the air freshened and the scent of flowers reached them. Edith breathed deeply and smiled. She didn't feel so nauseated. She *could* smile.

"You have an oasis here, Mrs. Sydenstricker," Charlotte said.

"Oh, please, call me Carie. Yes, I have. It's taken a great deal of work digging up roots and planting seeds whenever possible. Everything eventually grows, and I do not know why more effort isn't taken to plant a little colour. It heals me, gardening." She bent to smell the beautiful bloom of a white rose.

"You do have amazing flowers," Mrs. Robertson said. "I suppose they remind you of home in America?"

Carie smiled a sad little smile, pointing to a flourishing bush. "This comes from the same white rose stock as the one I planted on the grave in Shanghai."

Edith exchanged a look with the others but had no idea what to say. What grave?

Carie waved forward a Chinese woman carrying a tray of teacups and cookies. "This is my dear companion, nanny, and helper, Wang Amah."

Edith nodded to Wang Amah when the woman offered more tea. "It's wonderful and so gracious of you to come down to the dock and invite us to share it." She felt well enough now that the small cookies appealed to her. The first tasted so delicious that she accepted a second.

"Do you and your husband have children, Carie?" Gertrude asked.

Carie sat on a low stool and hugged her knees. She tilted her chin upward. "Yes. We have seven children."

Edith's eyebrows arched in admiration for a moment.

"Yes, three are in America attending school, and three are buried in Shanghai where foreigners are buried." Carie pointed across the river. "When my youngest died of diphtheria, we laid him to rest over on that hillside. You can almost see it from here. That grave is where the other white rose blooms and thrives." She dropped her shaking hand into her lap, her shoulders sagging. "I haven't had the same energy since."

"Disease is a terrible scourge in this country," said Muriel.

"Yes, and cleanliness undervalued. But never mind. We have avoided a very wet rainy season this year and the river is calm right now, so your journey upstream should be smooth." Carie straightened her back and offered a bright smile.

"Are the inland Chinese people very different from those in the city?" Edith asked.

Carie nodded in the direction of Wang Amah. "Few are so very loving and loyal to foreigners. Many hate Westerners and blame us for drought, war, disease, and famine. The others are simply trying to survive."

"Are you never afraid then?" Charlotte's eyes were wide.

"Allow me to tell you a story[8] of the time my husband was sent to a village on the Grand Canal. There had been a severe drought that summer. The people were starving and blamed us foreigners. Andrew was off on one of his village circuits, and one evening I heard the locals discussing how they would gather and kill me and the children that very night."

"You understood the local dialect?" Edith asked.

"Oh, yes. I understood their intentions very well. I couldn't allow that, so I had Wang Amah make pots and pots of tea and bring out all the little cakes she could find. I dressed the children, who had been asleep for hours, and sat them in the parlour. When I overheard the villagers gathering rowdily at the gate, I opened the door and invited them in." Carie and Wang Amah exchanged looks, then Carie laughed. "It would have been rude, you see, not to come in when invited. We hurried to serve tea. I apologized for not having chairs for them all. The children sat on the floor playing with their Western toys, and soon the adults found this so interesting that they began to drink tea and two of them played with the baby."

Edith exclaimed, "Oh, how brave a woman you are, Mrs. Sydenstricker."

"If only I were so brave when little Clyde was ill." Carie's head bowed in sorrow.

＊

When the ship's whistle blew, Ethel jumped up and the others quickly followed, thanking Carie for such a charming albeit poignant break.

Edith led the other three on their hurried trip down the steep slopes, her long brown skirts swishing about her ankles. Thank goodness her dress didn't drag in the dust! Will had considered it somewhat risqué for her outfits to be at the top of her heel rather than the bottom.

"It's just not practical, Will," she had told him. "We shall be walking a great deal, I suspect, and you know what's in these streets."

The sailors had unwound the ropes, ready to push off. Edith could feel the bounce of the gangplank as she hurried onboard, and they were on their way.

Seeing her husband, Edith waved. "Will, there you are."

"Yes, here I am. And here you are, looking like a new woman. Your cheeks are positively blooming."

"Oh, Will." Edith could feel tears threatening to spill. "I have so much to tell you."

＊

After two days, the steamer chugged into Hankou. Across the river, the bustling city of Wuchang quivered with the activity of innumerable workers.

Dr. Smith remarked, "Too bad the famous Yellow Crane Tower was destroyed in a fire twenty years ago. But there is the famous Guiyaun Buddhist temple, if anyone is curious."

The new missionaries examined with interest the mile-long, fifty-foot high stone wall along the waterfront.

"Is the city as attractive as this retaining wall?" asked Edith.

"Yes. There are English, Russian, German, French, Japanese, *and* Belgian foreign concessions," the doctor informed them. "And walkways along the waterfront are safe. Plenty of activities for traders here."

As the steamer made another sharp swing with the river, turning northwest, the waters churned and boiled.

"Erosion must be very bad along this river, don't you think, Will?" Edith again felt somewhat nauseated and tried to keep her mind on the geography. "Is this the area where the famous cliffs are?"

"Yes. We'll soon be approaching them. Apparently, near a city called Ichang, they are spectacular. Rolling hills come to the water's edge between what seem to be a series of mountains and valleys lying perpendicular to the river."

The wind carried the sweet chiming of small bells from the temples.

To Edith, the two-week trip felt endless. The sights were interesting, but in places she found the dark, craggy rock formations oppressive, and the obvious state of polygamy among the wealthy Chinese on board, disturbing.

1921

JUNGHSIEN

Edith dipped her pen into the inkpot. She wanted to finish her story in her letter to Mary, hoping to answer Mary's questions.

> We finally disembarked at Chungking. Already I could
> hear the difference in dialect. Probably not yet the *tuhua*,
> or earth speak of the rough rural Szechuanese dialect
> spoken farther north, but still more coarse than what we

used in the city. They spoke so quickly, I despaired of ever understanding the locals.

Here, two other missionary families met us, preparing to board for the trip back down the river to begin their furlough. The Sparlings and Endicotts had spent six years with the Inland Mission and would return to Szechwan after a year in Canada. It was a brief encounter, though we would get to know them in the future. Every one of us had reached the point of exhaustion from travelling.

Your father and I joined the Overland Limited, which provided sedan chairs for human passengers. Petite Chinese women hoisted bundles as large as themselves to carry on their backs, animals were herded into line, and our entire troop surged forward at a steady pace.

Inside the curtained box, I had to grip the lightly padded seat tightly, praying my insides wouldn't spill out. I attempted to study the countryside, but the jostling only made me feel more ill. I tried leaning back and closing my eyes, thinking of the new tune I had heard a few weeks ago: "From farthest east to farthest west, where human feet have trod, by the voice of many messengers, goes forth the voice of God."[9] It seems a very good tune. I wondered how meaningful to the Chinese many of our hymns from the West would be.

Fifteen

1907

CHENGTU, SZECHWAN, CHINA

Through the fall, Will and Edith persisted with their intensive language training at the mission in Chengtu. Will continued to read, keeping up to date with what was happening at home in Canada, while Edith became involved with the Baby Welfare Clinic and Sunday afternoon gatherings for Chinese women. The foreign men were not allowed to associate in any way with the Chinese women, but the missionaries' wives could. They served Chinese tea and the women shared their difficulties, exchanging advice and sympathy. Edith returned to their rooms in the Chengtu mission house, full of enthusiasm.

"The babies are so adorable, and the clinic is teaching me more about how to care for an infant here," Edith remarked to her husband. "We women have much in common, Will. We may not be preachers, but we can still evangelize the Chinese women, who need so much uplifting. They are valued less than beasts of burden in many cases. I was used to earthen floors in Western Canada, but some of the mud huts and earthen floors have been passed down generation to generation for hundreds of years with no sign of improvements."

Edith gazed into the distance, then quickly shook her head to bring herself back to the moment.

"Will, when you're at the annual meeting, can you ask if anyone is writing hymns for the Chinese? I don't mean just a translation into Chinese but hymns they will understand. Are there any Chinese Christians writing hymns in Shanghai or Foochow? I'd like more appropriate ones, especially for the adults."

He agreed to ask around, privately. Some scholars weren't keen on integrating the Bible with Chinese culture. But what did Hebrew, Greek, or Latin mean to them? Especially if they couldn't feed their family? It was a dilemma, for sure.

＊

After Edith left with Mrs. Smith for the afternoon Baby Welfare Clinic, Will settled to focus on his reading of an old November 1901 edition of *Acta Victoriana*. There were always interesting perspectives in the Missions and Religious columns.

In his address at the annual missionary conference at Victoria University, the Reverend V.C. Hart had explained that in the 1890s he'd undertaken the task of bringing ink and a printing press from Chicago all the way to Kaiting. After purchasing Chinese type for setting into the press in Shanghai, he'd had difficulties packing the press for shipping up the Yangtze River.

Since then, a mind-boggling number of tracts, Gospels, and New Testaments had been printed. The surprising thing now was how the press had been expanded to print scientific documents, which paid for the cost of printing the religious material.

Reverend Hart had frequently trained Chinese workers and added presses. He'd asked for the presses to be moved to Chengtu, the capital of Szechwan and a point where easier distribution could be made for the Western Methodist's missions.[10]

Will understood Hart's emotional plea for support. Any little thing to make the gigantic task of sharing the Word easier or more efficient helped. He so looked forward to the next week's council meeting in Chengtu, and meeting up with old friends to see how they were getting along.

He was among the more newly arrived and hadn't yet worked in an outstation, although he had gone on several rounds in the company of George Hartwell. He'd also met with some Presbyterians from Canada and Disciples of Christ from Texas. Having so many different denominations caused the Asians such confusion.

Surely there is only one Triune God, one Son, working through the Holy Spirit, he thought. *Why do we humans make it so complicated?*

Will left for the meeting room of the mission right after a meal of rice, cabbage, and a sliver of pork, nicely flavoured with spices still mysterious to him. Edith, now in her fifth month of pregnancy, had just raised her feet to rest for the evening when he went out.

He kicked his long black robe slightly sideways, as he'd been shown, in order not to trip down the steps of the residence. The long garment required for all teaching and preaching staff still felt unfamiliar to Will.

A Chinese woman carrying a baby stood in the centre of the compound looking around.

Will kept his distance, but asked, "Are you looking for the Baby Welfare Clinic?"

The woman bobbed her head and Will pointed to the steps leading to the clinic. She bowed. Will bowed. She bowed again. Will bobbed from the shoulders and moved in the direction of the meeting room. He wasn't sure how the system worked, but it seemed men didn't bow as often to women as women bowed to men.

He removed his long teaching garment and hung it on a hook, one of many already in use with the other twenty men's clothing. He entered the meeting room and greeted his colleagues, some having travelled days to attend this gathering. Several of the Vic Eight greeted him enthusiastically. It was always a pleasure to see a friendly face, and renewing friendships offered support.

Tension increased during the ensuing discussions, even about creating a dictionary, as some ministers tried to persuade the others of arranging a Chinese character dictionary alphabetically.

The chairman of the meeting, the Very Reverend James Endicott folded his hands on the table in front of himself. "I ask you, Dr. Smith, how else can new recruits, and indeed all of us who are searching out a word, find the character we are looking for?"

Dr. Smith wiped his forehead of perspiration with a white handkerchief. "But words are built by adding to the root of a character, and then by adding more. We should organize a dictionary by the root characters."

Someone Will didn't recognize raised his hand to speak. "Has anyone seen a copy of the latest translation in Chinese from the Episcopalians, and are there any available for purchase?"

"We have a printing press," Hart replied. "We could be ready to go ahead with at least the New Testament…"

"Have we any copies of Chinese hymnbooks?" asked Will.

Smith flipped his greying pigtail to the side. "Doris Yu has been working on one. I'm not sure if all the hymns would be appropriate. Do we know what doctrines she is preaching?"

There were so many considerations to make in distributing books and hymns alone.

Their decision to try to discourage the buying and selling of prayers written on red paper remained firm. The Buddhists and Taoists had a thriving business creating these for mourners and others who wanted to give respect to the small local gods tucked away in the corners of every town and village. Some Chinese, new to the faith, had been asking the ministers for them.

It is the last on the agenda, but not the least important, thought Will.

In the end, the meeting was considered a success, giving them further direction as to where missionaries would reside for the next two years, their duties, and new construction or acquisition of buildings.

The locals were most reluctant to rent or sell to the missions, though by law only the missionaries, of all the Westerners, were allowed to purchase land and build. No such privileges were extended to Western businesses or private individuals, unless they were in designated city concessions.

Endicott announced, "We're lining up outside for a photograph, everyone. Just your suits, no gowns. This is for the folks back home."

The photographer lined everyone up in front of the mission building. Will stood in the back row, his dark wavy hair parted more to the centre than when he had left Toronto. He was one of twenty-one men in Western suits, not a Chinese man among them.

One evening, Will and Edith took a stroll, walking the top of the city wall surrounding Chengtu. Wide enough for carriages travelling in two directions, it provided a broad view of the rolling hills rising in the west and fertile plains of the expansive valley in the east. From the inner parapets, a panorama of the city's ancient and modern buildings spread before them.

"Look at those magnificent gates, layers upon layers, not just a straight tower. How many gates are there?" Edith asked.

"Four gates in the wall, one in each direction. It's a way of keeping the city safe from attacking rebels as well as periodic flooding. They can easily close and lock the gates every evening."

"I love the way the corners sweep up so gracefully."

"Not all modern buildings follow the traditional rooflines, but I see many that do," he replied. "I believe that's the printing press. Hart must have done some substantial fundraising to erect a two-story building of that size."

"Who lives in those official-looking buildings?" Edith asked, pointing to a cluster of impressive edifices surrounded by walled grounds.

"That will be the viceroy's estate.

"Is that why I detect a less nasty odour, and no open sewer ditches running the streets?"

Will grinned. "Yes, probably, but the viceroy has been thoroughly modernizing Chengtu. They collect the refuse and build sewers to keep the streets cleaned up. Do you realize there are no beggars in this city? Do you know why?"

Edith smiled up at Will. "I suppose you will tell me."

Will nodded, a serious look on his face. "One night they rounded up all the beggars and took them to a reformatory where they were given baths, shaved, put into a clean uniform, and fed. Then they were trained to do jobs and put to work. Other cities should consider it."

People, carts, and carriers plodded through the narrow streets below them. "What's that tall brick structure?" Edith said.

"The water supply. It holds the city's clean water and is filled by hand. Probably a job for some of the former beggars."

Will took Edith's hand to lead her along the stone walkway. "Let's cross the road to see where the new rail line to Hankow will be built."

Edith stayed close to Will as they crossed the busy road running along the top of the wall. Never a shortage of people, all of them moving somewhere, filling any open space between the sedan chairs and fruit sellers. "A train would be so much faster than the route we took."

1946
KINGSTON

Mounds of the winter's snow refused to melt during the final week in March. Mary had the new season of the musical society to assist with, student reports were coming due, and she needed to catch up with correspondence. However, she wouldn't turn down an invitation to speak about missions to China.

"Welcome, Miss Sibley. What can you tell us about your life in China when you were young?" asked Mrs. Corbett, the buxom chair of the Chalmers United Church Women who had introduced Mary. A navy-flowered hat identically matched her navy suit, contrasting with her pale skin and rosy cheeks.

Mary ran her gloved hands down the side of her pencil-straight skirt and grasped the podium. She welcomed this opportunity.

Since Mao's lockdown in China, the country had been closed to most missionaries and almost all Western correspondence. Rumours had abounded ever since.

"Sometimes my nanny would take me into the city to shop," Mary began. "She did the cooking for us as well. My mother spent as much time with me as she could, but one time when I was about three and wanted to stay with her, I was not allowed. I remember being a little afraid because my mother hadn't been well. My nanny, Ming Lin, had given me a sweet to suck on and bid that I follow her out into the street. She used a mixture of signs and Chinese, as I couldn't always understand her dialect..."

1911
PENGHSIEN, SZECHWAN, CHINA

Ming Lin grabbed my hand as we moved toward the busy part of town. "Shopping. We go to the market and buy food. Hurry."

Mary didn't like to hurry. There were too many sounds and sights to take in. She liked the bright colours and shiny black material. She wanted a dress like Ming Lin's with the little collar.

Tiny bells tinkled in the distance. Mary turned in every direction to find where the sound came from. She followed Ming Lin through the crowds that shifted in many directions. Displays outside the shops drew her attention, but her nanny pulled her along the route she wanted Mary to go.

A wrinkled and bent woman lurched toward Mary as they approached a narrow side street. Ming Lin clicked her tongue in warning to the woman.

There, too, was the man who cut hair, Mary noticed. He carried his shears with him and stopped in the midst of everyone to shave an old man's forehead. They both stood during the process.

She bent down, trying to scoop up some of the black trimmings.

Ming Lin yanked her hand. "No. Dirty. Don't touch."

Tears formed and Mary cried. She wanted to feel the black hair. Her own hair had no colour, though her mother said it was gold. It didn't look like any gold she had ever seen. Sometimes Ming Lin would let her touch her black hair, but not often.

She wanted to sit, but she knew the street was no place to sit down. It even smelled bad.

Chains of small firecrackers crackled and snapped along the ground, sizzling their way toward Mary. She pressed close to Ming Lin.

"Oh. A bride and groom are coming." Ming Lin picked Mary up and stood to the side of the narrow street against a wall. "Look, Mary. See the pretty bride. Firecrackers for them."

Mary covered her ears with her hands, grimacing at the loud, surprising bangs. She did turn her head to look, though. The bride's painted red lips were stark against her pale, powdered face, and decorations dangled from the young woman's hair piled high on her head. Her red outfit was colourful and bright. Mary couldn't help but follow with her eyes, still clutching her ears.

"Come," said Ming Lin. "We need fish and cabbage. I will show you how to pick a fresh-caught fish, no?"

Mary's back prickled with heat and she wanted to stop and scratch, but Ming Lin carried on, half-dragging her. She tried to point out the man with the wheelbarrow. They could ride on that. It had a back and she could sit in Ming Lin's lap. Her mommy was very big and fat these days and didn't want to carry her around.

"I want to go home, Ming Lin. Please take me home for a nap. I'm hot and… and grumpy."

"Ha. Grumpy. Where did you hear that word? No nap today. We need to shop. I *maybe* will buy you a treat. Come, move away from those wooden boxes."

Mary followed, trying to keep up. She didn't like the hissing sounds some of the men made watching her.

"There goes a white baby devil," a man chortled.

Mary wanted to cry. "Ming Lin. I want to go home. Please."

The caregiver stepped with Mary to the side of the street. "We are not going home. Miss Sibley is busy. She is very busy this afternoon." She reached into a pocket. "Here. You have one more sweet, and I buy you another one when we finish."

Mary could hardly carry herself forward, but Ming Lin's arms were full of bundles. Mary had to follow, or she would be lost.

"You are a very good girl. Very strong. Here is a package for you to carry, then we will hire a chair."

Mary tucked the package Ming Lin handed her under her arm and pouted. Her lip quivered, but she grasped a fold of Ming Lin's dress and forced herself to drag along behind.

They stopped. Mary's head drooped, and her eyelids closed. She still clung to Ming Lin's dress and held the package, but she was startled awake when the man in front of her flicked her chin up.

"She's asleep on her feet," he said.

"I know, and so many afternoons she won't close her eyes, even with many songs." Ming Lin continued speaking to the man, too quietly for Mary to hear or understand.

Oh, the street was so noisy. Couldn't they just go home?

"Ming Lin," Mary said. "I want a mooncake. Please get me one."

"Mooncake for Autumn festival. Not now for a crying girl. You hush and we reach your home soon."

⁂

When Mary did arrive home in a rickshaw with Ming Lin and the bundles, the house was very quiet. Usually there was some activity going on, but today all was still.

Mary perked up as they entered the gate and she ran ahead up the stairs. One foot, other foot. One foot, other foot. At the top, she turned, still grasping the single, paper-bound package, and waited for Ming Lin to catch up.

"Mommy!"

The quiet unsettled her and Mary was scared when no one answered. *What's wrong?*

Ming Lin dropped her bundles. "Shush. Shush, child. Your mother is busy. Come and have your nap."

The woman picked Mary up, but now Mary was contrary to having a nap and wiggled from her caregiver's grasp. She scooted away toward her mother and father's room and reached for the handle. The brass knob turned easily and Mary dashed inside.

"Ah," said the girl's mother, startled by the intrusion. "Mary. I'm sorry. I'm not well."

Mary stood at the side of her mother's bed, staring at her red eyes. What was happening?

"I'm sorry, Miss Sibley," said Ming Lin. "She ran away from me. I will take her now for her nap."

Edith stroked the top of her daughter's hair. "Yes. Please go with Ming Lin. You can see me after your dinner. Be a good girl, now."

Mary puckered her face, ready to cry, but her mother's sad eyes prevented her. Her shoulders drooped and she allowed Ming Lin to take her to her room, where she would lie on her bed. But she wouldn't close her eyes. No, she would stay awake until dinner.

※

Mary stirred in her father's arms. Was this a new day? Why were they hurrying in the streets? "Where are we going, Daddy? Why are we bringing so many bags?"

"Shush, Mary. Go back to sleep. We are nearly there."

"Where, Daddy? Why are all these people rushing?" Carts and rickshaws pulled piles of baggage and people. The noise frightened her. Why was she smelling smoke?

Mary could see the tall, thick walls of a compound. Many of the adults carried things, and children were crying. She started to sniffle and hung on tightly to her father. Her mother was having trouble keeping up and Mary tried reaching out to her.

"We must get you safely inside, Mary. There are troubled and angry people out and about. Your mother is following us. Don't be afraid."

They entered the compound gates. Someone called, "Refugees this way. Hurry."

Sixteen

1946
KINGSTON

Nita and the two Wilder sisters settled in for an afternoon tea and another installment of Mary's narrative. However, Claire was to be at a girls' basketball tournament at the university and had a meeting with the Athletic Council afterward. She had taken a large briefcase and asked the others to wish her luck.

"She'll do just fine. I'm sure the men will respect such a *tour de force*," Mable said, smiling to herself after their friend departed.

"But that's the problem," Mary said. "They are all men, and the two student representatives are boys! What happened to the girls' representation?"

"Oh, it'll come. After all, we got the vote in 1926, didn't we?" The irony dripped from Mable's voice as so much honey from a productive hive's honeycomb. "Actually, women weren't considered persons in *la belle province* until 1940. Our aunt voted in a provincial election for the first time in August of '44."

"Yes, Mable." Nita elbowed Mable lightly in the arm. "We know how you feel about male dominance. So tell us, Mary. Did you get to come back to Canada for visits? What about your parents—did they take holidays?"

"Most summers they went high up into the mountains to Mount Omi and Cave Mountain. Each denomination developed their own summer camp where we cooked outdoors and lived in rough huts. The temperatures were so much more tolerable," Mary explained. "The missionaries were granted a one-year leave called furlough every six or seven years. The voyage home to Canada took weeks, if not months."

Nita started pouring the tea for the others. "I suppose it's a long boat ride."

Mary smiled. "Actually, the trip across the Pacific Ocean was the fastest part of the journey. The cart rides, the train, the riverboat travel took longer. The trip home to Ontario headed west around India, through the Suez Canal and the Mediterranean, then around to England. The journey was wasted on me as a three-year-old. And there was the waiting. During several periods it was deemed too dangerous to travel in China and permission had to be granted to sail by the British navy and the Home Office in North America. Some left anyway, chancing attacks by gangs of thieves and rogue bands of militia."

She accepted a cup of the tea without adding anything to the steaming liquid.

"At home, of course, we toured around the countryside raising funds," she continued. "On first coming to Canada, I was very disappointed not to have my father with us for long periods of time, as I couldn't understand why he had to be away from us at all..."

1912

Furlough in Canada and Chicago, Illinois

Days before they were to leave for their furlough, Will informed Edith of his acceptance to the doctoral program at the University of Chicago, Illinois. He grasped his wife's upper arms and lowered his head to seek her downcast eyes. It was the end of a long, busy day at the mission and it had been the first chance to discuss the situation.

"I know it's a sacrifice, but it's only two terms," he said. "And you know how missionaries are in demand to make appearances and presentations for fundraising. The thrust of the missions abroad has never been stronger. People flock to hear about our conversions and the culture. Can you do that for my sake?"

"But Will, Chicago is so far from Erin and Toronto or Vancouver. And I'm worried about your health. You're still so thin." Edith gently patted Will's sunken cheek.

"It's the only university that can accommodate our furlough and allow me to finish through correspondence. My brother's and sister's families aren't too far away from Chicago. You can come and visit. They would be happy to escort you around. And I'm getting stronger by the week. We'll have a lovely trip home."

Edith, still a little unhappy about the prolonged separation, frowned. "My father isn't too well, you know."

"Ideal then, for you and Mary to stay with your parents. She hasn't got any other grandparents, and this will be her first trip home."

"Of course. I don't want to steal your thunder, but if you're working on your doctorate, you won't have time to do the usual round of speaking engagements."

"You'll do a fine job. And Mary will be a bonus attraction for all the women."

Edith smiled. Mary was just at that age of being interested enough in what was going on around her to make her entertaining. "Yes, we have a beautiful daughter who has her father's eyes. Muriel Bowles told me their furlough involved over two hundred speaking engagements between her and her husband. Gertrude said she can't even remember how many they had booked."

1913
PENGHSIEN

The return to China was both sad and a relief for Edith. At the end of a wide range of speaking and fundraising engagements for her and Mary, the dissertation for Will's doctorate remained in draft form after a gruelling year of study. There would no longer be the casual gatherings of family and friends, women's groups, and enthusiastic congregations providing tables laden with a great deal more food than Edith had ever experienced before.

The guilt of so much choice and abundance had stirred at her conscience when she knew how little many Chinese in Szechwan had to eat. Not only could they not afford food for their families, there were some years when none was available; floods, drought, or locust swarms were the natural enemies, but warlords and their armies either devoured or burned fields of crops if the farmers didn't pay tributes. Fear, intimidation, and impossible taxes ground down the Chinese peasants struggling in the northern and central provinces. There were no modern industrial cities there.

"I hope they've had a good harvest this year," Edith remarked.

Will nodded. "We can pray so. I haven't heard of any particular disasters while we were away. I'm off to find Morgan. You could join me in a while for some fresh air on deck." He touched his daughter's cheek. "You look after Mommy, now, will you, Mary?"

"Yes, Daddy. Of course, 'cause I'm a big girl now."

"Indeed you are, Mary. See you both later."

Edith bobbed her head in agreement. She stood looking at her profile in the glossy mirror, placing her hands on her hips. "All my dresses have been let out at the waist, and you, Mary, have blossomed with a growth spurt. Your cheeks have filled out like rosy new apples." Edith brushed Mary's fine hair back and tied it with a ribbon. "We'll soon have to tuck in our tummies, though, won't we?"

Mary looked at her mother with wide, serious eyes. "Will we be hungry again, Mommy? Will I get tummy aches?"

Edith hugged her daughter close and buried her nose in the nape of the four-year-old's neck, breathing in and cherishing the sweet smell of a clean child. "Not if I can help it, Mary. Now, let's brush your hair before we join Daddy out on the deck for some fresh air. I think we'll need our coats, in case there's a wind."

※

While the Sibleys were on furlough, and despite the political unrest, the Renji Dental Hospital in Chengtu opened in 1912. Dr. Omar Kilborn, having seen the need to treat injured soldiers, established a Red Cross chapter in Szechwan Province.

While in Chengtu, Edith took the opportunity to visit Mrs. Kilborn at their residence, near the hospital.

"My, how you have grown, Mary," Mrs. Kilborn said, looking at Edith. "Things have changed so much while you were gone."

"I understand that the university closed after the communists' revolution and the Republic of China was formed," said Edith. "Have things improved in any way?"

"Well, I suppose you could say yes. The schools and university reopened and are now almost functioning at the same level as before we were evacuated. We'd dearly like to see a train connect from here to Shanghai, but it's very slow progress. It's nerve-wracking not to have a quick route to safety. There are still feelings of unrest about building rail lines. The land has been confiscated from tenant farmers who for generations worked the same fields. They've been pushed out of their houses and left without land to sustain themselves. And none of the political groups seem to care. Thousands have migrated south into the cities, begging for help or starving in the process."

"And the outlying missions?"

"More Chinese come to informal meetings." Mrs. Kilborn laughed. "All we have to do is serve tea and biscuits and whole families turn up to listen to speakers."

"How well accepted is the Christian Sun Yat-sen in Szechwan?"

"I'm afraid the countryside has been ravaged with the revolution and the political leaders tend to hide out in the coastal provinces, now the Empress and Little Emperor are dead."

Mary wasn't particularly interested in talk of politics or the progress of buildings. She wanted to see if her painting brushes and ink were still where she had left them. She had new paper pads from her grandparents so she could practice drawing Chinese characters. And she wanted to find Ming Lin and see if the garden had grown.

The mission school in Penghsien had excellent teachers. Edith over-saw a music program with groups of both children and adults, accompanying the hymn-singing and directing the youngest in their exercises to music. They practiced songs. Newly arrived orphans were often quiet during these interludes of recreation, not sure what was expected of them in this Western setting.

Mary was particularly attentive when the women gathered. The Chinese women would often act out their own stories, gracefully moving around the room in simple robes, their hands flowing about like birds in slow motion.

On the streets, never without the company of at least one Chinese helper, Edith always had a tight hold of Mary's hand.

"Mommy, why are there so many girls at the orphans' school, and not so many boys?"

"We'll talk about that later, dear. Hold on now and stay close. Here comes a crowd."

The line of dusty, downcast workers coming in from some mining worksite passed by. Cursing in Chinese under their breath and spitting in the direction of the Westerners and their children, they shuffled along the packed earth of the roadway to one-room homes and scant meals.

*

Within two years, the outbreak of a great war involving most of Europe brought unrest everywhere. Weekly news spread, even to the far reaches of the Chengtu Basin and the farthest missionary outposts.

Edith ran up the steps of their Penghsien mission home flapping the letter in her hand. "Will, my brother William is signing up with the Canadian Expeditionary Force to go overseas to Europe. How can Alice cope on her own?"

"Perhaps your mother will go and stay with her until William returns, now that your father is gone."

"He was such a carefree, almost wild lad. I can't imagine he'll be of any use in a war."

"I'm sure they'll find one for such a spirited young man; his skills as a mechanic and carriage hauler will be invaluable."

"It all seems so far removed from here, yet I worry."

*

Two mission board representatives from Chengtu, Gordon and Stephen, visited Penghsien later that year to check on the welfare of the staff. Although the world war in Europe appeared so distant, the effects infiltrated every aspect of life. And there was much talk of the Japanese government's demands of China in 1915.

Gordon pulled up his trouser legs as he sat down in Will's study. "Can you believe they had twenty-one demands extending their economic rights in Manchuria and Mongolia?"

Stephen pulled out a pipe and pointed the stem toward Will. "Mind if I smoke?"

"Not at all." Will retrieved a heavy stone ashtray from a drawer. He didn't smoke. "Arrogant to think the Chinese will agree with them all, including the joint project at the coal and iron complex. They're trying to squeeze China out of its own country."

Stephen puffed on his pipe, creating an aromatic cloud in the room. "Yes. I've been reading the papers, as outdated as they are. How can Japan demand China transfer to them all German interests in Shandong Province? The Chinese are developing very negative attitudes toward the Japanese in this country. Do you think we'll have trouble?"

Will shrugged. "Britain, France, Italy, and Russia announced they would support Japan's claims to Germany's possessions in the Pacific *if* Japan supported them in the European war. That *would* be trouble."

Gordon leaned forward. "But Lenin is making the Japanese nervous with troops lining the border on Russia's side of Manchuria. Both Russia and Japan want to keep the ports and Manchurian railway under their own control, not China's."

"That's been going on for decades." Will waved Edith into the room. "We must focus on the work of the Lord, each of us in our own small area. Look at the progress made with the Faculty of Religion opening at West China Union University."

Gordon nodded. "Quite right. The latest count is 177 of us in the Canadian West China Mission, making it the largest in Chengtu."

Edith passed around a tray offering a few sticky sweets and handleless cups of tea.

"That's wonderful," said Stephen. "But what of the rice supply? We hardly meet the needs of the resident students and orphans. If only we could obtain a secure supply."

Will's high cheekbones overshadowed his dark, sunken cheeks. "I know." He frowned. "We can't seem to purchase more than we need of any grain in good years, because it disappears, whether by pilfering or rats."

Edith shivered as she arranged a tray on the side table. "I'll just go and check things in the kitchen. Those in Canada don't know how the people here suffer."

"That may be true, though we've done our best to make them aware of the poverty and hunger," said Will. "Is Ma Ling feeling better yet?"

Edith backed toward the open door. "I believe so, but I want her to rest in her room until we are sure it's not typhus."

"Thank you, Edith."

Stephen said, "North America has its head turned to Europe and the war. I sure hope it doesn't last long. My wife frets about it daily."

Will was sure it unnerved Edith as well, though he thought she put on an admirable front.

Seventeen

Mary began her presentation to the women of the St. Andrew's Presbyterian Church. It pleased her when they had asked her to speak. Mission work for the church had changed since the war but remained so important.

"It's only within recent years that I discovered my mother gave birth to a stillborn son, William Edward. At that time, the infant mortality rate was extremely high in crowded cities from New York to Hong Kong. There were many diseases, few Western doctors or hospitals, and a scarcity of food in central China. Many missionaries' wives lost one child at birth. Others accidentally drowned or died from infections. Mrs. Goforth lost four of her five children. Three to diseases and one from a fall.

"For those reasons, many missionary families chose to leave their children in Canada at a boarding school, where they could be more certain of survival. It ripped families apart, but the work of the Lord came first. That was drilled into us. That, and the fact we often experienced hunger ourselves when supplies were low.

"Before they returned to China, my parents placed me in a boarding school in Toronto where other missionaries' children attended. I was fourteen, but many were younger. Since I had aunts and uncles within a short train ride, I could visit during holidays, and sometimes one friend or another accompanied me.

"The province of Szechwan where I was born is centred around the Great Red Basin. In 250 B.C., the governor began a tremendous public works program to control flooding of the Min River. By setting piles of hay on fire on top of the rocks, then pouring cold water on them, he broke through the mountain chunk by chunk to create a lake-sized reservoir. On a visit, I stood near this structure and imagined the huge river in flood washing away embankments that once had destroyed the rice fields below. Now, the gates regulate the water for a constant flow, as the same gates have for two thousand years. The history of it weighed heavily on my impression at the time."

"This is a country where inventions like the spinning wheel, silk, spurs, the kite, the umbrella, playing cards, and perfumed toilet paper..."

A few in the audience tittered.

"...were used for hundreds of years before being reinvented in Europe. It's hard for us to imagine how ancient are the ways of China. We talk of decades, but I've seen farmers stepping on thousand-year-old paddles raising water by buckets into a higher-level field. Despite missionaries trained as doctors, nurses, and clergy making huge progress with education and medical centres, I've seen children so thin they couldn't stand.

"Will the government of Mao Zedong bring a better standard of living to the millions of Chinese through communism? We will see. But one thing is certain: before they were exiled, Christian missionaries prepared the way for better living conditions. Since the expulsion of foreigners, the Chinese ministers, priests, and nuns have been left to care for anyone who is brought to their doors."

Mary took a deep breath as she concluded her presentation.

"Are there any questions?" she added.

A dozen hands flew up.

"Yes?"

Mary pointed to a young woman, who stood and nervously glanced from side to side. "What kind of diseases were there, Miss Sibley?"

"The four most widespread were typhus, cholera, diphtheria, and typhoid. Typhus is a bacterial infection from the bite of an infected bug. Typhoid and cholera are digestive tract bacteria. That is why cleanliness was—I mean, *is*—so important in all schools and hospitals. Diphtheria, spread by sneezing, is very contagious and harmful for children."

Mary nodded to a young woman in the back.

"Why did so many die?" the woman asked. "Couldn't the missionaries bring medicines when they went over?"

Mary sighed. "Doctors and nurses could distribute medicines, but they were hard to get and very expensive. People were too malnourished to fight disease. Also, many Chinese were suspicious of foreigners and their ways. They have their own holistic doctors who use traditional medicines. Conditions in the early part of the century were much like other impoverished parts of the world at the time.

"Don't forget, there have been millions of people in China for quite some time. Our own cities had the same diseases, but they are now more quickly contained, and many have become less common. Yes?"

She pointed to a smartly dressed woman in the front. Mary's lips twitched when she saw the notebook in the woman's hand.

"What was your opinion of Dr. Norman Bethune?"

Mary tapped the podium, considering facts and her opinion. "Canadians criticized Dr. Bethune for supporting communism, but he did save hundreds of lives during the revolution. The leader of the Communist Party, Mao Zedong, met Bethune *once* in 1939. Thereafter, Mao eulogized him as 'the great foreigner who showed the Chinese the way to true internationalism.'[11] His words. I wonder what he thought of the numerous other foreign doctors, nurses, teachers, and theologians who, during previous decades, had dedicated their lives to the humanitarian cause of helping the Chinese?"

Mary pulled her shoulders back defensively, knowing some would not agree.

"Whether or not Bethune's strong Presbyterian roots influenced him in ways he didn't acknowledge, I don't know. Mao Zedong claimed that Bethune died a martyr and showed China the spirit of internationalism, yet he is closing off relationships with the entire world." She sighed. "There *is* a case for foreign missions, and it's not just in giving the Chinese people means of physical survival."

Another hand went up. "Wasn't it more important to feed and give them medical care than to make them Christians?"

Mary nodded. "I understand what you're asking. People can't learn on an empty stomach. Or, if they are ill, they cannot work to feed their families. Even the smaller cities in China are crowded. Houses and businesses are all mixed together. Rooms behind stores often have no windows, no washing or bathing facilities. No toilets. Did you know that at one time Toronto had 187,000 outhouses?" Mary heard gasps among the rows and nodded. "Surprising, I know, considering how far North America has progressed in the area of sanitation. We must, at the same time, give people the hope of Christ."

Mary almost missed the woman timidly raising her hand only as far as her ear. "Yes, ma'am."

The woman looked from side to side, as though checking to make sure Mary had addressed her. "I understand that thousands of Jews were saved during the war in Shanghai and Hong Kong. Is this true?"

Mary was taken aback. There had been rumours. A friend in China had informed her of such.

"Yes, there were many who were able to get visas to China, specifically to Shanghai," Mary said. "It's not a well-known fact, but there were some wealthy Jewish families in Shanghai who tried to accommodate hundreds, perhaps thousands, until the Japanese arrested them. The Japanese didn't distinguish between Gentile and Jew, so many Jewish refugees were saved because they were German, a country friendly to Japan."

Another woman with a notepad on her lap raised her hand. "Have things not improved a great deal since you were in China twenty or more years ago?"

Mary grimaced. The recent news out of China had not been good. "Recovery from civil war and the Second World War has been neither easy nor fast."

Mary shuffled her papers together.

"Just one more question, Miss Sibley," someone said. "What happened to the mission buildings in Chengtu?"

"The buildings were expanded after the communist revolution, before the expulsion of Westerners. Many Chinese doctors and nurses as well as clergy were trained to prepare for that time. Everyone knew it was coming, and so the training went through to administration and custodial staff who learned of the importance of hygiene. I'm sure healing of all sorts is presently happening as a result of missions."

"I'm sorry if there are more questions, but we are past the time allotted for my speaking," she said in closing. "So I will turn it over to Mrs. Bartholomew to conclude the meeting."

Eighteen

1915

BINBROOK, ONTARIO, CANADA

The Reverend John Kitching sat in his ground-floor study in the manse looking at the letter from his brother-in-law. His hands shook. He left his study for the evening, joining his wife in the parlour.

"What's wrong, John?" Mary Ann's clicking knitting needles didn't miss a beat.

"It's a letter from your brother and Edith. He describes how one cup of dry rice has to feed a family of six. They add a little chopped cabbage or other edible greens and cook them together. No meat. No protein. And then they work twelve-to-fourteen-hour days from the age of eight upward to the day they die." He shook his head. "And there are so many of them. Farmers, rickshaw pullers, women who do laundry. He's asking us to see about raising more funds."

"It feels like a sieve. We keep sending money, clothing, hospital supplies, and yet it seems to make no difference."

"How can so little make a difference? It's hundreds of thousands, millions of people we're talking about. And the rich in China are impervious to pleas from the people. They are completely cut off and protected from the society that pays for their extravagant lifestyle. Will complains that the general population is always too busy at ordinary daily chores. They can't spare the time for reflection on their spiritual lives."

"But are the Western missionaries not teaching them about God's love? Can't it be better to have some hope than none at all?"

John twisted his moustache. "You are absolutely right, my dear. Our hope has to be in the Lord, because over and over again people disappoint. I believe we are going to be involved in something far wider reaching."

Mary Ann dropped her hands into her lap, still holding the long wooden needles and wool knitting project. "Please don't tell me the war is going to last another year."

John frowned. "All of Europe is in a turmoil."

"Perhaps it's the time for another church supper."

John nodded. "Good idea and I'll make an appeal to the congregations this week about mission funds. I feel people are being generous, yet it's not enough. Nothing will be enough."

Mary Ann tipped her head. "Didn't Jesus say we would always have the poor with us?"

John shook his head. "Yes, and I say the greedy as well."

1918

CHENGTU

Dear Aunt Beatrice,

I'm so happy to get your letter. They've been scarce these days. Don't tell Grandma Harrison what I'm going to relate to you. She has enough to worry about with Uncle William being in the war. It would scare her to know that we are being shot at. Well, the buildings are being shot at, and many Chinese have died. It seems everyone shooting is Chinese, but they are calling it a revolution. I thought it was a war.

They have a curious thing in the city of Chengtu, and in other cities too. Gates. The army can block off small sections of the city and keep out everyone attacking us. But when the bullets come through the walls and roof, it can be fearsome. The smell is very strong and stings my nose.

The boys' barracks were hit the worst. Some of the younger children cry at the loud bangs and booms, but I try to help keep them quiet. That is very important, because we don't want to be targets, Miss Broomhead tells us. She is our head English teacher and I love to listen to her accent when she speaks. Normally we only speak English in class.

Mother and Father are well. Are you well? And how is Grandmother Harrison and Aunt Alice? I hope she likes living in Kenora. She must miss Uncle William and worry about him being in the war in Europe. Like everyone else, we thought it would be over long ago. I think of you all every night in my prayers and ask God to keep you safe and give you a good life.

Your loving niece,

Mary Sibley

P.S. Have you accepted Reverend Thomas Reed's proposal yet? I'd like to think of him as my new uncle. Below are the new characters I've learned to write. I like practicing my brush strokes. It makes me feel relaxed and artistic.

Mary looked at her newly developing signature in cursive writing. She had practiced it many times over and hoped Aunt Beatrice would be impressed with it. Her Chinese characters were also improving with spending so much time indoors, where her teachers deemed it safe.

She patted the thin paper dry with an ink blotter and folded it to fit a regular-sized envelope. She copied the address in Chinese and English. Mother would have a stamp. She always had a supply of stamps and paper for letters because she spent an hour every day writing letters and mailing them. Who knew, though, when her letter would arrive?

1921
CHENGTU

Thick odours of spicy soup mingled with the steam lifting from the iron cauldron of boiling green bamboo. The carver Li Xing, an old man in his forties with a shaven head, wore a faded blue cotton work robe, girded tightly to keep it from interfering with his work. He scraped the chisel gently, evening the depth of cut between bunches of grapes, leaves, and characters, focusing on the nearly finished paintbrush pot.

Maybe not his most intricate piece of work, but the foreign missionary woman Mrs. Sibley required two brush pots. Matching. He never made an exact copy of anything. He was an artist. The second would be similar in size and also decorated in grape vines, but each piece of bamboo suggested its own detail. As it turned out, they mirrored each other—similar, yet unique.

A precious bit of tung oil simmered in a small enamel dish, ready to be applied after he finished. It would be rubbed and worked in gently to protect the pot. The fee the company had negotiated—or rather, demanded—was ridiculously high, but Mrs. Sibley had been willing to pay without argument. She respected him and his work. He wouldn't see a quarter of it, but he was paid regularly, and that was needed to sustain his growing family. Bad luck that he had five daughters. No, four, he corrected himself. Dowries for girls were expensive.

Dozens worked in the shop of the Wang Chou family. Hundreds of tools were carefully organized in wooden cubbyholes along the walls and heavy workbenches were arranged in the middle of workrooms. Li Xing had followed in his father's footsteps, as his father and grandfather had assumed their fathers' place in the shop. All had worked in the artist's factory cooperative in Chengtu. Only the owner of the shop had changed. Since the Qing dynasty had settled into position more than two hundred and fifty years ago, a Li family member had been an artisan working with bamboo relief carvings. Their skills were developed from the time they could hold a small knife safely.

"Why do we make paintbrush pots for the foreigners?" Wu Chang asked his friend and co-worker, Li Xing. "They won't use them. The bamboo will dry out and crack."

"Hmm. Perhaps. But they will stand on a shelf and look pretty. They won't get stained with ink."

"Oh, you defend those foreign white people. When will you see that they are trying to make you think like them? They don't understand our ways or even the language. Did you hear that new black robe try to tell me not to take second wife?"

Wu Chang continued to chat, and Li Xing kept working. Some of his views were best kept to himself. He had to save face with his co-workers.

Despite the continued desire for works of art, peace did not hold across the country. Warlords battled for control over gangs of robbers and thieves, who terrorized the peasant farmers. When crops failed, some of the farmers and labourers joined the gangs. If a first wife didn't have a son, another wife was arranged. Many had children in hopes that a son or two would survive long enough to look after them in their old age.

So it had been for centuries.

In the meantime, Li Xing's boss took loads of artwork to the port cities where he could sell them for exorbitant prices.

"Those religious Western people only want to spread their imperial poison," said Wu Chang. "We don't need another king to support."

"Stop complaining, you foolish man. Don't you know that without the foreigners buying so many things to take home, only one of us would be working here?" Li Xing rubbed the paintbrush pot hard, working the oil into the bamboo around the relief carvings. It was shaping up well. His father would be proud. No, his father would say it was adequate, but inwardly he would think Xing had done a fine job.

Li Xing said, "You know, the Westerners at the mission church are as thin as we are. They don't keep any extra food for themselves and their children. They hand out small packages of grain if people go asking when they've become desperate."

"That's a bribe. They want you to come in and listen to their foreign ways and talk. They hope to steal your children and use them for body parts. They make big money selling children's body parts to the place they call a hospital. I know two doctors were arrested for that."

"Yes, and then they were let go. I've seen how they help sick people. And when was the last time you met a Chinese person who would give something away for nothing?"

Wu Chang laughed. "Last night. My mother gave me soup and didn't ask for anything in return."

Li Xing laughed too. "She knows to wait until the next time you visit. She will have some job that needs doing."

Nineteen

1921

CHENGTU

Li Xing moved along with the crowd in the street toward home. His mouth watered thinking of the fried vegetables and rice waiting for him. Rice would fill his grumbling stomach, at least for a while.

As Li Xing entered their tiny windowless home, his wife Yu addressed him in a quiet voice. "Xing, please. Our daughter Wen is ill. I cannot stop her from heaving. It is the intestinal disease and Auntie Shu has done all she can. Please take her to the hospital of Western medicine." Her black eyes steadily held his gaze.

Li Xing sighed. And sighed again to signal his displeasure.

His own mother was of no help, enshrouded in her opium fog as she always was at this hour. He dared not ask how she financed her addiction. *Do I have to work long hours every day and get no peace from my wife when I arrive home?*

"Is the meal prepared?" he asked. "I need to eat."

Yu looked at her husband, pleading with unshed tears. No lines in her face revealed love, worry, or discouragement. Would it make a difference to him if one of their four daughters died, joining her ancestors? Hadn't they already sacrificed one daughter, selling her into serfdom?

"Go and see her," Yu said. "I'll serve your soup, so you can eat quickly."

Xing nodded. He pulled the door hanging aside and scrunched up his nose at the foul smell coming from the slight figure on the mat. His daughter's thin arms and frail hands shook and her sunken eyes made her seem already like a ghost.

He shivered. Would those foreigners know what to do? He would put off eating for now. He picked up Wen wrapped in a thin quilt and carried her out into the street.

Xing hurried past workers heading toward him and wove his way around those going in the same direction. Sedan chairs vied for space in the narrow street, hemmed in by overhanging balconies and vendors selling their last few items of the day. He thrust his daughter out in front of him, holding her as far from his nose as possible. Pedestrians, recognizing the foul odour of the diseased girl, parted before him.

He walked on past the edge of the city to a brick wall. The wooden sign showed the funny letters of the Western language, the Chinese characters below that, imperfect in their meaning, with the rough grain of the wood having caused uneven strokes.

The building was intimidating. Tall and imposing in its design, it reflected modern Western ideas, with two stories of glass windows and tall steps to reach the wide, solid wooden doors. Rebellious Chinese Nationalists had burned down the first hospital and trashed the foreigners' schools and missions fourteen years ago, but the foreigners were insistent. Sometimes they were even useful.

"Help me. Please let us in. We need the doctor," Xing called. His daughter weighed so little, even with the quilt wrapped around her quivering body.

"Yes. How can we help?" A very tall, pale woman dressed in a grey, midcalf Western dress surveyed the gate and path behind him, anxious.

"My daughter Wen is sick. Please help." Xing pushed past the woman the moment she opened the door another foot. "Show me where."

"Bring her in here. The doctor is out on a call, but I expect him back soon. Can you set her on this examining table?"

The woman drew her lips in tightly, perhaps trying not to breathe in the ghastly odour. She pulled a white apron off a hook and picked up a basin. "I'll get some boiled water to clean her up. How long has she been like this?"

Xing could see a softening around the woman's eyes as she turned to look at him openly. Had she been Chinese, he would never have faced her, a woman, directly. How old was she? He couldn't tell. Young. Perhaps she was a student.

"She has had nothing to eat or drink all day or last night," he explained. "She is shaking."

"Has anyone in the family had similar symptoms?"

Her fumbling attempt at using his language would have been humorous if he'd had no other worries. "No. Everyone else is well. Can you give her medicine?"

The woman gravely shook her head. "The doctor will have to see her before he can treat her. Won't you sit down and wait here?"

She carried on with cleaning his daughter, covered her with a white sheet up to the chin, and then, using a new basin of clean water, dabbed at the child's forehead.

Xing looked around for some sign of their god. Was the bleeding man nailed to a wooden cross somewhere? Or would the wooden cross be empty, a sign, he had been told, that the man Jesus had overcome death? He shivered to think that the ghost of this man might be hovering in these rooms of the hospital.

A giant of a man threw open the door of the room where the young girl lay. "What is that terrible smell?"

Xing jumped up off the wooden chair. "Can you help my daughter, please, Doctor? She will surely die if you do not treat her." He bowed in respect, knowing this man could choose to help or not.

"Sister Dale—I mean, Nurse Dale—have you not cleaned this young lass up?"

"Doctor, I have, only she is in delirium and not in control of her bowels. I suspect diphtheria."

"Yes, thank you for your prognosis. I shall see to her in a moment, after you have cleaned her up again."

The doctor spun on his heel and stalked down the hallway.

Xing hung his head. Had his effort been wasted in bringing Wen, youngest of his four daughters?

It seemed like a few moments passed. Someone shook his shoulder.

"You can go home if you wish, Mr. Li," said the nurse.

Xing started, confused at being caught napping. *Who is Mr. Li? Me. Nurse Dale is speaking to me.*

"Your daughter has had a treatment and will need to stay for another night or two. I'll see you to the door."

"Thank you, Miss Dale. I will come back tomorrow." He trudged through the gateway.

What kind of magic did these foreigners use? Mr. Sibley had tried to explain about a special man who was the son of God. But wouldn't the father be more powerful than the son? Xing didn't understand these people at the missions. Some said one thing, others proclaimed another, and none of it fed his family or kept them from harm.

At the next corner, he deviated from his path home. A small temple sat hidden between two ancient buildings. It wouldn't hurt to call on the help of another god. Just to appease them all.

He paid the young boy taking care of the incense for a stick to burn on the stone altar of the Daoist temple.

※

When Mary turned thirteen, her mother had taken her to order some wood carvings from the workshop of Wang Chou in Chengtu. Two dozen craftsmen worked in various rooms of the shop, and Edith had ordered several items months in advance of their sabbatical leave.

During one of the last days before they left for Canada, Edith led Mary firmly by the arm. While they were in Chengtu, Edith insisted that Mary should have one last look at the market stalls, hear the sounds of the local singsong dialect, and smell some of the more pleasant odours coming from the jars and bottles of the herbs and spices displayed by the street vendors.

"Mother, can we buy one of those satin jackets? They are so beautiful."

"Mary, we can't carry many more gifts. We ordered some carved brush pots and such from Mr. Wang's shop. Let's pick them up first and see what we can fit inside each. Embroidery work and fans would really appeal to your aunts."

Mary let her hand slide away from the sleeve of the jacket hanging up for display. There were so many things she would like to get. It would be years before she could return to China. If she were to become a teacher, maybe even a year at university would be necessary to get a position. She could come back and teach English to the Chinese. Being fluent in Mandarin would be useful, but she wanted to teach children. Not necessarily as a missionary, but as a real teacher.

※

Li Xing observed Mrs. Sibley and her daughter entering from the narrow side door. He lifted the two finished paintbrush pots onto his workbench and made a show of polishing the bamboo carvings. It was unusual for foreign women to enter the shop, but maybe her husband was too busy.

Li Xing bowed deeply. Mrs. Sibley and her daughter bowed from the shoulders, as a person of wealth might do. His face remained blank as he watched for her expression.

"They are lovely, Li Xing. Thank you. I am pleased with your design." She fingered the writing on the one she had picked up. "Passing over bridge, feels like autumn." She tipped her head to the side. "Am I right?"

Li Xing nodded vigorously. "Very good," he replied. "This is an ancient poem, well-known in early Song dynasty. It's a favourite of the dowager empress."

It wouldn't matter if she translated it awkwardly. The beauty of the poetry would be lost to most Westerners anyway.

"The grape vines are perfect. My family will appreciate them very much. Will you carry them, Mary? I'll pay Mr. Wang."

Li Xing bowed as they left. He sent a silent thanks to their god, who encouraged such extravagance. The extra coins the daughter had discreetly passed to him would help feed his family and buy medicine for his sick daughter.

For a moment, it pained him that the pots would go to Canada, away from his country. Would anyone ever know what the words said, other than Mrs. Sibley or her daughter?

Mary sat on the deck chair of the ocean liner with a book. The initial excitement of leaving China had fizzled. Now the days seemed long on the way home. Their stay in Yokohama, Japan had been brief.

"Mother. Do you think anyone will be meeting us in Vancouver?"

Edith smiled at her daughter, running her fingers through Mary's fine, light brown hair. It whirled gently in the breeze. "Probably not. It's too far for Grandma Harrison on her own. Anyway, it would be too much of an expense for anyone to meet us. We still have to be careful of our money, though I expect we will eat better."

"And not have to worry about the drinking water? Or disease?"

Edith nodded. "Do you remember coming to Canada nine years ago? You were only three."

Mary shook her head. "I don't remember much, but I remember thinking you had to do the things Ming Lin used to do for me. Like getting me dressed and brushing my hair." She thought for a minute. "I remember being afraid of the hot water coming out of a tap. That was new to me."

"I'm sure you'll notice many more things this time." There was a little sadness in her voice.

Mary took her mother's tanned hand. "It's going to be wonderful, Mother. Let's be happy so I can have good memories of our year here together. Just think—a whole year!"

Twenty

1922

In September, when Mary studied the photo of herself and her parents taken the week before their furlough ended and her parents returned to China, she was pleased. She had worn the string of pearls her mother gave her for safekeeping, the pleated raw-silk blouse in a pale rose colour, and she had her hair pulled up and pinned into place. Very mature-looking and appropriately wistful. It suited her. A copy had been sent to her Grandmother Harrison. And her dear parents.

She held the photo close to her chest, folding her arms around it. How could she not cry? When would she see them next? Heavy teardrops rolled down her cheeks. The earliest furlough would be granted sometime after 1928. She would be twenty. She would be in university by then, if the scholarship came through.

"Mary, what have you got there?" Her childhood friend from the mission school in Chengtu bounced onto Mary's single dormitory bed, rolled onto her stomach, and kicked up her heels.

"A photo." Mary swiped at her tears and turned the framed photograph so Viola could see it.

"Ohh. How chic you look. Very mature." Viola looked at Mary, who turned to wipe her eyes again. "You look lovely, Mary. It's a wonderful keepsake. We don't all get professional pictures like that, you know."

Mary turned and smiled at her friend, knowing a limited number of dark, distant shots a few inches square were all the photos Viola had of her parents. "I do know. I'm so fortunate, and aren't we lucky to be on the same floor as each other? Here, look at this picture." Mary dug in her desk drawer and pulled out a self-framed photo in sepia of her two cousins. "Isn't this a hoot?"

Viola studied the two children dressed in magnificent, wide, white-lace-trimmed collars. "Who are they? Are they brother and sister?"

Mary threw her head back with laughter. "No. They're two boys. We're all cousins. John Kitching is the tallest, and this is Carmen. He's three. This was taken at the manse in Tyrell."

"He's a boy? But the picture is so old-fashioned."

"It was taken about ten years ago. They used to dress boys and girls the same. I guess they never cut Carmen's hair before this photo was taken."

The two girls giggled in fits, pointing to the ringlets, the pantaloons, the collars. "The family must have had money to be able to do this," Viola said.

"I think my father's family got an inheritance when their parents died. Both my father and his brother went to university to become preachers, and three sisters became teachers." Mary placed her arm around Viola's shoulders and gave a squeeze. "I'm so happy we're on the same floor," she repeated.

"Do you think there was *influence* used?"

They laughed, having heard the word bandied about by some older girls giving them sideways looks.

"Of course there was. One look at the handsome Reverend William Sibley and they would do his bidding," Mary said, only half-joking.

Viola smirked. "Right. Now tell me, which teams are you going to join? What are you doing at Christmas, and are you writing to anyone in China? Do you have a beau?"

Mary gasped. "I'm fourteen, for goodness sakes. I have years and years before I can think of a beau. I want to learn as much as I can and be a teacher."

"Me too. I want to teach drama." Her friend hopped off the bed and flung her arms out in a theatrical pose.

"I'm hoping to be in the choir, and I think I'm getting tall enough to be on the basketball team. Do you think I'll qualify?"

Viola contemplated her seriously, hands on her hips. "Mary, I believe you could do anything that you set your mind to. Will you join the dramatic group?"

Mary scrunched up her nose. "I'm not cut out for that. Not like you are. I'll join the music club."

"I think it's called the glee club. Oh, Mary, I'm so excited to see you here. You know that our Chengtu classmate Ben had to go to a private school in Vancouver. He won't know anybody there."

"Ah, too bad. He'll miss his sisters."

"So are you ready for a snack?" Viola asked, patting her tummy. "There's so much to choose from here."

"I don't eat snacks. Besides, I feel like I just ate lunch."

Viola looked at her in surprise.

"Don't look at me like that," Mary said. "When I think of how little my nanny Ming Lin ate, I'm ashamed to have such huge platefuls. Let's go for a walk. I'd like to see more of the facilities."

"Facilities, eh. All right, let's go. Maybe my stomach will stop growling on the way."

After closing the door, Viola and Mary linked arms, both happy to have an understanding companion in this strange, bountiful country they would now call home.

As December rolled around, Mary found herself standing in line, shifting her weight from left to right and back. Ahead of her, a young girl faced the wicket. Mary watched her shoulders slump as the postmistress shook her head.

It's so hard not hearing from your parents for months on end. Mary moved a step forward as the girl turned away. *Oh, please, please let me have a letter this month.*

She hadn't had any letters for a few weeks, but that was to be expected.

Her turn arrived. She stepped forward. "Mail for Miss Mary Sibley, please."

"You're a lucky one. A parcel from China, and letters besides." The woman smiled kindly.

"Thank you." Mary had only a moment of guilt as she took hold of the small parcel and stack of cards. "It's like Christmas." She laughed.

"Do you save those stamps?" the postmistress asked. "I have a nephew who collects them from all over the world."

Mary lifted her gaze from the reddish stamps on the parcel to the woman's hopeful face. "Oh, sorry, yes, I collect them all."

She headed off to her dorm room to spend a delicious afternoon opening her mail. She always took her time, carefully lifting sealed flaps or cutting the ends open, reading and rereading every page of every letter. Now she would pin these new cards on her corkboard for display. Her roommate never bothered, but she could go home twice a month, not living too far away and the family having the luxury of a chauffeur-driven car.

Mary ran her fingers over the definitive red stamps. One featured a junk on the river, and another, a reaper on a field before the Temple of Heaven. Both stated in Chinese and English, "Republic of China." They were new issues and not familiar to her.

She pictured her mother with a small brush, placing a dab of homemade glue to the small paper squares and attaching them to the corner of the envelope. She would have wiped away any excess glue before letting them dry. Her mother would have taken the envelope to the local post office and handed it to an official, who would check that it had the correct amount of postage for Canada and pound an official imprint across the stamps. Her mother would then smile and give a quick bow as she turned away to return to the mission.

The letter would have been stuffed with hundreds of others into a heavy, waxed leather bag. The full bag would be collected by a pole carrier or backpacker who trotted out of town toward the city. There it may have been collected at the main post office before being placed with thousands of other letters into the saddlebags of a mule driver who proceeded to Chungking.

Mary knew the post office officials were trying hard to utilize every railway that had been built to move mail faster internationally, but there was no rail line yet between Chengtu and Chungking. The next step would be for the bags to be transferred to a Yangtze River steamer, now under official Government Post Office control, where it would make its malingering voyage downstream in the seasonally low water.

Then it would be transferred to an oceangoing iron steamship bobbing across the Pacific Ocean to Hawaii, then Victoria, British Columbia. Her letter would have been sorted by hand, the Chinese writing scrutinized, taken by ferry to the mainland, placed on a CPR or CNR mail-sorting car, jostled between sidings, stations, and stops all along to Toronto.

What a journey you have travelled, dear letter, Mary thought, pressing her lips to the envelope and breathing deeply of the faint hint of spices.

November 5, 1922
Penghsien, Szechwan

Dear Mary,

I hope my package arrives in time for you to have it for Christmas Day, so you will have a little something to open with everyone else. I'm sending this letter beforehand, so you will at least have it. Father sends his love. His days are filled to the brim with tutoring as well as preaching. They have built two new outpost church buildings for the villagers, and the attendance has been good.

As usual, we often have a few expecting to receive a handout of food, so we have taken to providing a potluck type of affair after the service and everyone goes away happy, though many are puzzled. They can't yet understand the giving and sharing we Christians do just because others have need of it. Some are quite stuck in looking out only for their families, for whom they would do anything, including lie or cheat. They don't see that these things are unnecessary and that everyone would be happy if they shared lovingly. The wealthy are the worst, at times, because they want to know what they owe when they come to church. God's love cannot be bought.

After hearing that three passengers carrying measles were held in quarantine in Vancouver after our trip, I was so thankful to know that you have not contracted a case. Now that you are safe in Canada, I can relax a little, knowing the school will do its best to keep the contagious diseases under control.

Ma Ling is continuing to serve us in her dear manner. I try every day to compliment her on some dish beautifully prepared, or some flower arrangement she has made. She bows in humility and modesty overcomes her, the dear woman. She has been a true companion. Her tiny feet give her more pain than she ever lets on, and I agonize over the effects of that cruel tradition. I do thank God regularly. It is one thing which has nearly stopped. Ma Ling would have liked to be in the nursery with the babies, but the work proved too much for her. She is very committed to finding baby girls who might otherwise be abandoned, or worse. The orphanage is half full of orphans who found their way there through her contacts, cajoling, and concerns. On her afternoons off, she visits to check on her children. She truly is a fine mother.

The housing for new missionaries has made great progress since you were here. I take solace with other missionaries' wives who have sent their children back home to Canada, Britain, or America. We all have that cross to bear when we send our precious ones away or leave them in the care of schools. Some have buried more than one child and regret not sending their children to a safer environment. Recently, the Bowles children were bitten by dogs set on them by some vicious neighbours.

I want to assure you we are safe and sound, as you have probably read of troubles in Szechwan. Penghsien has not had any more outright attacks. Thankfully, the locals are not tolerating the rebellious youth who light fire to Christian buildings or break down walls in the night that were constructed in the day. They are beginning to understand our desires to improve everyone's lives.

Some are very strong now in their beliefs, placing more value on all lives and showing compassion to those with no homes. Still, the youth are unsettled. You remember the old Chinese saying: "Heaven is high above and the emperor far away." These things are sent to test us.

We have completed an outer wall and have tall, solid gates again. We can leave them open in daylight hours, otherwise the compound can feel like a prison for the children. They enjoy their time working in the gardens, and often members of the church come to assist. There is plenty of help when it comes time to harvest, and I try not to notice the bulging pockets as the helpers leave, sometimes carrying their "share" out in the open. We try to be flexible, but it means we have less for the babies and children later on.

I trust the Lord to keep you safe, and pray you are finding joy in doing the many things you are privileged with.

Please send our love to Viola. Her baby brother and parents are doing well, and we all feel it a blessing that you have each other. I have written to your Aunt Mary Ann and Uncle John, and they are most happy to have you spend the holidays with them, and of course young John, now that he is over the worst effects of polio. We all wait for the day a vaccination can prevent such a horrible disease. He will appreciate your company. He finds some of the younger boy cousins too rambunctious, his mother says.

May you receive God's blessings every day to carry you forth.

With much love and affection,
Mother

Twenty-One

1925
TORONTO

Mary opened a letter addressed to her in her mother's neat handwriting. Mary had never been this neat, but at least her English handwriting was legible. Even her Chinese characters were passable, and she felt it relaxing to practice drawing them, like making pictures but also choosing a style from Chinese artists she admired.

> November 3, 1925
> Junghsien, China
>
> My dearest Mary,
>
> As there has been quite some activity these past few months regarding the Chengtu mission, and since you have asked, I'm going to try to elaborate on them.
>
> If you remember me speaking of the Reverend Stanley Annis and his wife Agnes, he is suffering from some health issues since their return from Ontario. Agnes shared with me a lovely photo taken before they left Canada. The four children all look well, even young Harold, who, as you may remember, suffered severely

from malaria. He spent three months in hospital, and although he tires easily and has a worrisome cough at times, he is better. The three oldest children are resettled into the Chungking Canadian School along with nineteen others. I must say, dear, despite the painful separation, that I am truly thankful you are away from the dangers of Szechwan.

There has been the usual discussion over how much say the Chinese should have in the type of church buildings that are planned. Let them design them all, I say. After all, it's their country and we won't be here forever, but, as a woman, I have no opinion. Mary, if you ever decide to marry—when you're older, of course—make certain that your opinion matters. Now that women have the vote in Canada, you are a Person. You'll soon be able to vote yourself!

James Endicott Senior is insisting there be regulations regarding the Harrison Memorial Fund from your grandmother. I'm sure that you will get full benefits and believe it is a generous amount. With the formation of the United Church of Canada, it seems that we are receiving less, and cuts are being made across the board. Not only in China, I believe, but other missions as well as at home in Canada.

The south China missions are returning to normal after the upheaval of recent times. Ichang was the least disturbed. The dear, loyal Chinese gateman and neighbours were able to prevent looting at the compound, and there was little damage at the upper medical building, but there was havoc in the Chungking bungalows. Fowchow Boy's Middle School will stay closed. It's a dilemma that, although the feeling is the church should be thoroughly Chinese, missionaries are still wanted. We must leave it in God's hands, though I wonder when the words of the hymn "In Christ there is no east or west" will come true.

I've just had word that Mrs. Endicott died yesterday, November 28. I hadn't known she was ill. It was most providential that their son James and his new wife had arrived before the fall term at the university. He has taken up a position at West China Union as a professor of English and Ethics. His father is very pleased. Rumblings are heard that young James has befriended Zhou Enlai. Missionaries are generally discouraged from any sort of involvement with local politics or politicians, but the young ones coming over are not so cautious. At least he could be with his mother during her illness. I'm sure James Senior will miss his wife and all her vigorous activity among the women, once he realizes how much she contributed.

Your father is looking thin, but he won't rest in the heat as he should. Temperatures this fall have been moderately cool and not as wet as some years. We still head to the hills during the hottest month and can enjoy a reprieve then. We expect our next furlough to be in three years, but we may apply early.

I so miss you, and pray that you are well, happy, and contributing to the Lord's work in any way you can. I am glad that you are participating in basketball and other sports because that will invigorate you during your long hours of study and music practice. Your father sends his love and will write to you himself before long.

You are ever in my prayers and thoughts,
Mother

1946
KINGSTON

Mary realized that tomorrow would be Nita's last night staying at the house. She would be leaving for her mother-in-law's place with David to wait the arrival of her husband. Nita buzzed with excitement.

"Will you give us another installment tomorrow evening, Mary? I'm going to really miss our radio evenings. It's helped me contain my excitement and impatience. I can't believe I'll see Leonard next week!" The pitch of Nita's voice had climbed, along with her hand clenching and waving.

Mary studied Nita. "Are you sure you want to try to sit still all evening?"

In a few days it would the twentieth anniversary of Mary's mother's death. It wouldn't be fair to dwell on those thoughts on Nita's last night.

"I know what we can do," Mary said. "How about I make some special Chinese dishes and sweets as a treat? We can talk about Chinese celebrations. And how do you think David would like a few firecrackers?"

Nita gripped Mary's hands. "Oh, would you? That would be so special, especially for David."

"He's been such a good boy, playing quietly while we talk most evenings and going right to bed when you say." Mary released Nita's grip and patted her hand. "If I hurry, I can get down to the corner store where the Wong family stocks a number of items I'll need."

Mary started planning the menu in her head. She thought of chao fan, a fried rice dish in which she could use the leftover pork roast.

I'll look for chow mein noodles, make kung pao chicken, maybe char sui to flavour the pork...

She wouldn't have time to make wontons for the soup. She might find an eggplant, but maybe not at this time of year. Perhaps she could get canned chestnuts. She already had the ingredients for egg tarts and almond cookies.

"I'm off to shop, and Nita, don't you do a thing toward tomorrow night's meal. We'll make it a real celebration."

She could wear her red cheongsam dress and tortoise shell combs, though with her fine hair they never stayed put for long. She'd ask the others to dress up too, for the party.

Mary popped on her hat, grabbed her purse and crocheted shopping bags, and pulled her gloves on. No need for anything but a light jacket on such a warm late May afternoon.

The meal planning and preparation would distract her for now, but she couldn't help remembering those awful days after receiving news of her mother's death…

1926

TORONTO

Mary grabbed her nightdress. She'd need a few days' clothing. Not her school uniform, but a black dress. Did she have her black dress here, or would the grey suit be better? What kind of funeral would there be? The message gave no details.

> Mother deceased. Possible return on next available vessel. Father.

The headmistress had been as shocked as she. Last week's letter from her mother had indicated that everything was going well. They had been making progress at the mission, though funds were tight. Why had her quiet-spoken mother had to die?

Here she was, barely eighteen, and so far away from both her parents, missionaries in China. She imagined the slow, rough ride in the donkey-drawn cart, then onto the Overland sedan chair, down to Chungking and a Yangtze River boat, over the American rail line from Hankow to Canton, aboard a ship to San Francisco, followed by a cross-country train journey to Toronto. She had travelled this route when she was thirteen, accompanied by her parents on their furlough. It had taken weeks.

When would she see her father again?

William Edward Sibley, thirdborn child and oldest son, had not followed in his own father's footsteps of being a cooper. He'd become a preacher, to the delight of his aunts. He had gone further, though, heading right into missionary work at the height of the rush to Christianize China. The Boxer Rebellion had been squelched, but periodic arson attacks struck the missions. Had her mother's death anything to do with that? Why hadn't he explained how Mother had died?

Mary took her black dress off the hanger and folded it slowly, the weight of it so heavy in her fumbling fingers. With the addition of a nightdress, a few personal items, including her writing kit, the little brown cardboard suitcase was full. Mechanically going through the motions, she smoothed down the fitted jacket of her grey suit, flipped the lid closed, and clipped the two latches.

A black sedan awaited her outside the school's iron gate. At the manse in Hornby, Aunt Mary and Uncle John Kitching would meet her and draw her into the warmth of their home. Her cousin John S. would try to lighten the grief, of that she was sure.

Twenty-Two

JUNE 9, 1926

HORNBY, ONTARIO, CANADA

John flicked the drape aside in order to see out the window of the manse. The carriage had arrived. His cousin Mary stepped down while his father paid the driver. He watched as she lifted a small cardboard suitcase off the floor of the open carriage, holding it close in front of herself. Protection from grief.

John brushed away a drop. No good shedding tears. The tragedy of his aunt's death was still sinking in. He had returned home—or rather, to the present manse in the middle of nowhere—from the University of Toronto the day before. The closest station was three miles away at Rockwood, and this was where his father had gone to pick up his cousin.

"Come in, Mary, come in." John's mother placed an arm around her niece's shoulders and patted the girl's arm gently. "There, there, now. Let's get you into the kitchen for a cup of tea, shall we? John, take Mary's suitcase upstairs to her room, will you please? Take your time."

John nodded and took the suitcase, glad of the opportunity to get rid of the excess water building behind his eyes. Also annoyed. Just a little. Of course he would take his time. What else could he do going up two dozen steps to the second floor with his gimpy leg? Since struck with polio six years ago, he'd worked hard to walk in a normal fashion, but steps were always a challenge.

Then a thought occurred to him. His mother might want extra time so she could comfort the poor girl.

＊

Mary leaned into her aunt's shoulder, allowing the sobs to shake her. It was a natural release of the numbing grief which had frozen her since she'd walked out the gate to the black De Luxe motorized taxi which the headmistress had ordered.

The ride from Branksome Hall on Elm Street in Toronto to downtown Union Station had brought her past the market square, but she hadn't taken any interest in the sights around her. Even the countryside swirling past as the train hurled her down the track had done little to loosen the self-control she had strained to maintain.

Not until her Aunt Mary Ann had put her arm around her had she stopped fighting the tears.

＊

John set Mary's lightweight suitcase on the dressing table chair. He opened the window a crack to freshen the stuffy room. It was usually closed up, except for visitors. A lacy embroidered cover overhung the ends of the dresser top. A tortoise shell hand mirror, brush, and comb set was lined up on the enamel tray. It would probably be comforting for his cousin to be here with familiar furnishings while she waited for her father's arrival.

Tears swelled in his eyes. Horrible, horrible. He could still hear the tremor in his mother's voice as she'd relayed the news to him yesterday in a rare phone call. He had managed to leave right away from the University of Toronto's School of Hygiene's Connaught Lab, where they worked developing rabies vaccinations. He caught the last train of the day from Union Station in Toronto.

Arms outstretched, his mother had immediately greeted him, almost overbalancing him. This was an exceptionally emotional action from his very reserved, controlled mother.

"It's an awful thing, John. Will has asked us not to share all the details with Mary when she gets here." She wiped at her eyes with a hankie. "We knew there was trouble with the people in the streets in Szechwan during the rebellions, but they led us to believe things had settled down." Mary Ann rested her hand on John's sleeve. "You'll not be teasing her now, will you?"

John frowned. "Of course not, Mother. It's such a shock, and Mary hasn't seen her mother for three years." He swallowed hard.

"Her father wants us to keep Mary for the summer. You'll carry on working at the laboratory in Toronto?"

"Yes, they've accepted my application. I start next week as a paid assistant for the term. What will Mary do while she's here? There isn't much around Hornby."

"We'll manage, what with the ladies group and family. So many of them will want to come for the funeral—I mean, a memorial service. We'll have to plan for all that. It will be months, maybe, before Will can get home. Hopefully Mary can keep up her piano practicing. Maybe bring out some of those old duets you two used to have fun playing." Mary Ann tsked. "I can't believe it."

John descended the steps one at a time to the landing, his gimpy leg first, his other following, as he gripped the rail. Going down proved far more difficult than going up.

"John, come into my study for a moment, will you?" John's father held the dark, varnished door open, inviting him to enter. "Have a seat."

What more news could his father have? It was a bit like being called up before the headmaster.

John Senior closed the door and indicated the chair across from the desk. They both sat down.

"I haven't given your mother all the details, but your Aunt Mary was beheaded in the street. Then a group did further desecration to the body, kicking it and rolling her…" His father coughed and swallowed hard. "…the head into the ditch. Today's *Toronto Globe* just says she was murdered with a knife. It was a broadsword. Too gruesome to print the details. I wanted you to be aware, but I'll leave it up to Will how much he shares with Mary."

John picked up the folded newspaper. The large, uppercase headline stated "Canadian Woman, Wife of Missionary, Slain by Chinese." The secondary lines were in smaller print: "Mrs. William E. Sibley is struck down in Streets of Chengtu, Assassin Captured."[12] The article itself was short, not giving many more details.

"'The motive for the crime has not been established,'" he read aloud. "The Nationalist Party's aim to unify all of China is motive enough." He slapped the newspaper onto his father's desk. "Is Uncle Will returning to Canada? Surely he won't want to be staying in a country that doesn't welcome foreigners after a tragedy like this."

"I have no idea, but the call to bring the Word of God to the heathen is very strong in your uncle. Has been for years, as it has for all the missionaries. So many years of learning the language and writing it, trying to understand their way of living." The Reverend John Wesley Kitching's normally gaunt face drooped farther, his heavy moustache swooping along the sides of his mouth and curling back up, the style of the day. "Your mother will be a comfort to your cousin. Be gentle and thoughtful with her, will you please, John?"

"Of course." John was thoughtful and gentle, but he also liked to tease and pull pranks. It had been his way of healing after the ravages of disease, and studying medicine was another way to fight the enemy.

"I'll go and take that frog out of her bedside table drawer." He cracked a half-grin at his father's look of dismay. "No, Father, I'm joking."

"Well, that's what I mean. We need to be *sensitive* around Mary, and your mother too."

John nodded and rose from the armchair. "I will. Is that all, sir?"

His father nodded and John dismissed himself, wondering how well he might be able to control his remarks. It was a defence against sensitivity in himself, not a genuine desire to hurt or be mean. And maybe, just maybe, he had a bit of a naughty streak in him.

An hour later, Mary was seated in the corner of the sofa twisting a hanky in her lap. John stood, resting his forearm against the mantle as he made a point of studying the ornamental pieces lining the polished timber above the fireplace. A deep blue Moorcroft vase held sagging lilacs, their perfume now edged with the sharp odour of decay. Two carved bamboo paintbrush pots reflected the afternoon sun, their warm amber colours soothing the eyes.

"These came from China with you and your parents in '21, didn't they?" John said.

Mary glanced up at her handsome cousin. "Yes, we bought them and so many other things from the shops around Chengtu."

"Do you know what the Chinese characters mean?"

She stood and walked over to the mantle. Picking up one of the pair, she said, "It's a poem and so not easily translated into English. This one says something like 'Moon giving birth to the forest at dawn. Pass over the bridge, feels like autumn.' This column of characters is the year, in the Chinese calendar, of course."

She set it down and took the one John handed to her.

"This one is harder," she said. "The author wrote it by the side of the lake next to a stone chair, maybe? This column has the word for 'neighbour.' Then there's *du*, which could be 'pity' or 'community.' And this column translates as 'far,' perhaps the idea of thinking or recalling a lotus flower. And then *Pu*... I think it's a place name." Mary looked off into the corner of the room. "I don't get many opportunities to speak or read Chinese."

"How do you like your corner of Toronto?"

"You know, it took a long time to adjust to the school and city of Toronto. I rather enjoyed the British school for missionaries' children in Chengtu, but of course one has to have an education to accomplish anything worthwhile." She bowed her head, pursing her lips. "It's funny. That was something Ming Lin taught me at Junghsien. 'If it's not hard to do, then it's not worth doing.' Quite the opposite of what some think."

John fiddled with a silver jug. "Have you made friends at school all right?"

At this moment, he was wishing he had made a point of seeing Mary more often, though university took precedence and he worked hard. Holidays were the only time they met, and those were usually shared with half a dozen other cousins.

"Yes, I've met several students from Chengtu in different years, but I have two very close friends in the same dorm. They've been away with the geography class on a three-day excursion to New York State. Audrey and Viola." Mary straightened. "Still walking the 'hallowed halls' of Banting and Best in the medical department?"

John smiled. "They *are* revered, especially by the medical students. Their developing insulin has changed medicine and the future of diabetics." He glanced over at Mary. "We interns don't exactly tiptoe, but there's a feeling of awe in the labs."

Mary returned John's smile. "You enjoy it then? Not finding it too strenuous?"

John shook his head. "No."

There was a silent pause.

"Mary, I'm so sorry about your mother. Is there anything you would like me to do for you?"

"Thanks, John." She shook her head and allowed her chin to rest on her chest. "There isn't anything that can be done."

John turned away and frowned. He couldn't believe that his quiet, unassuming Aunt Edith had been killed. Would his Uncle Will return to Canada? Surely he wouldn't stay in those deplorable conditions, where unrest among students and violent military types seemed to be contributing to the political conflict.

⁂

A few weeks later, John stepped off the train from Toronto. He recognized two of his mother's sisters, their husbands, and several of his cousins disembarking from a carriage farther down the platform. Aunt Edith's mother and sister had travelled from British Columbia and were staying with his parents. This was one of the few times Mary had met her maternal grandmother. The last time she'd visited with her Grandmother Harrison had been over four years ago when her family had returned to Canada on furlough.

"Carmen, Aunt Margaret, Uncle Thomas. I didn't realize you were on this train too." John gave his aunt a hug, then shook his uncle's hand. As he grasped Carmen's hand, he leaned in and said, "Time to behave, cuz. Mary's still pretty broken up about this."

"And Mother and Father, too," Carmen said. "Oh, look, there's the others. Hello. Where's that new young brother, John Junior? We haven't met yet."

"He's hiding behind mother's skirts," said cousin Norah. "He's simply exhausted from the long trip. Is Mary at the manse, John?"

"Yes, along with aunts and Grandma Harrison, Edith's mother. She's taking her daughter's death with stoic bravery. You're all staying at the farm?"

"That's the plan. I suppose we'll see you tomorrow at Aunt Edith's funeral," said Norah.

John grimaced. No real funeral, no burial. There had been no chance of bringing her body back to Canada. The gathering was really for Mary's benefit, though she hadn't asked for any fuss. Perhaps it was a way to let others show they cared. In any case, it would be a dreary affair.

Twenty-Three

On the twenty-seventh of March 1927, Will Sibley walked down the gangplank of the *Empress of Asia* to the dock in Victoria, British Columbia. The journey from Hong Kong had been long and arduous, a sense of failure and grief burdening his heart and mind. He was departing at the same time so many others were also leaving because of the political unrest. It felt like desertion.

After many days at sea, he swayed slightly, though now on solid ground. This return to his homeland was so different than the previous furlough in 1921. Edith's death weighed heavily on him. How would he face his daughter, Mary, now a young woman of nineteen?

Will stood at the bottom of the steps to the entrance, studying the ivy and greening shrubs of Mary's boarding school. Compared to the dusty, dry streets of Chengtu and the treeless schoolyards in Szechwan, this was heavenly. He breathed in the fresh spring air.

Yes, we made the right decision in leaving Mary here in Canada, where she was safe and had the best training possible. Edith and he had often discussed the wisdom of leaving her on her own so far away, though she had relatives not far off. *It was our own selfish desire to have her close.*

Edith had missed her so often, but the sacrifice of not watching their child grow up had been necessary to be able to focus on spreading God's Word. They had forfeited much, and the gain may have seemed negligible, but he'd felt that even his few converts would grow in number and the Word would spread. In the meantime, thousands were cared for who might otherwise not have survived.

Will waited in the headmistress's office while she located Mary to bring her to him. He fiddled with his hat, until the door opened, revealing a much taller, more beautiful young woman than he remembered. Dark circles under her eyes alarmed him.

"Ah, Mary. There, there, dear girl. We mustn't grieve so in public." He glanced up at the headmistress and raised his eyebrows.

"I'll leave you now, Reverend Sibley," the headmistress said. "And please, my office is at your disposal. Help yourself to water and biscuits as you need."

With that, the headmistress stepped out the door, eyes pointed at the floor.

Will held his sobbing daughter in his arms, tentative in the unfamiliar pose. He patted her back, then stepped away to scrutinize this young woman who had matured so much in the past few years. He held her by the shoulders as she took a hankie from her pocket and blew her nose.

"Father, it's been so hard. So hard. I try to keep the sadness bundled inside, but it hasn't been easy." She wiped her eyes. "Oh, you're so thin." Her shoulders sagged. "You must be heartbroken about Mother."

She began to weep a portion of the many tears she had bottled deep inside. Sobbing, she clung to him, even as he tried to seat her in the office's leather wingback chair. He dragged a second chair closer to the first and wrapped his arm around her.

"Oh, Father. I wanted to see you so much, to hold you. I've waited so long." Mary again reached into her pocket for her hankie. "Why Mother? Why did that man hate Mother so much? What had she ever done to him?"

"Oh, Mary. Your mother simply happened to be in the wrong place at a time when the peasant could stand his burdens no longer. It wasn't your mother he attacked. He struck out at her because she was a foreigner. Even those of us who have proven we want to help them, give them hope of a better life… even we are linked to those foreigners who brought and spread the opium trade, who have taken their little pieces of land without compensation for the building of railways…"

"But surely they must see the benefits of the schools, churches, and hospitals."

"It is safer for them to attack foreigners in their frustration than the Chinese gangs of Mao Zedong and Chiang Kai-shek's militia. They don't know who will arrive next, and they all turn up with demands."

Mary nodded in understanding and agreement but burst out in fresh tears. "It's extremely confusing and dangerous, and I've been so alone, Father. I don't want you to go back and leave me again."

He patted her hand. "I've taken an early furlough and won't return for a year at least. You're ready to begin university in September, are you not?"

Mary wiped her tears. "Oh, yes. Miss Moore says I should study English and would make a wonderful teacher. I'm looking forward to going, but I want to think about the home economy classes. That would be fun to teach. Where will you be going, Father? Can you stay in Toronto?"

"I will, Mary. In fact, I hope to complete my doctoral thesis at the Vic along with supply work. I've thought about us boarding together."

"That would be wonderful!" Mary hugged her father with a burst of joy. "Oh, how I've wanted you to stay here. What will you do until then? Could we look for a little apartment to rent?"

Will nodded slowly. "We can see what the cost would be. I'm not much of a cook, you know. There was always a cook and someone to help with the garden, and your mother... well, your mother usually looked after the household affairs."

His head dipped. He truly missed Edith, her music making, her smile...

He brought his head up quickly. *I have a beautiful, intelligent, loving daughter, and I need to get to know her.* He squeezed Mary's shoulder.

"Mother was happy in Szechwan, wasn't she?"

Will pressed his lips together hard to block the tears. After a moment, he said, "She missed you terribly, Mary. Not a day passed without your name being mentioned, but she dedicated every bit of her energy and soul—and, as it turned out, her life—to help as many of the orphans and families of the town as she could. Despite the rebellions, the threats from the Boxers and Red Lantern Society, she never allowed any of it to dampen her enthusiasm for doing the Lord's work."

Mary tightened her grip on her father's shoulder and hugged his sleeve, and a fresh pouring of tears soaked into Will's rumpled suit. He allowed his own tears to flow, dripping onto his daughter's smooth, light brown hair.

⁂

At the end of the term, Mary moved her things into the boarding house where her father had rented rooms for them. Money had never been plentiful, but she had learned to be frugal as a young girl in Chengtu. Her father was often asked to speak at churches about missions in China, as the demand was still high. Interest carried on, despite the church offering less financial support.

"Do you think our landlady Mrs. Fullgate would like help in the kitchen, Father?"

"I'm not sure. She may regard that as interfering, but you could discretely ask. Are you bored, Mary? Would you like to continue piano lessons?"

Mary thought for a minute. "Yes, and I would like to join some sports team. Maybe tennis?"

Will nodded. "Good. There's a club only about four blocks south of here."

Mary didn't like to argue with her father, but this was the first summer she didn't have to be at boarding school or travel around the countryside visiting relatives. "There is a court in the other direction, a few blocks northeast of the school where some of my friends play."

Her father studied her while she concentrated on eating her lunchtime soup.

"I can still walk there," she added. "The fees are very reasonable for lessons."

Will shook his head as if in disbelief. "You are perfectly right to ask," he said. "Here you are, a grown woman at nineteen, not the thirteen-year-old we left alone at school. Of course you would like to meet up with your friends. I will have meetings many days, so certainly we should sign you up where you would like to play. I'll withdraw the fees from the bank tomorrow morning. We'll start your piano lessons next week with Miss Vida Coatsworth. She's not far away."

"Can we afford it, Father?" Mary watched her father for signs of displeasure, but he was smiling.

"Your scholarship fund has been growing, thanks to the generosity and hard work of your Grandmother Harrison." He looked away from Mary's intense gaze. "I stopped by Annie's while I was in Vancouver. I felt I owed it to your mother."

Mary could feel the tears building. "Oh, I'm glad, Father. How is Grandma Harrison doing? She seemed to be well at the memorial service, even after the long trip across Canada. Did she... was she able to understand why you couldn't be there?"

Will nodded. "She's coping. She's had some time to deal with the circumstances, but she will come east again to Ontario late in the summer. She dearly wants to get to know you better." He pursed his lips. "She allowed them to use our family photograph in the Summerland newspaper. It was quite a wonderful article about your mother and missions. Apparently, it stimulated donations to missionary funds from all over the town."

"That's wonderful news that she's coming to Ontario. Oh, I'm so glad. I can show her the school and some of the town. Will she stay with us?"

Mary began making plans for an August visit with the only grandparent she had left. They had first met when Mary was four years of age and quickly become friends.

Her bristly, whiskered Grandfather James had been courteous but intimidating. Her mother's younger sister and she had become allies quickly. Then, when Mary was ten, her grandfather had died, leaving her grandmother alone. She never complained, though the loss of another daughter would be very hard, as Mary's Aunt Ellie had died at age twenty-five.

Mary wondered if it was worth marrying and having children. She had seen so many orphans while growing up in Szechwan, perhaps she had hardened herself against wanting her own family. So many hundreds who needed care and love filled Christian orphanages in China. Their parents couldn't feed them, or maybe they wanted an honourable son to care for them in old age.

Mary knew there were many neglected and mistreated children even in Canada. Being a teacher would give her the opportunity to help some, so she didn't need to bring more into the world to do that. Many of her teachers had been spinsters.

Nothing wrong with dedicating yourself to a career.

Twenty-Four

1928

<small>Toronto</small>

Mary scrutinized her father facing the minister at the front of the church. Oversized bouquets of full pale blooms, positioned on pedestals at either side of the altar, sent a heavy fragrance wafting through the pews. Will's betrothed walked up the aisle with unexpected poise.

The arrangements seemed to have come about suddenly, near the conclusion of Will's furlough in June. Was he having second thoughts about getting remarried to Vida Coatsworth, or was he simply somewhat nervous before the formidable judge and his fiancée's clan?

Mary sat between her Aunt Mary Ann and cousin Nellie, listening to the wedding vows. Vida's niece, in a lovely yellow dress reflecting the bridal bouquet of roses, and the son of a cousin in his smart blazer characteristically twitched, displaying signs of restlessness, as most children six and seven years of age would.

The satin streamers dangling from Vida's bouquet fluttered gently in front of her full skirt.

It seems a little fancy for someone her age, Mary mused. *But maybe with it being her first marriage...*

"Unto death do us part." Her father's clear, firm voice overcame the implications of the vow. His eyes remained focused on the minister's face. He fished in his pocket for the ring he placed on Vida's finger.

He's holding onto her hand. Mary swallowed hard and blinked. *He wants to be married.*

"You may kiss the bride." Will leaned in and Vida met him, their lips meeting briefly.

Mary puffed out a breath in relief. It hadn't been as awkward as she thought it might be.

Seated beside her, Nellie twisted her long rope of beads draped around her neck. "Do you think they've been practicing?" she whispered near Mary's ear.

Mary pushed her new large-framed glasses back up her nose. "Of course they have. What do you think?"

She really did hope her father and Vida would be happy. Some people simply wanted to be married.

When the Sibley side of the family gathered near the trees in the back garden of the Coatsworths' spacious backyard, Mary stood behind her father as the photographer brought out his camera tripod. She wanted her father and Vida to be front and centre. Some of the younger cousins sat in the front row, cross-legged.

I hope I'm not squinting with that sun in my eyes.

"Mary, I understand you are attending the University of Toronto this fall," said Aunt Margaret. "What program are you enrolled in?"

"It's more of a general program to start the first year, but I hope to take an honours degree in Home Economics."

"Oh, that will be most practical. Certainly useful for when you get married and raise a family."

Why do people assume I'm going to get married? I don't think I want to. "My real desire is to be a teacher, Aunt Margaret, like Aunt Helen."

"Oh, but she's a career person." Her aunt tipped her head, studying Mary. "I suppose being the intelligent young woman you are, you might want to be one too."

Mary smiled. "Yes, Aunt Margaret. I'd like to teach the older students in secondary schools. Home economy is quite the science these days."

"Yes, I understand the University of Guelph has an entire department devoted to the subject." She laughed. "I didn't think being a housewife and mother was such a science. Mostly it's just natural or learned from our mothers." She drew her hand up to cover her mouth. "Oh, I'm sorry, Mary."

"It's all right, Aunt Margaret. You lost both your mother and father early on too, and you've done a wonderful job with your family. I've gotten used to doing things without my parents around."

Mary searched the mingling groups for her father. Vida had her hand through his elbow and still carried her bouquet.

"You know, I'm happy that Father has someone to look after him while he's in China," Mary said. "It seemed the single doctors and missionaries were more often sick than the married ones. Keeping house up to Canadian standards is extremely challenging, and not something of which the men really take notice."

Aunt Margaret shook her head. "I don't know how people do it. Such a foreign place and so many strange customs. I wouldn't want to. Isn't there enough work in this country? The price of everything is rising sky-high. I'm just glad we've had the farm."

"Yes, it's a hard life, but at least you always have something to eat. I hear there's drought out west."

"Yes, several years of drought off and on. I can't imagine the heartbreak of seeing fields stay dry and brown and the seeds blowing away with the dust."

"Let's get some lemonade, Aunt Margaret. I want to say hello to some cousins. I'm sorry John couldn't come until later."

Her aunt followed her to the tables where glasses of lemonade and an array of sandwiches had been spread out. No one here could complain of going hungry.

❋

After her father and Vida's departure and her Grandmother Harrison's visit, Mary threw herself into the entire school curriculum, from her classes to the sports teams through the glee club and Christian fellowship group. Keeping herself busy would ward off the sadness of missing her father and help prove she was worthy of the scholarship paying her way at the university.

I'm going to be the best student I possibly can.

The ache of separation had been breathtakingly painful again. Mary could still physically feel the tender sting of her parents' first departure.

They are leaving me in a foreign country, she had thought. *I'm here in a place I didn't grow up in.*

Then it occurred to her: they had left the country they'd grown up in and loved, to go out into a foreign place where they knew no one.

Mary wrapped her arms around herself in a resolute hug. At least she had some family and friends.

1932

WHITBY, ONTARIO, CANADA

After obtaining her master's degree in Home Economics, Mary felt she was finally on her career path—teacher's college. Frankly, she was surprised at the wide range of activities provided by the Whitby Ladies Teachers College, though she had no interest in horseback riding or archery. She might join in the dramatic and choral group, depending on the presentation they planned.

The May Day celebration pictured in the syllabus revealed the May Queen dressed all in white, followed by the little girls from town, also in white, holding the train of the Queen. The procession held a prominent place in the brochure's enticing photographs of the college.

Chills went up and down Mary's spine as the hired car turned into the long driveway between the imposing brick gates. The grounds were made safe at night with spotlights facing the base of the school buildings, lighting up the ivy-covered walls.

The main structure, she knew, had been finished in 1862 for Nelson Gilbert Reynolds and sold to the Methodist Church in 1874 for a school.

What a grand building for a church to own, and I'm lucky enough to attend here.

She had been instructed to go to the office to meet Miss Maxwell, the dean, before heading up to her rooms. She hoped she could leave her luggage with a porter near the entrance.

The driver took the two large trunks up the steps one at a time, and Mary followed with her tennis racket, hat box, carpet bag, and shoe bag. It was everything she owned in the world, unlike most of the girls who came with only the things they needed, having left most of their possessions at home.

Stop feeling sorry for yourself, Mary. Yes, it's another move, but maybe I'll meet old friends and make new ones.

Miss Maxwell's office reminded Mary of the boarding school's headmistress's office, plain and business-like. However, Miss Maxwell did not remind her of the stiff and formal headmistress of her former boarding school.

"Good morning, Miss Sibley. I trust you had a safe journey."

"Lovely, thank you, Miss Maxwell. I appreciate being met at the station by the driver. I'm afraid I do have quite a lot of luggage."

"Well, of course you would, not having a home in which to keep most of your possessions. We have storage rooms in the basement of the dining hall, should you like to sort out what you will need and what you may want to put away. Let me show you to your quarters. You can leave your things in the office for the time being, and a porter will take them to your assigned room later. Come this way."

Mary was impressed by the formal dining room, the gymnasium, and auditorium. "I'm amazed this was once a private residence," she remarked.

"Yes, quite," said Miss Maxwell. "Although there have been many additions since its inception as a school. Now, here are the change rooms, which you may use for any outdoor activities, and then we will climb the stairs to your room. Do you still speak Chinese, Mary?"

Mary raised a questioning face to the woman. "Not often, but I understand Szechwan Mandarin very well."

"We have an international student coming from central China, and I wondered if I might call upon you to help her fit in. You'll be sharing a room. We are only beginning to offer places to students outside of North America."

"I would be delighted," Mary said.

Oh, it will be a challenge. What memories will it bring to mind?

Twenty-Five

1932

WHITBY

Mary felt that the lace curtains were a little fussy for the size of the room, though the windows reached up twelve feet. It had been a grand mansion once upon a time, and the bedrooms had been subdivided for dormitories.

When she first met the new Chinese student, she had doubts. The young woman's expression was unreadable, despite Mary's cajoling and use of her own language.

"What is your Chinese name, Ruth?" she asked.

Ruth was an odd choice for a Chinese person, simply because the *r* sound didn't exist in their language.

The woman's black eyes widened. "I am told to speak only the English when in Canada."

"You will, of course, but I do speak and write Chinese. Where are you from?"

"Chungking. Do you know this place?"

"I had very little opportunity to visit anywhere outside of Szechwan, except when we travelled back to Canada for furlough. I don't believe we passed through there on either trip."

The student looked at the floor. "My Chinese name is Li Ping Yung."

"Well, Ping Yung, we will work together to make you comfortable here. Are your plans to return to China or stay in Canada?"

"My adopted mother wishes me to return and teach at her school. She take me in as a baby, left on the streets. Now I must have career. No rich man want one with big feet."

She lifted her ankle length dress to reveal size-five feet, never bound, and Mary smiled.

"You have small feet for Canada, and you will have to use them to walk everywhere," said Mary. "We are a big country with a small population, and there is much snow in the winter. I'm glad you have 'big' Chinese feet. You will find they are much better."

Ruth followed Mary around for the first few days, but on Sunday she refused to go to the chapel for church.

"Is your adoptive mother not a Christian?" Mary asked.

"Oh, yes. She go to church but want me to choose Confucius or Jesus, and I go with Confucius. Man on the cross too scary for me."

Oh dear. Poor girl. No one explained the sacrificial lamb.

Mary smiled encouragingly. "We can talk of this later. I would like to show you the chapel sometime, but not today. I will see you when I return from the service."

After the Methodist minister concluded the hour-and-a-half service, Miss Maxwell approached Mary.

"Good morning, Mary. I was expecting Ruth might be here with you."

Mary met the dean's eyes. "She preferred to stay away this morning, Miss Maxwell. It may take some time to convince her to attend a Christian church."

Miss Maxwell drew her head back. "Really? I was assured in her mother's letters that Ruth was a Christian. We have had many applicants with strong Methodist beliefs who might have been better candidates."

Mary squared her shoulders. Her height was an advantage in this case. "Miss Maxwell. With all due respect, I think this is a perfect opportunity to show what Christianity has to offer, but it won't happen by force. She must come to see the hope and love Christ offers on her own. I'll encourage her, and I anticipate opportunities for her to experience it herself. She must be surrounded with love and acceptance first."

Miss Maxwell offered no words to argue with Mary's reasoning. The heat rose in Mary's neck.

Have I gone too far? Am I wrong about this?

"Well, Mary, I see you have the missionary spirit of your parents in you. I'll be watching, but you appear to have a better understanding of the young woman than I do." She nodded slowly. "Yes, I believe you have the strength in you to bring this girl to the faith."

Mary relaxed. "Thank you, Miss Maxwell. I will be making every effort to do so."

Her doubts began as soon as she walked into the bedroom to smell the leftover whiffs of burnt incense. The profusion of ornaments and items on Ruth's bedside table had her taking a deep breath. A black lacquered box sat in the centre.

Patience. Patience. I can do this with Your help.

"Hello, Ruth. I'm glad you have some of your things out." Mary's eyes were drawn to a small stack of books. "Oh, I see you have a book by Lu Zun. Do you like his writing?"

Ruth turned her lips up, almost forming a smile. "Yes. He is the greatest modern author. I read many of his books."

Mary pointed to one. "May I?"

"Please, yes. He writes with the Chinese characters, but he says that, for a modern world, we cannot continue with characters."

"Does he suggest the world use the pinyin system with the Latin alphabet to translate the characters ?"

"No, he still writes with the characters."

"And the black box? That looks interesting." Mary didn't want to pry but wondered what idols Ruth might have brought with her. To Mary's surprise, Ruth smiled.

"That is game of Ma Jung. You know it?"

Mary bit her lip. "Isn't it a game that is rather frowned on?"

"Oh, no. It so much fun, many play games all day. No worse than your cards." She opened the box for Mary to examine the tiles.

"Oh. *Bei*, *dong*, *nan*, *xi*… the four directions."

Ruth appeared pleased. "Yes, four winds. I teach you to play?"

Mary hesitated, then nodded. "Yes, but maybe not on Sundays, and no money involved." It shouldn't hurt to learn a new game, one that Ruth showed keen interest in. Whatever she could use to make Ruth comfortable, she would. Besides, it might be fun.

1932
WHITBY

Mary had borrowed boxes of cleaning supplies she wanted to use in her classroom demonstration. Hers would be the first presentation to the class of Home Economy, so she had nothing to compare it to. Had she done enough work? Was she putting too much emphasis on using actual materials? She lined up the boxes of Hudson's Soap extract, Gem Soap Flakes, Borax, Brillo Pads, and the bottle of Clorox. Mother would have loved to have had even a small portion of these available to use in the nursery. Even simple cleaning supplies were nearly non-existent in the schools, Mary knew. Sometimes teachers were able to add requisitions to the hospital supply list, but often they had to use boiled water and elbow grease.

Upon finishing her presentation lesson, Mary sat down and waited for the critique that would follow.

The instructor, Mrs. Stanton, took her place behind the podium, bending to enable her to see her notes over her ample bosom.

"Well, Mary. You have set a very high standard of presentation for the rest of the class to follow. It was a thorough demonstration of a student lesson. Your organizational skills are evident, and the use of hands-on materials an excellent device." Mrs. Stanton carried on with specifics, then asked, "Do you have a medical background? You seem to have almost an obsession with cleanliness. Not that it isn't vital, but I just wondered."

Mary could feel the defensive attitude boiling up in her. Should she try explaining?

She cleared her throat and stood, as was required when answering in class. "I grew up in western China, where disease was rampant. Typhus, diphtheria, and cholera were constant threats, especially to infants and children. Many died, including the children of Westerners. The hospitals were supplied, but the poverty among most people was unlike anything we have ever seen in this country, even in the past few years with drought and the depression."

Mary took a breath and then continued.

"Most people in Szechwan were farmers, barely even able to feed their families. Their floors were dirt, the streets used for toilets and garbage. Lice and bugs were rampant. Westerners tried to explain, to demonstrate, that it was necessary to boil any water that would be consumed. I learned from an early age how cleanliness meant survival."

She was glad that Ruth wasn't in this class. The explanation would have embarrassed her.

Two other student teachers were of missionary parents in China. They joined in with Mary and Ruth in discussions and language practice.

Most times they helped Ruth with English, but they enjoyed trying to remember their Chinese and distinguishing various dialects.

Sometimes Ruth laughed at their pronunciation. "You use *tuhua*, earth speak. In Chungking, that is thought to be crude."

The others shot glances at each other.

Molly said, "My nanny taught me a few words, and when my father heard them, he got all red in the face and then angry. I think the boys would find out some of these words and use them."

Mary smiled. "I'm sure that happens in every country where boys try to outdo each other in getting away with using *bad* words."

"You're right," Molly agreed. "Lois was telling me her brother could get away with saying things that have never crossed her lips. Her father is a businessman, not a preacher like ours. How is your father and his wife doing these days, Mary?"

How much to say? "They have rebuilt in Penghsien after last year's fire, but they feel there is dwindling support from the West, and they don't know how depressed the economy is here. Apparently, there have been anti-Japanese parades and threat of civil war again. They beg for the Chinese to return to Chengtu after training in the West."

Molly was nodding. "So, the usual then?"

Mary tipped her head sideways in reply. Ruth remained silent. What must she be thinking?

"Ruth, have you heard from your adoptive mother lately?" Mary asked.

Ruth nodded. "Yes. She says things are very bad in the city. There are military and troops crowding the streets and squabbling breaking out. Some not very nice things are happening." She averted her eyes at their looks of concern. "But you know old Chinese saying: 'A crisis is an opportunity riding the dangerous winds.'"

That was an expression new to Mary, but she understood its significance. "Well, let's put on warm clothes and go out in the new snow. Soon it will be too deep."

It was a very busy year for the women at the college. They had opportunities to train with working teachers and at times prepared and taught classes themselves.

Christmas came with a reduced staff and many would leave for holidays with family and a much-needed break. Mary had been invited by her Uncle John and Aunt Mary Ann to their Paisley Street house in Hamilton, now that Uncle John was retired. Her cousin John would be home from Toronto, of course. He always lifted her spirits. There was a mischievous streak in him that his staider parents had not been able to quash.

Mary placed her carpet bag on her bed and flipped it open, ready to pack for the holidays. Her purchase of gifts had been small, considering her limited funds. She looked forward to a time next year when she would have her own salary and could freely spend the money she wished to on gifts.

She glanced over at her roommate. "Ruth, are you happy going to Molly's for the holiday?" she asked. "You're looking a little sad. Are you not satisfied with the plans?"

Ruth studied her hands, clasped in her lap. "I have not very nice gifts for Molly and her family. What will they think of receiving only a handkerchief or scarf?"

"Oh, Ruth, you don't need to worry about gifts. They will appreciate what you give them, no matter what. They understand you are a student, the same way I am a student and feel that my gifts to my aunt, uncle, and cousin are inadequate. They'll know this and understand. When we are working and receiving our own salary, we can go shopping."

"But Christmas is all about sharing gifts, is it not?"

Mary sat beside Ruth on her bed. "Ruth, there are many gifts that have no price value but are more important than anything we can buy.

God's gift of Jesus to us can never be repaid with any sort of gift-giving. Our love can be shown with a smile, or helping hand, or an appreciative comment. We don't need to keep score, but we give freely to show our love."

Ruth turned to Mary with a puzzled look. "Is this true in only Canada?"

With an arm around her shoulder, Mary hugged Ruth. "No. This is true everywhere, North America or Asia. Jesus asked us to love one another."

Twenty-Six

1936

KINGSTON

Mary heard a tapping on the front door outside of her room and voices as the landlady answered it. The next tap was at her door. Mary opened it and stiffened. A telegram. She nodded her thanks to Mrs. Hardcastle and closed her bedroom door. She opened the envelope in a hurry, then relaxed. The telegram from her father announced his and Vida's safe arrival in Los Angeles from Honolulu on March 10. At least they were on the continent. They had waited in Honolulu for over two months to get safe transport back to North America.

Mary pictured Honolulu and the tropical vegetation, the chickens roaming freely around the countryside, and warm ocean waves rolling onto sandy beaches. She had seen the postcards and smiled. How hard would waiting there be? Of course, after nine years on the mission field, where recent tensions made life even more arduous for Westerners, they deserved a little relaxation.

Vida's parents had invited Mary to their Etobicoke home for Easter weekend during the second week of April. She looked forward to the break. It would be a joyful reunion for her, knowing her father would remain in Canada once and for all.

After much anticipation, Easter weekend arrived, and the joyous reunion they all had hoped for materialized. Will's own tearing up surprised him, whereas Mary's did not. At least they were happy tears.

The meal was superb, as the Coatsworths made an extra effort in celebrating their daughter's safe return from a country they considered dangerous. Vida's older widowed brother and her spinster younger sister joined them.

The conversation inevitably swung around to the slow invasion of the Japanese military.

"What? You mean that little country is taking on the giant of China?" Judge Emerson Coatsworth bellowed.

His deafness resulted in some very loud conversations and made Mary's ears ring. Vida and her sister were looking crossly at their father, either because of the subject or the volume. Mary wasn't sure which.

"China may appear much bigger on the map, but the Japanese have a tremendous population, which is bursting at the seams of its borders." Will wiped his lips with his linen serviette. "The Japanese have allowed some conspirators among the Guangdong Army to create supposed Chinese attacks on Japanese residents and workers along the Manchurian railway. This has been happening for years, going so far that now Korean-Japanese armies are moving in from South China."

"I thought the Chinese Nationalists published a goodwill mandate, banning the anti-Japanese movement," the judge said.

Will cleared his throat. He didn't like to argue with his father-in-law, but the issue was so complicated, the news in the media so persuasive, that he didn't have a hope of explaining what was truly happening in Manchukuo.

"Yes, they have," Will said. "And there have been Japan-China trade associations established. We can pray that things will settle down."

How could he explain the tensions between Russia and Japan, between the Nationalists and Mao Zedong, the armies, subversives, private trade, and the League of Nations? *He* didn't understand it all, though he had lived among all the strife for more than two decades.

Vida's mother, Helen, broke in. "Shall we change the topic, Emerson? Do you remember our last trip to Britain together in 1924, Vida?"

Vida smiled. "I remember it well. You were directing the porter to load our trunks onto the dolly so we could flag down a hackney at the front of Paddington Station. It was chaos. There was no one to meet the train. Uncle Harold couldn't drive anymore. You said, 'I wonder if I've done the right thing in taking you girls traipsing around the globe. Neither of you seem content to find yourselves husbands and are enjoying careers as teachers far too much.'"

Vida smirked and worked on finishing her dinner.

Mary said, "I'd love to go to England and Scotland someday. It would be lovely to see all the places we read about."

"Well, it was a busy trip," Helen said. "You girls never seemed to have your pocketbooks open."

"Oh, Mother. We adored travelling. We learned so much going on those trips," Vida's sister said. "I am thoroughly satisfied with my life as a teacher." She glanced at Mary. "You are, aren't you, Mary?"

Mary smiled and nodded. "Very much so."

"And to think you, Vida, have spent all these years in China." Helen shook her head. "What will become of the churches you left behind?"

Mary caught the exchange of looks between her father and Vida. Some would never understand the draw the Orient had for Christians wanting to share their faith. And yet Judge Coatsworth's home was decorated with artifacts from around the world: decorative plates, sculptures, and artwork. Even a pair of carved bamboo paintbrush pots, so like the ones her Aunt Mary Ann and Uncle John Kitching displayed proudly on their mantle.

Vida clasped Will's hand. "We had promises from Dr. Sun and Reverend Wang. They will keep things going, no matter what. 'Even if we have to run to the hills, we will continue your work,' they said."

＊

The summer holidays of 1937 rapidly approached. Mary had made time to read the Pulitzer Prize-winning American author who was becoming her favourite: Pearl S. Buck. She had read *The Good Earth* before Christmas and was completing *Sons* at the moment. She understood why the author was so renowned and had won awards.

Mary had difficulty hiding her anticipation of the summer. On the final day of classes, paperwork and departmental discussion kept her very busy. Mary and Miss Shand, one of the other home economics teachers, were assigned to clean out the fridges, the top and bottom cupboards, the stoves, and the closets. Nothing was left untouched, and a strong odour of disinfectant permeated the air of the classroom kitchens.

Mary polished the taps and sink with satisfaction, standing back to view her handiwork. She had just concluded her third year of teaching at the Kingston Collegiate Institute and Vocational School.

"Do you have plans for the summer, Mary?" Miss Shand asked.

"I do, and I'm very excited. My mother's sister has arranged a touring party of Yellowstone Park, and I've been invited. My three teenage cousins will be accompanying us. I'm taking the Canadian Pacific train, the *Dominion*. I'm catching it here in Kingston, and we'll arrive in Vancouver two days before crossing over to Washington State."

"My, that sounds like a wonderful trip. Pardon me for asking, but is it expensive? I've thought of travelling west."

"Well, it is quite pricy, but I've been saving for three years and it's my first vacation, not counting my trips to Toronto to visit my father and his wife."

"You speak of his wife. Is she not your mother?"

Mary quickly shook her head. "My father was widowed more than ten years ago and remarried Vida."

She kept wiping and polishing, hoping to avoid any more conversation in the uncomfortable direction this was proceeding. Miss Shand was a colleague who rarely engaged in friendly banter.

Mary tidied the remains of the cleaning supplies under the sink. She needed to make a quick getaway to prepare for her trip.

"I'll take this bag of garbage to the janitor and then be on my way, Miss Shand." She was too wound up to stand around making conversation.

Miss Shand checked her purse before removing her sweater and apron from the hook behind the door. "I hope you'll have a wonderful holiday this summer, Miss Sibley."

"Thank you, Miss Shand. And I hope you'll have a wonderful holiday yourself."

She gathered her aprons, placed them in her cloth shopping bag, and walked down the empty hall to the boiler room to deposit the last bag of garbage.

Mary wanted a total break from routine and looked forward to this outdoor adventure with the cousins she barely knew. She would postpone thinking of any concerns over the destabilizing of the Chinese currency. The Japanese forcing warlords in northern China to break away from the Nationalists could only mean they intended trouble, and she had no idea where the communists stood in all of this.

What would happen to the children in orphanages? Would they be fed? What about older people who were failing to earn their way, women like Ma Ling and others who had worked for the missions. Some of her 'mish' kid friends had returned to China to join their families as missionaries. Now they were being ousted by the Chinese government. All she could do was keep in touch with friends and support them, but for now she would focus on her planned trip out west and the luxury of riding aboard a sleeper right across Canada.

She hurried to her boarding house, where her trunks and suitcases had been half-packed for days.

"Mrs. Hardcastle, would you have a few minutes to show me where I can take my things to place in storage for the summer?" Mary asked.

Since she would be away for two months, the boarding house owner's daughter Celia could have her old room back while home from her nurse's training in New York.

An hour before the train was due to arrive, the driver dropped Mary and her suitcases off at the Kingston train station. The weather was fine, so she waited outside on the bench after checking the punctuality of the train bound for Detroit-Windsor.

During the long train ride west, Mary studied the brochures for the outstanding American national park. She shuffled through them. Two caught her interest: "Plants of Yellowstone National Park" (1936) and "Trailside Notes". She also located maps for the hiker. She'd packed her walking shoes and long pants, thinking that even if her Aunt Beatrice and Uncle Thomas didn't want to hike, her sixteen-, thirteen-, and ten-year-old male cousins and Uncle Thomas's other nieces and nephews would want to go.

A third brochure caught her eye—a new publication with a photo of Old Faithful on the front. Another with an attractive cover was a pamphlet titled "Early History of Yellowstone National Park and its Relation to National Park Policies" (1932). Mary had read of the Folsom-Cook expedition of 1869, the main point she'd taken from the booklet being that the park's discovery linked it to expeditions of settlers prospecting for gold.

The entire family crossed the border on July 6, 1937. They would all stay in Yellowstone, walking the trails and enjoying the outdoor camping. Thrills of anticipation tingled up and down her spine.

Throughout the trip, the smells of pine trees and cooking fires reminded Mary of Camp Quentin on Mount Omi. For a month each summer her parents' anxieties had fallen away and they focused more attention on her, laughing and enjoying the warm weather without mission concerns.

Here in the wilderness with family, Mary experienced new pangs of loss. Not the immediate loss she felt with her mother's death, but the absence of shared memories, of toughing things out, of sharing laughter and love with her parents at important times of her life.

＊

After Mary's return from her holiday late in the summer, she paid a visit to her father and stepmother. Will dozed off in a comfortable chair in the garden of the manse, allowing Mary and Vida time to connect.

"Aubrey, my youngest cousin, was the most troublesome on the trip," Mary said. "I don't know whether it's because of his nature or the fact that he's youngest and seems immune to grasping the rules, but he certainly gave us a scare, I can tell you. The wardens, Uncle Thomas, his brother, and I all went searching for him on the mountain where we had followed the trail just an hour earlier, in the full light of day. In the darkness, we had to follow the headlamps of the wardens and watch our steps. We each had a small tin-framed candle holder which we held in the air, hoping to cast a bit of light amidst the trees."

Vida sipped a tall, thin glass of lemonade. "Your Aunt Beatrice must have been frantic."

"Somehow she seemed resolute, but I think she was counting on us finding him. Which we did an hour later."

"Was he hurt? Had he gotten lost?"

Mary shook her head and laughed. "He'd fallen behind. I had done my best to keep an extra eye on him, trying to follow him all along, but somehow, at a rest stop, everyone lost sight of him. As it turned out, he had gone off the trail when he heard the sound of a waterfall. Only by God's good grace did one of the wardens check a favourite lookout where Aubrey sat huddled in fear, having seen a bear."

"*Could* he have seen a bear?"

Mary grimaced. "Yes. There are bears in the woods of Yellowstone Park, which is why everyone was warned to stay on the marked trail." She smiled. "Otherwise it was a most wonderful experience, and I'm so glad I went. A wonderful memory I will cherish forever."

"My mother always thought travelling was the best education. She took us on quite a few trips before I married your father." Vida glanced over at Will, his head tipped to the side, his eyes closed. "I hope to convince Will we could travel to England sometime soon."

Twenty-Seven

1939

KINGSTON

The letter from her Grandmother Harrison was propped between the cast-iron ashtray and inlaid jewellery box on the hallway table where Mrs. Hardcastle placed the post for the three lodgers. Mary smiled with anticipation. Her grandmother had made great effort to write to her twice a month with updates on the immediate family and friends. She often included notes about missionaries in China, and this letter, by its thickness, probably included a clipping from the newspaper.

With the letter and a pot of tea on a tray, Mary retreated to her room where she could prop her feet up on a footstool to relax in a civilized manner. She tipped the teapot of steaming liquid through a strainer, expertly aiming it into the delicate white and blue painted porcelain teacup.

Things had worsened in China since the Japanese invasion in July of 1937.

> My friend Ruth Carter told me about her daughter who works at the China Inland Mission Hospital in Chengtu. She met Jean Ewen, who was accompanying Dr. Bethune to the frontline to attend the wounded. The

hospital was preparing for siege as the Japanese army was only ten miles behind Dr. Lim's Chinese Red Cross Unit, with whom Jean and Bethune were attached. They had travelled gruelling miles by foot and rail. Jean was resolute and matter of fact. She didn't appear to let Dr. Bethune's frustration at not being able to treat more of the wounded or being delayed trouble her.

There is a great deal of stress because of shortages of doctors and medical staff, despite new Chinese trainees. Mission schools in outlying areas are being sold and many missionaries are taking furlough. Disruptions from government attacks on mission schools are forcing closures. There was a mob attack in the city and two Japanese newsmen were killed. People are angry. Reliable news is not getting through, as most printing presses have been taken over by the government.

I am glad to say that the Harrison Fund is still active and paying for the education of missionary children residing in Canada. Will sends word about the fund from what is reported at the meetings, even since he and Vida have returned to Ontario.

Mary read the other news of her nieces and nephews. Her Aunt Beatrice also kept her up to date. They had grown much closer after her trip out west. Beatrice included her as she would a younger sister, warming Mary's reflections on the family expedition to a great extent.

She went back to the description of Jean Ewen. What had happened to her after Bethune's death? On the one side of Canadian opinion, Dr. Bethune was a traitor. The other side agreed with Mao's eulogizing Bethune.

What about everyone else who had given their lives to serve, and the people around the world who had for a century financially supported the missions, hospitals, schools, churches, and universities in China? Of course, they weren't communists. Had missionaries been such unwelcome guests?

She slapped down the letter. *What's the matter with me? Here the Japanese have walked into China, promising this and that to Germans and Koreans in the cities, while Russia hovers at the border like a hungry dog ready to pounce.*

Mary opened the latest newspaper, dated Friday, September 29, 1939. Not a day since the beginning of the month had there been anything on the front page but news of the world's second great war. Germany and Russia had divided up Poland between them. Chinese villagers were being massacred by the Japanese and given little help by the military. Boatloads of Jews were being turned away from North and South America, but thousands were being given visas to Shanghai, ending up within the one square mile of the Restricted Sector for Stateless Refugees...

1939
HONGKEW, SHANGHAI, CHINA

Lawrence Kadoorie glanced at the line of refugees along the eight-foot brick wall of the entrance to Hongkew.

It's a bit like hell, he thought. *They think they're being rescued, but at least here they have some chance of survival.*

He knew their clothes would become tattered and worn to shreds after a few months of wearing the same thing day after day.

Lawrence stopped in front of a man he assumed was a rabbi. Perhaps he would be good at leading the arriving group to settle in.

"*Hela freynt,*" he greeted the rabbi in Yiddish.

The long-bearded, bespeckled man drew his head back in surprise. Lawrence glanced down at his own blue trousers, stained and rolled up revealing his handmade rattan sandals. How far he had come from silk three-piece suits, custom-made in the latest fashion.

"Are you the leader among this group?" Lawrence asked, carrying on in Yiddish. He was trying to establish a helpful attitude to acclimate this group to the realities of living in Hongkew.

"Yes, I suppose the people in this group expect me to guide them," said the man. "We are just off the ship from Vienna. Where are we to go now? Do you know? Forgive me. I am Rabbi David Isaac."

"Call me Lawrence, please. You and your people will be in shock. Please tell them to keep all of their belongings close. Others who have been here for months or years will try bartering useless things for something warm to wear in the colder months."

"Is there a hotel nearby? We have several women in the family way who need a bed to rest on."

Lawrence shook his head at the irony. Six years ago, his father had owned the best hotel in the city. Now the Japanese officers had established themselves there, crowding into the lavish rooms, tearing down anything Chinese, and pinning up maps and grainy photos between the gilded art deco light fixtures. That was in another world, another part of the city.

"Here we have more than a hundred thousand Chinese, Jewish, and other stateless refugees crammed into one square mile of bombed buildings. It doesn't matter if you have money or had it. Everyone will need to share accommodations. This street will be filled with vendors early in the morning. You will need to make a grab for what vegetables you can. Find a cooking pot you can share and look for blankets at a reasonable price."

Rabbi Isaac's face lost its colour as his eyes widened with horror. "Where will we find Kosher foods?"

Lawrence gave a disheartened laugh. "The good Lord will forgive us, I'm sure, if we must eat other food to keep alive. You will see."

He surveyed the group, beckoning them to follow as he and the rabbi walked next to each other. He would lead them to the most spacious building, which could be fixed for suitable quarters for the forty or so people gawking from side to side, pressed together against the crowded flow of gaunt Chinese carrying everything from soup pots to bags of bedding.

"Will there be toilets and clean water where you are taking us?"

Lawrence shook his head. "No. Outhouses are used. The water systems were destroyed with the bombing. Any water you get must be boiled and boiled. If not, you can expect dysentery."

The rabbi's shoulders drooped, but he called back to encourage the others to keep pace, to stay together and hold onto their belongings.

Lawrence turned down a refuse-strewn alley to an open doorway and pointed up the cement steps. The building had been filled with sewing machines and bolts of fabric, housing a prosperous business before the Japanese had arrived.

He grasped the sleeve of the rabbi and pointed across the alley. "I live in that building and wash my son's diapers in the courtyard. I'll come back tomorrow to help you."

"Is there any Red Cross or health organization? Isn't the United States assisting refugees in Shanghai?"

Lawrence bit his lip. "There are a few nurses who try to help the thousands, but we never see any financial assistance. I'm sure it's diverted by the Chinese military to support the war effort."

"Should we expect to be arrested?" The rabbi peered nervously up the steps. "Is the Gestapo anywhere near?"

At last, Lawrence could say something positive for these newcomers. "No need to worry about the Gestapo. The Japanese have only arrested the very wealthy Jews in the city, so they might confiscate their homes and businesses. Most of us are in this concession. The Japanese are keeping the Germans far away from the Jews. They don't agree with the Nazis' politics."

The rabbi nodded at Lawrence as he directed people up the stairs. "Thank you. You have given us hope, where before we had none."

1939

PEKING, CHINA

When Sung Shangjie had stepped off the boat in Peking in 1927, he'd never dreamed he would be evangelizing to crowds everywhere he went. After receiving his doctorate in chemistry in Ohio and teaching briefly, he'd had a spectacular conversion and switched to the Union Theological Seminary.

Unfortunately, he had then grown troubled and signed himself in for psychiatric treatment.

After a period of rehabilitation, the authorities had returned him to China where he entered into an arranged marriage and soon had children. He loved to read aloud from the Bible and bring the characters alive with his acting skills.

This particular gathering hummed with excitement as he perched on a stool, addressing the audience from the church's platform.

"The good news of our Lord Jesus Christ is that you can be saved," he spoke. "You can break the bonds of tyranny while on this earth. You can free yourselves from fear and threats of war. You can find hope in God right now." Shangjie—or John, as he was known to many—carried on. "Go to your churches. Speak with your priests and ministers. Follow God's love and love your neighbour. When you have sinned, repent."

He bowed and stood, having delivered his message to hundreds of local citizens.

His wife brought him a bowl of fresh water, their youngest son slung on her hip. His other four children stood close together, not minding those around them but watching their father curiously. His passion for Christianizing his people—all people, in fact—had taken him far and wide away from them.

On this day he was surprised that his wife, Jin, had caught up with him.

"You found me."

"Your name is everywhere," she replied. "And the people are happy to direct me to your side."

"Have things been well?"

Jin looked at him with large eyes. "We have survived. The Japanese noose is tightening around those in the north. I worry about your father. His church is in danger. War is coming to all the world."

"The only war that matters is with Satan. We must reach the people with the Gospel before it's too late."

"It may be too late for some already. Please come home with us."

John nodded. "I will find you accommodation. Should the city become unsafe, you can come to the village here for refuge."

"Your friend has sent this note and a list of places where the people are asking for you." Jin lowered her eyes. "You must come back home and take care of yourself." Just above a whisper, she added, "And us."

He enjoyed acting out the parables on stage, but John knew his wife was right. He needed surgery—again.

"We will go. I have a meeting tonight with some of the elders at the Presbyterian church. Then we will go home." He tousled the hair on his youngest son's head. "Do you remember the story of Jesus and the children? 'Come unto me,' he said..."

1939

CHENGTU

Shelling sounded in the distance and smouldering ash sent odours of destruction swirling around the hospital through broken windows.

Dr. Whang summoned the gatekeeper to come inside. "We must prepare to receive more wounded."

Pen Chi Lin threw his head forward. "But we are full, Doctor. There are no more bandages and no more beds."

Dr. Whang pulled on Pen Chi Lin's sleeve toward the staircase. "Have the nursing sisters tear up some old clean sheets for bandages. Help your son who is up on first floor to move patients with diseases to the second floor, and we will put bags of straw here on the main floor for the newly wounded."

Pen Chi Lin wondered how Dr. Whang knew that more wounded would be arriving. Was that what the meeting with the soldier had been about? He was somewhat puzzled by the insignia on the man's tan uniform.

Pen Chi Lin hurried up the steps, glancing at the crucifix on the wall before he turned the corner to ascend the next flight of stairs.

Do you see what's going on, Jesus? he prayed. *When will this end?*

He felt that the local government was useless. What did they know about bombed-out buildings and wounded survivors?

Spotting Fong helping a man to his bed, Pen Chi Lin shouted at his son. "Fong, put a gown on and wrap your face with a cloth. We are taking the dysentery and typhoid cases from downstairs and bringing them up to the second floor."

"Why? There is no room."

"Dr. Whang's orders." Pen Chi Lin turned to go down the stairs.

"Father, cover your face with this." Fong handed his father a thin piece of sheeting. "Wrap it twice and sterilize your hands."

Pen Chi Lin huffed. "You are not a doctor yet."

But he took the sheeting and smiled inwardly. His son would be a doctor one day, thanks to the Westerners' hospital and university. The missionaries had been forced to leave behind their buildings, schools, and fortunately some trained Chinese teaching staff. He couldn't worry about which political group would organize the country. Any of them would need hospitals; even if they brought back ancient medicines, there would be a place for modern surgery and a high standard of cleanliness.

He hurried down the steps and into the first room on the main floor, searching for men who would be able to get upstairs without assistance. Then he would organize a stretcher to carry some of the others to the second floor. It would make some space on the main floor for the incoming wounded. Treating them was another matter.

What would he do if the doctors were to become sick and wounded? The bombing had been heavy. Brick buildings had been flattened to piles of rubble, broken sewage drains were sending wisps of dreadful fumes into the air, and dusty, bedraggled children were shuffling around with blank faces. War.

Twenty-Eight

1948

Kingston

Mary exited Chalmers United Church through the side door. It had been a delight to see Mable at the May evening meeting, and they had agreed to catch up over tea next week. As she made her way down the cement steps in front of the building, a young woman hurried to catch up.

"Miss Sibley," the woman called, waving her notebook. "Yoohoo, Miss Sibley!"

Mary stopped and waited for the woman with a smile.

"Miss Sibley. I would very much like to interview you for an article with the *United Church Observer*. I'm Betty Watson, a freelance writer."

After agreeing to meet at the diner on Princess Street for lunch on Saturday, Mary made her way back to Nelson Street through the slush and muddy sidewalks.

✳

Mary checked the booths and recognized Betty immediately. Her hair seemed shellacked into place, an unnatural sheen to the black bob, her berry-red suit fitting smartly across the broad padded shoulders and down to a slim waist.

Very modern, thought Mary.

"Hello, Betty. My, that's a smart looking outfit." Mary took off her long, brown woollen coat and hung it on the triple-pronged hook between booths. Then she smoothed her hunter-green wraparound dress with matching belt and seated herself. It would be as private a setting as a family restaurant could be on a Saturday.

Mary ordered an omelette, passing up pancakes or the farmer's sausage on a bun. Casual conversation ensued through the meal until coffees were served, and Betty got out her notebook.

Mary watched the woman take seemingly innocent glances around them. She got strong vibrations of secrecy from Betty and shivered in response.

The waitress came by with a pot of coffee and filled their cups. The milk pitcher was still half full, enough for several more cups, should they choose to stay. The rush had slowed, and the rowdiness calmed so they could now hear each other speak.

Betty leaned toward Mary in a conspiratorial stance. "I have a confession to make, Miss Sibley."

Mary straightened as she stirred her coffee in the heavy ceramic mug. "Oh?" was all she could bring herself to say.

"I actually work for a political organization. Please don't tell anyone. It's the Communist Party. I just wanted your views on China's political situation, you having been a 'mish' kid and all."

Again, the only response Mary could summon was "Oh." She gave one last stir and put the spoon back on her side plate. "Do you wish to quote me, or can I give you my honest opinion?"

Betty laughed. "Oh, good. You have a sense of humour. Well, you don't have to go on record, but I really wanted to know about the conditions in China and how it will work when Mao Zedong forms a communist party."

Mary nodded as she sipped her still hot coffee. "Well, that's a good question. I'm not sure I can answer it. I haven't lived there for decades."

"Just whatever you think. You must have contacts. Tell me more about China."

"Well, from a foreigner's perspective, there are many Chinas, in the same way there are many geographical areas, many cultural differences in Canada." Mary frowned. "Do you want a perspective as a Christian or politician? Or an ordinary person?"

"As a Christian, an ordinary person."

"All right. Well," Mary fumbled, "there are so many considerations, and I'm not sure I can even begin to tell you what I think. Perhaps I can tell you what a few people I know in China think."

"I understand James Endicott is not pleased with Chiang Kai-shek and the Kuomintang," Betty said. "What do you know about what happened at the West China Union University last winter?"

Rubbing the knuckles of her right hand vigorously, Mary considered. Most of what she had heard came from news reports, but she had heard a few things from a friend at the university—in privately coded letters. Things were not good.

"You know, we children of missionaries were always advised to stay out of politics, warned that religion and politics shouldn't be mixed. But there were thousands of dissatisfied students from five universities in Szechwan, and they rallied at the West China Union University. The western missionaries built, staffed, and expanded this university. The Chinese students wanted reform. They wanted peace and a better life than their parents. Most of all they wanted fairness and a coalition government that would guarantee fundamental freedoms, democracy even."

Mary tipped her mug up, but the last cold drops didn't appeal to her.

"What I understand is that James Endicott saw the police ready to surround those on stage and jumped up to prevent them arresting anyone by making a speech. Four students had been killed in the previous month, but he took a chance the police wouldn't jail a foreigner. He understands there is a rising tide of unrest, especially among the farmers and agricultural workers who account for about sixty percent of the population."

"That seems like a high number," Betty remarked. "Are you sure?"

"Yes. Only a small percentage of people live in the cities, and, prior to being expelled, almost all the foreigners. Outside of missionaries, doctors, nurses, and teachers, the cities were full of rich foreigners and Chinese businesses, legal and illegal."

"Like Shangdai du Yuesheng and the Kadoorie hierarchies? All those fabulous hotels and clubs we hear about?"

Mary's eyebrows rose. She'd heard of the gang leader Shangdai and of the vast wealth Jewish families from Baghdad had gained and lost in Shanghai and Hong Kong prior to World War II.

"But how does the Christian faith work into this feeling of rebellion?" Betty asked.

"Christians want to see justice, fairness, and a government that isn't suppressive and dictatorial or riddled with corruption. They wanted the people to freely choose Christ, unimpeded by crushing taxes, suspicions, and tattle-telling. The youth are the ones who hope communism will change their lot in life. They saw their agrarian parents and grandparents lose everything during the rebellion. Farmers have always been notoriously poor in this world, and so dependent on weather conditions. Underappreciated, usually."

Betty nodded but went back to her specific topic. "I understand Endicott believes there will be a revolution, that the united front of Chiang Kai-shek and Mao is collapsing."

Mary reluctantly nodded. "He may very well believe that." She stood, pulling on her overcoat. "Well, I should be off."

Betty stood. "But which side will come out on top?"

1952
TORONTO

Mary recalled the meeting with Betty before deciding to give her father a call in Toronto. It meant spending a tidy sum for a few minutes of live connection, but she knew he would be up to date on, and maybe fretting about, the developments in China. She had been reading *The Toronto Star*.

"Hello, Father?"

"Mary. How are you? Is everything okay? You don't often call."

Mary frowned at the lethargic tone she was hearing. "I'm fine, thanks, Father. I heard about the final expulsion of missionaries. Is that in all of Szechwan, or China? Have you heard from the Canadian School in Taiwan?"

"Smith wired from Taiwan to assure us that everything's stable for now. They've settled there along with the Nationalists spreading across the island, not just Taipei. But we're finished in China, dear. Even the most recent arrivals have already shipped out. It's a sad end to so much of our work, so many lives given for the sake of Christ."

Mary heard the deep sorrow in his voice, the sense of having lost the battle.

"Father, you mustn't think of having been defeated by the communists. There are thousands, maybe millions of Chinese Christians, and they'll remain faithful to Jesus. The communists can't stop what people think. People will find a way to get around the rules. They always have."

"But the West China Mission has closed, and Chinese missionaries are leaving the country in droves since the Korean War."

"Father. Those Chinese missionaries were converted by a Christian at some point. Even if they are leaving China, they'll continue to evangelize in other countries. Canada has started to receive Chinese missionaries. Look at the new Mandarin-speaking congregations popping up in Toronto and Vancouver. You should attend one to see how God's Word has spread."

"You're ever the optimist, Mary."

"Thank you, Father. I was taught well. We have to be positive about this seeming backstep by China. You know, they finally started working on the railway from Chengtu to Chungking. Wouldn't that have been handy forty years ago?"

"Oh my, yes, wouldn't it have," he said. "Such little regard for the human condition. Women and men carrying all the luggage and passengers." Her father tsked in regret.

Mary sighed. "I haven't heard anything from friends at the hospital, but I'm sure it's even more difficult than it was before the war. We'll pray, won't we, Father? Give Vida my love."

Mary dropped the receiver into its cradle on the wall.

After her light dinner in a rented room, Mary checked her back issues of the University of Toronto newsletters. There were notes from several Chinese pastors being imprisoned, along with idealists and political activists against the communist regime. Mao struck hard and often. The prisons were full.

She would not write again to her friend at the hospital until she heard back. It might make matters worse, even if it passed the censors.

Mary fought tears gathering in her eyes and searched for a dry hankie. Hadn't she suffered enough for the cause after losing her mother at such a young age? At the time of her mother's death, she had felt her faith was being tested.

She should focus on other things. The twenty-five-year-old Elizabeth Windsor had ascended the throne, now that her father was deceased. As in so many situations in life, the joyous celebration of her coronation next year would be tempered by the loss of a king.

Twenty-Nine

1949

WOLFE ISLAND, ONTARIO, CANADA

Mary adjusted her glasses behind the podium at the United Church on Wolfe Island. Her prior addresses had paved the way for a flurry of groups inviting her to speak about Chinese mission work. She was determined to shine a positive light on the situation.

"I'd like to tell you the story of the first Chinese woman to graduate from a Canadian university as a nurse. Hers is a most inspiring story…"

1910

FATSHAN, CHINA

Chan Ah Fung stood beside her mother in her best dress. Its colour had faded and the edges were frayed. Her five elder sisters had worn it and now, at six, only she could still fit into it. She didn't understand why everyone was being so kind to her today, even though she remained hungry. Something special was happening, and it wasn't her birthday.

"She will grow strong." Her mother's voice trilled through the Mandarin words. "She is a good Chinese daughter."

Ah Fung peeked around the skirt of her mother and frowned. She didn't know this woman who stood tall on wooden shoes. She was shiny. Her fan shone, her dress shimmered, and the beads dangling from her hair sparkled. There was no dust anywhere on her. Why did Ah Fung's mother push her toward this woman?

"Follow me," said the woman. "I am your new mother. Serve me well and you will have enough to eat."

The stranger took tiny steps to turn herself in the other direction. Was Ah Fung to go with her? She turned to look back at her mother, hoping she would shake her head; instead her mother cast her hands from her waist, waving Ah Fung toward the other woman. Then she rotated and disappeared into the crowd.

"Madam. Madam. Wait for me." Ah Fung caught sight of the tall woman moving away from her through the groups of people, step by tiny step.

She managed to get closer and skirted around two young scholars to get directly in line behind the woman. Once there, she had no trouble staying within arm's length.

They hadn't gone too far when the woman turned into a gate, which was opened for her. Ah Fung couldn't see who opened it. She simply followed.

The green shrubs smelled delicious and the gate shut out the street noise. The woman waved her hand to an opening between two buildings. Ah Fung relaxed. She was being directed to the kitchen.

"In there. Cook's helper will direct you what to do."

The woman carried on past the buildings and disappeared down a path of black, worn stones behind the yellow flowering bushes.

Ah Fung's bottom lip trembled. Her steps toward the steamy entrance of the kitchen were hesitant. Hopes of some scraps to eat forced her forward.

"Ayee. The new help. What did they get a scrawny little thing like you for?" The cook's grotesque belly wobbled as he laughed. "Assistant, Song Peng! Wrap her in a clean smock. Tie it tightly so she doesn't trip. What's your name?"

"Ah Fung," she whispered.

"Speak up. I can't hear you." The cook's own voice boomed over the clanging and banging of kitchen activity.

"Ah Fung," she repeated, still afraid of speaking too loudly. She rarely spoke at home, and never with any volume. Usually a nod and a bow were all the communication she needed.

"Wash these greens in that basin over there," said the man. "Peel the onions and give them to Song Peng. Then bring in fresh water to soak the salty pork. After that, you can stoke the fire with sticks from outside."

Ah Fung threw her eyebrows up and would have burst into tears with so many directions had Song Peng not placed a hand on her arm and said quietly, "Start with washing the greens."

Ah Fung tried forcing her eyes to stay open as she spooned the broth into her lips. She felt weak and her knees had nearly given way before the kitchen staff had finished making, serving, and cleaning up after the evening meal. It would be dark before she got home.

She jolted awake when the bowl was removed from beside her head.

"You'll learn to eat faster tomorrow. You should sleep now. Dawn comes quickly." Song Peng helped her stand and pointed under a big table not far from the clay fire hive. "Lucky you. You get to sleep by the fire where it's warm."

Ah Fung could hardly wade through the humidity toward the door. "I'm not cold."

"Oh, no, Ah Fung. You sleep here. It's a new mat. You will like it in the winter when we really need the fire's warmth."

He pushed her under the table where a small but clean sleeping mat had been placed.

Ah Fung resisted with what energy she had. "But my parents will be expecting me."

Song Peng laughed. "What? Did you not know you have been sold to this family of traders? You stay here now. They own you."

Tears formed and dribbled down Ah Fung's cheeks. Of course. Yesterday and this morning had been her last day ever with her birth parents and five sisters. They had all been hungry, their clothes were stitched together from scrappy bits of fabric, and her grandmother had died, leaving all her jewellery to her son. Her daughter, Ah Fung's mother, had received nothing. Ah Fung had been sold to feed the family and pay for her father to have the new suit he needed for his work.

Once Ah Fung had quietly sobbed out the shock from her system, she was able to reason with herself. She had a cleaner mat here than at home, and she was in a kitchen and would be fed every day. She could learn to do the chores she was asked and then maybe the family fortunes would change, and she could go home.

Within a week, Ah Fung's hands were raw and bleeding. In two months, she had developed callouses and the bleeding had stopped. In eight months, her upper arms had developed muscles from carrying pails of water from the well. On her eighth birthday, she received a new clean mat and a longer dress and smock, neither of which were new.

When she was ten, she noticed Song Peng watching her guardedly. He would sneak a glance whenever the cook wasn't looking.

One night after she crawled under the table, weary from sixteen hours of work, she was startled to feel Song Peng's body close to her own. She stiffened.

"Peng, go away. There is only room for me on this mat."

"I'm cold, Ah Fung. Let me lie here."

Ah Fung heard shuffles coming across the dirt-packed floor.

"Get out from there, you surly lad. Leave her alone. Are you asking for trouble?" It was Cook's voice, and he was pushing his foot against Song Peng's back. "Did you not think I noticed you looking at Ah Fung? You have no home but here, and we can't have you degrading the slaves. Get out."

It was the first time Ah Fung had heard herself called a slave. She lay very still, thinking about her five sisters and birth parents. Some new form of self-preservation formed inside her young heart.

The next morning, after the meal preparations were finished, Ah Fung jumped to see the mistress at the doorway of the kitchen, studying her.

At noon, the mistress returned and handed Ah Fung a slippery dress. "Put this on and be sure your face and hands are clean."

Puzzled, Ah Fung did as she was told. Why was she being asked to put on this dress in the middle of the day? How would she get her chores finished in time for the next meal?

The mistress waited while Ah Fung changed her clothes. No one else was present. The quiet unsettled her, but the mistress waved her hands. "Hurry up. We don't have all day."

Ah Fung followed her mistress out of the kitchen, along the garden path, past the sour-smelling rotting blossoms of the magnolia shrubs, and out through the gate. On the street, a small carriage had stopped, the driver standing stiffly, ready to move at a moment's direction.

Their destination was a larger home with a garden of magnificence. Its blooms had been nurtured, shrubs trimmed of any dead blooms, and the ground freed of debris and twigs.

Ah Fung wanted to ask, "Why are we here, Madam?" But that would have been wrong.

She clenched her fists with worry. The statue-like gardener in coarse blue clothing stood without expression.

A woman came traipsing along the covered porch, hidden by shadows until reaching the step closest to Ah Fung. Her face was made up with white powder, her hair piled high into rolls decorated with flowers and beaded combs.

Madam bowed, and Ah Fung followed her courtesy, also bowing deeply before the new woman. Madam then swivelled on a heel and headed out the gate, back to the carriage. Ah Fung wanted to go after her, but the made-up woman had reached out to her and gently pulled Ah Fung up the step.

"You are in your new home now," said the young woman. "You are forbidden to enter the courtyard. Walk only under the covered path surrounding it. This way."

Ah Fung blinked back tears and held the sick feeling in her stomach. She understood this was an ancient hutong, a courtyard house of someone important. Who were these people, and would she be made up to look like this young woman?

She was brought into a dark room and noticed the mound on a raised bed. It was an old man.

The young woman bowed and said, "This is the new one, Father."

Soon Ah Fung realized that her job as a servant for this old, ailing man would not be pleasant. The odour of his decay was trapped in the wall hangings as Ah Fung carried trays of tiny dishes of food, emptied the night water, and watched for signs that he needed fanning. From early morning to late at night she worked, running to and fro until she dropped on her mat.

Surely this was worse than going hungry at home or having raw hands from cleaning the vegetables. She hardly had time or energy to eat.

The next morning, the old man lay still on his bed and Ah Fung found out that things were indeed not better. She stood a long time, waiting for his grunts and demands to begin serving him his breakfast.

The old man's daughter came in to see what the delay was. She shrieked and hollered. "He's dead! Father... Father, why have you left me?"

The funeral rites and burial took place in swift action and then crates were packed. The old man's son-in-law shouted orders at the servants, who disappeared one by one, slinking away to some unknown home, never to return.

Ah Fung ran as directed.

"Put this in the packing crate. Take this to Madam Yen. Take this to the kitchen. Get rid of this. Do this. Do that."

She moved as quickly as possible but never seemed to get everything done. After three days of mad packing, everything was ready.

"You girl, Ah Fung. Come with me."

Ah Fung had to follow orders. She knew that she was being sold yet again. She had no choice but to follow. Didn't anyone want her?

*

Ah Fung sat in the kitchen of her new home, waiting for Cook to put something in the cracked ceramic bowl in front of her. Cook bustled back and forth, screeching directions to the gardener for harvesting vegetables. She had been to market, bringing back strange items Ah Fung didn't recognize. Finally, Cook seemed to notice her and splashed a dumpling into the bowl. Ah Fung grasped the slippery morsel and chewed noisily.

"Oh my goodness, Cook. This is delicious. Why are we celebrating?"

Cook paused and frowned. "You do not know what is happening, do you, Adopted Daughter? You are going with the family to a place far across a wide blue ocean."

"Are you coming? Will I be able to eat more dumplings?"

"Only family members are allowed to go." Cook turned back to the fire and added a few sticks.

The next day, a messenger came to the gate. The second son ran to his father with the news that all their papers had been found to be in order. Soon rickshaws arrived and the family's luggage was loaded.

"Come, Ah Fung. Climb in here beside me." The mother of the two boys patted the seat next to her. "We are moving across the ocean where there is plenty of food and money. We'll be rich."

The rickshaw jolted forward, and they were on their way.

Thirty

1910

VANCOUVER, BRITISH COLUMBIA

Ah Fung didn't feel well. She was hungry but couldn't eat. Many were feeding the fish with the remainder of their dinners; she only wanted to lie down, but there was nowhere except on the deck. Up here she could at least breathe. Below smelled horrible and made her gag.

She tried reading the English sign again. It said, she had been told, *No Steerage Passengers Beyond This Point*. Why was that? She frowned. It looked as though there was plenty of room on the other side of the chain.

Nearly three weeks passed before the cry came.

"Land. I see land!"

The mother grabbed Ah Fung by the sleeve of her garment. "You must tell them you are my daughter. Your name is Fang Ah Fung, same as mine." The woman pointed to her husband. "He is your father, Fang Guy Do. Remember."

The line moved forward very slowly and each person was questioned. Ah Fung needed to use a water closet, and she was hungry, but the mother dragged her along.

"Don't worry," the woman said. "There will be lots to eat and many things to wear. Everybody is rich in Canada."

They waited in long lines which moved so slowly that most people sat on their bundles and slid forward as the line shuffled forward. Ah Fung stayed close to the rest of the family, ignoring the boys poking her. Finally, the mother took her to an indoor water closet. It was such a relief. She pulled the chain as the mother instructed and jumped back as water swished into the bowl and left.

Their bundles and the father had almost reached the narrow gate where men in soldiers' uniforms talked to people as she and the mother returned. They hurried into line, and the father went searching for the boys.

It was her turn. She shuffled to the desk and kept her eyes down.

"What is your name and how old are you?"

Ah Fung had no idea what that meant, but the mother had given her instructions. "Fang Ah Fung."

The man checked his paper. "Who is this?" he asked, pointing to the father.

She raised her eyes to the man's shoulders. "Fang Guy Do."

The mother pulled her forward and waved the boys to the desk. They stayed with the father while she and the mother were led into a room with people in white coats. Other women were in various stages of undress being poke and prodded.

The round metal piece made her shiver as a man placed it on her chest and back. He nodded and urged her to the next available chair. A smiling young woman in a stiff white dress and small cap came to her and spoke kindly. Ah Fung had no idea what the woman said, but she kept her eyes on her smile. Such white teeth. The woman ran little sticks through her hair.

They're looking for lice, thought Ah Fung.

She was nearly asleep by the time they exited the building with a big cart piled high with their belongings. She looked up the street. Where were the rickshaws? The people were mostly Westerners in Western clothing. She looked at her dark pants and padded vest. She was the foreigner now.

When they arrived at the building where they were to live, Ah Fung thought it was amazing. Huge. As big as a temple. But when the family was shown the two tiny rooms where they were to stay, Ah Fung felt confused. The room where they were to cook was the same as where they were to eat. Only one sleeping room meant that all five people would have to sleep in one place.

"Ah Fung, no time to ponder," said the mother. "Go down the steps to bring our luggage up the stairs. Hurry."

The packages were too heavy for Ah Fung and she had to stop at every landing to rest. The boys carried one between them while the mother stayed upstairs to receive the items. The father stayed below to direct the boys.

Ah Fung's stomach rumbled. How could she hurry? Why should she hurry?

"Get moving there, slow one," said the second son. "We have many more to move."

The second son slapped her on the head as he followed his brother down the stairs.

Each time she came through the apartment door, the mother would grab the parcel from her and shoo her back out. "Go. Go fast. We haven't got all day and night. Your brothers are doing so much of the work. You should be ashamed."

Ah Fung didn't know how she would make it back down and return even one more time without fainting.

The father shuffled the remaining parcels. "Here. Take this one."

Ah Fung's mouth gaped. This parcel was the same size as she was! How could she carry it? She stepped toward the parcel, wondering if maybe she could drag it.

"Pick that up, Ah Fung. It's not as heavy as these others. Go. Get a move on."

It may have been lighter, but Ah Fung could hardly balance it, and she didn't see her brothers coming down the steps as she made her way toward the building.

"Watch it there, little sister." The first son gave the parcel a bit of a push and Ah Fung fell back onto the ground, the parcel bouncing down on top of her. Tears streamed over her hot face. All she could hear were the two sons laughing and guffawing loudly.

Within a week, Ah Fung realized that she would be in serious trouble if she stayed with this family. She was a slave, doing whatever bidding the other family members demanded. The mother was often angry with the father and shouted at him. He would only pucker his lips and turn away from her.

A kind white woman had handed her directions for a place called the Chinese Rescue Home. The name on the paper was written in Chinese characters, with the rest in foreign writing. Ah Fung had nodded but tucked the paper away, since she had no way of knowing how to get there.

At night, the two sons would slide over to her mat to torment her. The second son covered her mouth while the first son would put his hands all over her, in places she knew they shouldn't.

One afternoon, after making a necessary trip to the outdoor toilet, Ah Fung skirted around the back of the building to a side street. She moved stealthily along the edges of the buildings, avoiding people's looks. She kept her head down.

A few doors along, she spotted a white woman speaking with an older Chinese woman.

The white woman turned and spoke to her, but Ah Fung didn't know what the woman said. Since she was still too close to the building where her adopted family lived, she kept moving, hurrying along several familiar streets.

Once she reached unfamiliar territory, she slowed and pulled out the directions to the rescue home. An old woman smiled at Ah Fung, giving her the confidence to hold out the paper for the woman to read.

"Oh, yes. You poor dear. I can show you the way. I'm sure they will take you in."

Ah Fung didn't understand the words the woman said, but she understood the kindness.

Ah Fung couldn't believe how good she felt. Washed, clean, her hair cut and combed, a cotton night dress on, and she was a new person. The missionary people were kind and caring.

In a few weeks, Agnes, as Ah Fung was now called, could read and recite the English alphabet, write, and count to one thousand. She beamed with happiness at her good fortune. She had come to the right place, and though the wooden cross in the large room with benches troubled her a little, she had enough food every day and was learning a new language.

Agnes worked hard and excelled in her schoolwork. During her years of elementary and secondary schooling, she became fluent in English and developed a dream.

In her final year, Agnes stood before the school matron. "I would like to become a nurse."

"Come into my office, Agnes, and we'll talk."

Agnes followed, smoothing her skirt down and straightening her back the way she had been encouraged to approach a challenging situation. As she sat, the matron smiled, and Agnes relaxed.

"There is a way, I believe, for you to qualify as a nurse. Your school marks are good, and I have contacts at Women's College Hospital in the School of Nursing, but it's in Toronto. It will be a demanding journey, and you will have to prove yourself."

"I understand, Matron. Women have a more difficult route, and Chinese women have an added challenge. Thank you for giving me hope of seeing my dream happen."

1949
WOLFE ISLAND

"I had the distinct pleasure of meeting Agnes after she attended the Women's College Hospital School of Nursing in Toronto," Mary said as she stood at the United Church podium on Wolfe Island. "Of course, everyone was abuzz with the acceptance of the first Chinese applicant. She graduated in 1923 but returned for an alumni gathering after further studies in Detroit, Michigan.

"She spoke about her desire to help the people in China, especially young girls who were still seen as a commodity. Upon learning of her story and the hardships she'd encountered, any resentment I had at being left alone to grow up in a safe country dissipated. Having parents who worked hard to save children from being sold, to save girls from having their feet bound or dying from disease and hunger, came to mean more to me than my own happiness. If the orphans become Christians, it is a joyful bonus.

"To know that Miss Agnes Chan returned to China as a Christian nurse to carry on mission work has been gratifying. Over the years, I have heard of so many other Chinese Christian mission workers and educators who have returned to their homeland to carry on good works. It fills me with utter exultation."

Following the light luncheon and tea, Mary made her way to the parking lot with the president of the Wolfe Island United Church Women. Mrs. Brisbane had a car and Mary had the good fortune to be transported back and forth between Kingston and Wolfe Island in it. Perhaps she would consider getting a car when the prices came down a little more.

Smartly shifting gears as they entered the hardtop roadway, Mrs. Brisbane said, "That was a most illuminating story, Miss Sibley. I'm surprised you never married."

Mary tucked her head down. "Two world wars have limited the field."

"That's very true, Mary. I don't know how you are such a cheerful person, with a big smile for everyone, when you have seen such misery."

"I have a great deal to be thankful for, Mrs. Brisbane. I believe I appreciate so many things in this country that other people take for granted. Few have known the hunger that starving people in China have experienced."

"Are things much better now, do you think?"

"Are we to believe the Nationalist reports, or the Communists? The world is still recovering from the war, but the civil strife in China has not been settled. Struggles for basic accommodations and food are still going on." Mary smoothed her blue gloves over her hands.

"What do you think would be most helpful for the Chinese people? They won't accept missionaries."

Mary tipped her head. "True, but I believe it's time for Chinese Christians to become more independent. Mao's communists have taken control of nearly every province. They are trying to establish their right to be considered the ruling party of China."

"Do you think the communists have a chance of gaining control of the whole country? Or of being accepted as a nation?"

"I know they have the Nationalists on the run, and the United States is withdrawing their support out of frustration with the two warring factions. The Nationalists are begging for American financial support, but Mao is engaging in talks with Lenin."

"Oh, heavens. If those two join forces, what will the rest of the world do? We've just had our second world war in the last thirty years. I pray there will not be a third."

Thirty-One

1956

TORONTO

The Victoria Day weekend was coming up quickly and Mary looked forward to visiting her father and Vida. After returning to Canada from their holiday in Britain, the couple had landed in Quebec City and then taken the train directly to Toronto. They would have passed through Kingston on their way home, but there would have been no point in their stopping, given that it was midweek.

At eighty-three, her father was still a substantial figure, but his days weren't as long as they had been, now that he was rising later and heading for bed in the early evening.

Vida would have all kinds of photos from their latest adventure now that the cost of developing the negatives was more reasonable.

When she arrived at their home in Toronto, Will clung to his daughter. "Mary, it's so good to see you."

Is he steadying a quiver, a sign of old age? she wondered.

"Vida, dear. Here's Mary." He took her elbow to head down the hall to the kitchen.

"My suitcase, Father?"

"Oh, just leave it there. We can take it up after dinner." He smiled. "I'm so glad to see you."

"And so glad to be home, I bet." Mary spoke the words quietly in his ear, knowing how much Vida had wanted to go on this trip, and how much her father had dragged his heels.

"Good to see you, Vida." Mary gave her stepmother a peck on the cheek and smiled. She had kept her father young.

She's been good for him. How would he have managed those last years in China without her?

"How was your journey here?" Vida asked, stirring something in a pot.

"Crowded. By taking the later train, I thought I would avoid most of the holidaymakers. It's warm for May, but I'm glad to be here. How are you both?"

Vida looked up from the soup pot. "We're fine. Somewhat tired, but we've almost managed to get over the time change. You're looking well, Mary."

After a hearty bowl of soup, the three sat chatting at the table until Mary noticed her father's eyes fighting to stay open.

"Well, it's been a long week and a long day for everyone." Mary gathered up the bowls and cutlery and placed them in the sink. She pushed up her three-quarter-length sleeves, prepared to wash up.

"Oh, just leave them there until morning, Mary," Vida said. "I'll do them with the breakfast dishes."

Mary could hear the tiredness in Vida's voice, so she swished the bowls in a quick rinse and dried her hands.

"Good night, Father, Vida. I'll just use the washroom down here and then get my things upstairs and head right to bed."

Mary pondered her father's jowls, baggy eyes, and sagging shoulders. He had never looked old before. But she patted his upper arms and smiled. She felt such joy in seeing him, no matter their age.

After reading a chapter of the Bible left on the bedside table, Mary put out the light.

I wonder what it would be like to own one's own home, to furnish one's bedroom and the living room, she mused. *I'd love a house with a big picture window to look out. I've never lived in a house we owned.*

Her father and Vida's house here in Toronto didn't feel like her home. Kingston was definitely home to her, but as fun as rooming with other women could be she'd never had the kitchen to herself. A little garden would be nice. The garden on Nelson Street was too shaded with big trees to grow any sort of vegetables.

Mary lay in bed the next morning, luxuriating in not having to rush about getting ready for school. This weekend had come as a welcome break. She was pleased she would be in a higher salary category next year—six thousand five hundred dollars. A fortune, if she used it sparingly.

It seemed only moments later she could smell bacon frying. "Up and at 'em, Mary old girl," she said to herself, throwing the covers off and putting on a lightweight, multicoloured dress and flat shoes.

"You look rested, Father," she said upon emerging into the kitchen. "How are you this morning, Vida?"

"Well, don't you look cheerful in that light blue. I think it becomes you, Mary. It's never too late for a suitor, you know," Vida said, winking at her.

"I believe I've settled down to being single. Forty-eight years of age, and I'm set in my ways. This is my twenty-second year of teaching, if you can imagine. I'm very involved in the community and quite happy, you know."

Vida momentarily stopped poking the bacon, which had crisped quite nicely. "I do believe you are."

Mary went over to the oilcloth-covered table and kissed her father on the cheek.

He grabbed the hand that rested on his shoulder. "Are you, my dear? Happy, I mean?"

"Yes, Father. I am. I have a handful of close friends, a very satisfying job, wonderful colleagues, and dozens of students. And there's the United Church Women's group at Chalmers and the New Symphony Association besides. We've organized a second concert this year. And I have you and Vida, of course. I am well and truly happy, Father."

Will nodded, seemingly gratified with Mary's productive life. "I'm sure you are a blessing to so many of your students and friends. You are our cherished, smiling daughter, I hope you know."

Mary patted her father's shoulder, a little surprised at his unusual expression of fondness. It was a rare occasion.

"Please have a seat, Mary, and I'll dish out breakfast," said Vida. "Not fancy, mind you, but the butcher shop had a special on back bacon this week, and it looked very meaty."

"We have a surprise for you, Mary. On Sunday, we're taking you to an afternoon Presbyterian church service." Her father waited for her reaction, and she responded with the smile she knew he had hoped for. "The best part is—it's a service in Chinese."

Mary's smile grew wide. "Really? So they have enough of a Chinese population to hold a service in Mandarin?"

Vida nodded. "Toronto is a growing city. Now, if you'll say a blessing, Will, we can eat while it's still hot." She closed her eyes and bowed her head.

Midway through the meal, Mary brought up the latest news from Shanghai. "It seems that since the war the Chinese have been busy constructing so many new buildings. I was really sad to hear the Xiban Gate was destroyed to harvest the bricks."

Will frowned. "It doesn't concern most of the population. They've torn down and rebuilt on the same locations time and again. Ancestorial burial grounds are far more significant for the Chinese. Something that should be said in their favour is respect for their elders. They feel such responsibility for their parents' welfare when they're old."

Mary quickly raised her eyebrows. "What are you suggesting? I should come and look after you?"

Will shook his head. "Heavens, no. I'm merely observing the prevalence of these places for older folks in Canada they call 'nursing homes.' What's wrong with hospitals if you're sick? And if a person isn't, someone can take care of them in their own home."

"That's why you have me to take care of you, dear," Vida said, Mary catching the twinkle in her eye as she spoke. "We need to plan that trip to the Canary Islands we always said we would do. I can't think of any place more pleasant to be in January or February than somewhere temperate."

Mary agreed. "And just think. You could fly there in a matter of hours, rather than weeks or months." She had no inclination to fly herself, but Vida might be able to convince her father to go on such a trip.

※

The service was crowded. The three accounted for the only occidental faces among hundreds of Chinese. Mary felt a shiver of anticipation. She didn't pine for her youth in Szechwan, but unbidden impressions of church services in Chengtu came rolling forth in bubbles of sound and colour. The musician joyfully hammered away at the upright piano, sending forth old hymns that Mary recognized.

Was the pianist trained in China? I recognize that tune.

It took her until halfway through the service to relax enough to let go of the words she didn't understand and focus on the words she did.

After the sermon, the minister announced prayers for the thousands of Christians imprisoned all over China. An elderly Chinese minister and his entire family had been sent to a work camp for "retraining." Prayers continued for the imprisoned Catholic bishop of Shanghai and the many priests who had refused to join the communist-created Chinese Catholic Patriotic Association.

More prayers were offered for independent Christians being threatened or imprisoned, as well as for the incarcerated Watchman Nee, still evangelizing prolifically enough to be noticed by the Chinese authorities. The minister named several who had refused to join either the Catholic or Protestant Patriotic Associations. Many disappeared. Some were returned to their families, shadows of their former selves.

After the service ended, two smiling young women invited Mary, Vida, and Will outside to a table filled with glasses of lemonade. They spoke to the trio in English and were surprised to learn that all spoke Mandarin.

Vida and her father explained about their work as missionaries in China, and Mary drifted off toward a very petite woman standing alone under one of the horse chestnut trees. Their early blooms spread a heavy fragrance in the warm May air.

"Hello," Mary said. "Can you tell me more about the people who were imprisoned? Are they being treated well, and can they receive visitors and packages?"

She'd see if her friend Ruby Chang could visit with some supplies Mary would send over.

"No. No visitors allowed. We hear only that Bishop of Shanghai, Kuna Pin-Mei, was taken to a dog-racing stadium during a *struggle* session with communists. They forced him to make a confession in front of thousands of people." The woman gave a hint of a smile. "We heard that he shouted, 'Long live Christ the King. Long live the Pope,' and all the people echoed his call to stay strong. Then they dragged him away and no one has heard of him since."

Mary had heard whispers of such things. "How do you know this happened?"

The woman looked Mary straight in the eye. "I was one of many people there. We didn't think they could arrest all of us, but they broke up the crowd with their sticks, and some were also dragged away. My son lives in Canada, and he brought us from Hong Kong."

"Did all your family come?"

The woman shook her still-black hair, cut in a short bob. "My husband threatened to report my daughter and me to the city authorities, so I left with her right away. I already had our passports hidden on my person. We left with a little money and nothing else. My husband would be happy not to be burdened with us." She pointed to a middle-aged woman drinking lemonade with two other women. "My daughter."

Hands gripping the sweaty glass, Mary leaned in to observe. The woman was a smiling, middle-aged child with the syndrome identified by Dr. Langdon Down. "That must be very difficult for you."

The woman touched the back of Mary's hand. "My son takes very good care of us. We are safe, and we can love God without worry about people reporting every activity we do."

Mary sighed. What Mao announced to the world would be what Mao wanted the world to hear. The converted would be in hiding for now.

Thirty-Two

1959

TORONTO

Mary breathed a sigh of relief as she stepped off the stuffy bus to Toronto in early July. She would be taking the train back to Kingston in two or three weeks rather than the overcrowded, slow-moving bus. Nothing like the heat and noise of some Szechwan modes of transportation, of course, but something she wasn't used to.

She looked around the parking area and spotted her stepmother.

Mary lifted a hand. "Vida. Here I am."

"Oh, Mary. It's so good of you to come down. Your father hasn't felt well enough to drive all that much."

Mary smiled to herself as she picked up her suitcases from the undercarriage of the bus. The new turquoise set included a round carrying case for toiletries and hats. Vida was her usual vigorous self, prepared to help carry it over to the old 1948 Chevy she had been driving since Will's retirement. Mary had never seen her father drive, although he claimed he could.

"Will is so looking forward to your visit. He's trying to take it a little easier these days and limit his preaching engagements. How was your trip?"

"Warm and slow. We had so many stops that I've decided to take the train back. How are you doing, Vida?"

Vida settled into the vehicle behind the steering wheel, her sturdy pumps pressing down the clutch and brake. "I'm fine, thank you, Mary. You look very smart in that colour of suit. Such a fine, slim figure."

"Well, I have a reputation to keep up in the Home Economics department. It's expected, even though my salary limits me, to a certain extent. I've been teaching for twenty-five years now, yet every year I look forward to working with the youth. They're so enthusiastic most of the time that they fill me with energy and hope for the future."

Vida focussed on getting into the line of traffic headed along busy streets to their Wendover Road home, but Mary realized there was more to her worry-lined face.

"Is everything all right, Vida? You seem uneasy."

"It's your father, I'm afraid, Mary. He isn't well at all." She glanced at Mary but quickly shifted her focus back to the road in front of them as they chugged up the winding highway, switching to a lower gear without much grating.

"Has he been ill?"

"Nothing specific. I'm just glad you're here for a few weeks. It will maybe ease his mind."

Mary was relieved to sip a cup of tea with her father in the garden while Vida prepared a light supper. Mary's appetite was limited at the best of times, but the bus journey had unsettled her stomach. She wondered if the unhealthy glow of her father's face added to her disconcertion.

"Have you heard from Aunt Mary Ann or John and Ruth lately?"

Her father paused to think. "Yes, Mary Ann is fine. She complains of putting on too much weight and her knees hurt. She's fortunate that John and his wife live so close by. They are a great help, it seems."

"Are you wishing I was nearby?"

"You're settled in your school. At Whitby, is it?"

Mary eyed her father. "It's Kingston, Father."

"Of course it is. Whitby was that fancy women's college you attended." Will picked up a newspaper and tapped it. "The Presbyterians in Shanghai lost a big supporter when Eric Liddell died at the end of the war. I thought you might be interested in reading the news from China in the latest post. They've expelled more missionaries."

Mary recalled the famous runner who had preached while imprisoned. "I'm sorry to hear that."

Her father shook his head. "We scattered the seeds, Mary, but it took a long time to stop being territorial and work together."

"You mean, under Mao and the communists."

"If we hadn't gone in and withstood the attacks, there wouldn't have been schools and churches. I wouldn't be surprised if there are thousands, if not hundreds of thousands, of Chinese who are secretly Christian, and many in the regulated churches who try to follow the way."

"Father, it would have been so much better to accept more of the Chinese customs from the start."

"We didn't know, Mary. We only went with our little bits of instruction and our Bibles. It took years just to learn the basic language and then more years to speak the dialect."

"But—"

"You were born there, dear. You didn't come into the country with a great deal of Western baggage attached. You know, in '34 there were still four of the original Vic Eight serving in Szechwan: Smith, Jolliffe, Morgan, and myself." He nodded. "In my desk is a photo album I want you to see. Top desk drawer, righthand side. Would you bring a fan as well, please?"

Mary went in and retrieved the album and took a fan out of the display case. Her father's head had dropped to his chin. Was he asleep?

Will's head popped up as soon as she came within sight.

"Ah, yes." He flipped through the well-thumbed black pages of the old photo album. "Here I am in May 1918. I was all in white, even white shoes. Half of us wore white. We had been told by missionaries to Africa that white was cooler than dark colours. We didn't know white was the colour of death for the Chinese. This was our first preparatory conference of our West China missions in Junghsien. Thirty-six Westerners and twenty-three Chinese. Here's the Union Bible Training School, Chengtu in 1920. You remember that building?"

Mary smiled. Indeed, she did. Its balconies had always been her favourite place to look over the countryside from a place of relative safety.

"The Chinese are wearing their traditional long robes, and the men are in casual suits. The pith helmet was going out of style, and the Western teachers have straw hats, which were locally made. Forty-six were in training that year. Here, during the war. Only four Western staff at the Renji Hospital. That's less than ten percent." Will shook his head. "Mary, the famine camps were where emergency relief was brought in and the sick taken care of. They grew larger in the mid-1930s. Aggression chased the population up and down the country. By the time the people reached refuge in Szechwan, they were nearly dead from starvation."

"I remember the bell ringing for church and people would come running from every direction," Mary said.

"There were no watches or clocks anywhere in most villages. We had to be sure to keep our own watches wound. I loved all the ancient, Oriental-style buildings. It was strange to see the Western-style businesses in Shanghai on our way home in 1936."

Will wiped at the beads of perspiration on his forehead with a shaky hand before continuing.

"Yes, the Anglicans had large churches and large populations of Chinese businesspeople, who supported the Western ways until the revolutions. Here, what do think of that?" He pointed out a photo of the

Szechwan Chinese Christian Association annual meeting on February 9, 1939. "What do you notice?"

Mary examined the photo closely. "Still, only half are Chinese."

"It was wartime. What else?"

"There are women." She smiled. "Most are wearing traditional dress. Look at this picture. The length of that man's braid. My goodness. I don't remember many Western men wearing their hair like that."

"The rules changed when you were too young to remember. The braids were called queues. That photo was taken before the revolution. The rule of the Manchu was for men to wear their hair in a pigtail, or queue, with the front part shaved. All the Westerners in China had to follow that rule at the time. The men and women wore mandarin collars on their robes as well. They said it made them feel like Catholic priests." He tapped another photo with the tip of his finger. "Here. Remember the Kwanksui rope bridge?"

Mary looked at her father. "No. I wasn't with you on that trip." She sighed. "I wish I could have gone back with you and Mother instead of staying in Toronto."

"You know it was too dangerous." Will's voice quivered.

She knew the topic was finished. Her mother's brutal slaying had never been discussed after Will's initial return to Canada in 1927. A few days after their reunion in Toronto, Mary had learned not to bring the subject up. The painful incident was neatly bottled most of the time; she and her father had had each other.

"I hear some rail lines are now running to and from most of the major cities across China," Mary said.

Will shook his head. "The world should have paid more attention to what was happening in China when Japan tried forcing their demands on them. It started with the Manchurian railway, opening it up for the Japanese to get in there and start putting pressure and controls on the surrounding area." Perspiration beaded on Will's forehead. "The League of Nations should never have allowed Japan to get all the German possessions in China, and why the United States kept supplying them with aviation fuel, I don't know."

Mary nodded. "Well, it did them more harm in the long run with the Pearl Harbour attack." She understood more of the concerns her parents and the Chinese had had during the two world wars.

"I've often wondered what happened to Arthur Ozawa. We dropped him off in Japan and never heard from him again."

She patted his arm. "Don't worry about it, Father. The real concern for most of the Chinese at present is this Cultural Revolution of Mao's. We've been so cut off from even our closest friends in China. We can't really say what's going on."

"We can pray. And we can continue to train Chinese Canadian Christians so they might someday return and continue our work."

Mary pursed her lips. "Perhaps the people within China will find ways to work around the rules. And besides," Mary took the photo album from her father and closed it, "it's time to let them test their mettle. They will become stronger in their beliefs for taking a stand."

The very next day, Mary's father remained in bed, not eating a single meal at the table with her and Vida. They guessed it was near the end. Mary made a call to Claire to let her know she would be in Toronto indefinitely, as her father was failing. Claire promised to drive to Erin when the time came and bring Mable. It gave Mary comfort to have close friends at hand.

Cousin John and his wife Ruth accompanied his mother to Will's funeral.

"It's so good of you to come, John, Ruth," Mary said. "Thanks for bringing Aunt Mary Ann. She's looking well."

John said, "I'm so sorry, Mary. I had no idea your father was in poor health."

"Thank you. Vida's been vigilant in caring for him, especially these past few years." Mary smiled. "I had wondered how it would go when they married, but they seem to have enjoyed each other." *Vida's heartbroken under that veiled hat.* Mary swallowed her own tears and put on a cheerful face.

"How are the Miss Wilders?" Ruth asked.

"Miss Emma is frailer by the week, but Charlotte appears robust. The young Miss Connie Krug livens things up at the boarding house, though it's not the same since Nita, David, and Mable left. Claire brought Mable with her today. We've all stayed friends over the years."

Thirty-Three

1962

KINGSTON

Claire had already been to the lawyer's office during her afternoon break between classes and tennis practice.

"I've signed, Mary," her friend said over the phone. "It's up to you now, and then 68 Richardson is ours! Imagine, at this stage in our lives we're homeowners."

"I'm heading down to the office just as soon as I get the last girls on their way. I'll be there in plenty of time to meet the five o'clock deadline. Thank you for the call."

Mary replaced the receiver in its cradle and glanced out the window of the Home Economics office where she could keep an eye on the girls' activities. The same two ninth-grade girls who had been giggling uncontrollably earlier in the afternoon were at it again.

Mary stepped out of the office and approached the two at the sink, suds overflowing onto the counter and a puddle on the floor.

"Girls." Mary placed one fist on a hip and looked at them sternly. She pointed to the offending suds and puddle. "You will need to wash the floor as soon as the dishes are dried, put away, and the counters and sink polished. And I expect this to be done by four o'clock, which gives you fifteen minutes."

The two giggling teens straightened in surprise, facing each other with a look Mary understood. They weren't used to Miss Sibley being quite so direct, but they'd had plenty of warnings. She didn't often have to be so sharp, but the students' behaviour was wearing on her a little more than usual today. Perhaps the tension in purchasing the house?

She returned to her office with a grin. Yes, they were being silly, making a mess, and had been warned, but they were having fun and had successfully made a broccoli dish with a smooth cheese sauce to add to the dinner. A number of boys in their grade had been invited to taste-test the results of the class's cooking that afternoon, and emotions had peaked and ebbed like the sound of a pump organ. Silliness was one result.

At four-fifteen, Mary strode in the direction of Princess Street where the lawyer's office was situated. *Are we doing the right thing? It seems like a good investment, but neither of us have owned homes before. What if we can't manage it?*

She had reviewed all her doubts with Claire in the days before closing the deal and been rebuked on every single objection.

"You're just nervous, Mary. We'll manage very well. We're both capable of looking after a nearly new house, and if we run into trouble with hydro or the plumbing, we'll call a handyman. You've learned to drive and keep a car in the past five years, so what can be so hard about maintaining a house?"

Mary took a deep breath. They had placed a substantial down-payment, what with her small inheritance from her father after his death three years ago, Claire's even smaller inheritance from her mother last year, and both their savings. They would have the mortgage paid in five years. Mary's school principal indicated she would be at the top of the grid next year, with a salary that just topped $10,000. And as Claire had pointed out, better to pay a mortgage than rent.

After signing all the papers, Mary returned to her room on Nelson Street. Miss Charlotte Wilder had outlived her sister Emma, but another widowed sister had taken her place. In 1949, Mable had gotten her own apartment and since married, leaving Claire and Mary with the two aging Wilder sisters and a new younger boarder, Connie Krug. Mable often popped in for a visit bringing her two young children.

Once at her desk cradling a hot cup of tea brewed with her own supply of China tea, and using a new electric kettle, Mary studied the latest *Toronto Star*. She reread the article on the barley and wheat Canada had supplied to China. The comments didn't match the latest letter from Pearl in Chengtu. Pearl, a Chinese doctor at the Inland Mission Hospital, now renamed the Provincial Peoples Hospital, had been an orphan Vida and her father befriended. Ever grateful for the opportunity to survive and thrive, she had kept in contact with the family.

Oh, I must remember to send her my new address. A shiver of excitement went up Mary's spine. *Our own house.*

She opened up Pearl's latest letter.

> My dear Mary, friend,
>
>   As you know, the diet of the Chinese is not large, so how could anyone go hungry? For the past two years, dry weather has not helped the grains grow, and the small diet is much smaller, but no one has ever died from lack of food. You know that Chairman Mao began the Great Leap Forward and things have moved along all right.

Mary set the letter down. They used codewords to exchange news that would not have passed the scrutiny of China's Communist Party personnel, should their letters be opened. Pearl's use of *all right* meant that things were not going well. And when Pearl used the word *some*, it meant thousands, as in the next passage:

> Your good man Hamilton has ensured that the Canadian
> Wheat Board shipped some tonnes of grain, both barley
> and wheat. They have assured us there will be more as
> long as this drought lasts, but it is still dry.

Was the grain even reaching Szechwan? Mary knew that the Great Leap Forward had been a disaster, and she could only imagine the poor in the countryside being unable to provide enough food for their children. She also had read in the papers that Canada had yet to decide who was the real power in China. Would the newly formed United Nations recognize the Republic of China at all?

She recognized the names of second-generation missionaries who had found positions with the Canadian government because of their ability to read, write, and speak Mandarin. She had met many of them and their parents. She hoped they were also acting as Christians with wisdom and understanding.

She carried on reading.

> We are facing wonderful new instruction now the
> communists run everything according to their plan to
> unite the country. Businesses are reviving in the western
> ports of China.

Mary understood this to mean that if you did not declare yourself a communist and go along with their policies, you would be in trouble.

Might this be Pearl's last communication with her? Pearl had the safety of family to consider.

Mary carefully folded the letter and placed it into the envelope. Often she sent stamps to her nephew in British Columbia, but this letter she would keep intact.

1970

KINGSTON

Mary reached up and pulled on the string to draw the overhead projector screen down, then secured the loop over the hook to keep it in place. Nothing caused more tittering than to have the old screen whizz upward with a great slapping sound.

As she turned, one Chinese student was making a nasty face at the only other Chinese girl in the class.

"Julie Wong. You will see me in my office before you leave this room." Mary's anger was barely concealed. "And Lilly, please remain at your desk when the bell goes."

Lilly's head barely made any motion as she nodded. Julie sat facing the screen without any sign of acknowledgement.

Mary's hands shook slightly as she straightened the overhead projector to centre on the screen she had pulled down. She would retire soon, hopefully soon enough to avoid any sort of blemish on her record.

She carried on with the lesson as planned, but acid roiled in her stomach.

Julie entered the department's office as Mary sat down at her desk.

"Please close the door, Julie."

Mary pushed aside a pile of marking and placed her forearms on the battleship-linoleum-topped desk before pressing her fingertips together. She didn't speak Chinese to Julie, having made that mistake when Julie first arrived in her class. Mary's Szechwanese Mandarin was a little rusty and had done nothing to aid her effort in making Julie, from Shanghai, feel welcome. Julie had told her, "I speak only English in Canada."

"What were you doing making such a face at Lilly? What is the problem?"

"She is only a farmer's daughter," Julie replied. "Stupid round face."

"Julie, that is no way to speak about another person. What has happened between you two? I thought you were becoming friends."

"She is no friend. No friend of China. My parents. They are friends of China."

Mary paused, thinking over the term *friend of China*. Did the Chinese Communist Party have some kind of hold over Julie and her parents? Julie was extremely well-dressed and usually wore some kind of jewellery, whereas Lilly dressed more plainly in clothes that might be second-hand and without adornment.

Mary studied Julie's face, holding her gaze. "In Canada, Julie, everyone is given an equal opportunity to achieve success, no matter whether you are born here or in China. We try to get along despite our differences, and we do not make cruel remarks that hurt others."

Julie stared at Mary stonily, arms crossed.

"I thought you both went to St. Andrew's Presbyterian Church's youth program?" Mary pressed.

Julie stiffly shook her head, her long ponytail swishing side to side. "No. My parents say it not good for me to go there with her." She uncrossed her arms and pointed with a jab in Lilly's direction.

Mary frowned. The churches were often instrumental in getting new immigrants settled. The Chinese regularly attended Presbyterian or United churches. "Do you go to the Anglican church then?" Before communism, the Anglicans had been a strong influence in Shanghai.

"Churches for poor people. We don't need help."

Mary grimaced. *Yes, you do. Everyone needs God's help.*

But she said nothing more about that. It wasn't her place to teach religion, though ethics and morals were part of growing up well.

"We shouldn't look down on people without the same financial means we have. I don't wish you to make Lilly feel uncomfortable, and I will have to speak to your parents if I see you being unkind to anyone in class, or in the school." Mary studied Julie. "Do I make myself clear?"

Julie nodded. "May I leave now? Please."

Mary smiled. "Yes, and I don't expect to have any more trouble between the two of you."

She watched Julie leave the classroom through the office window, then went out to see Lilly, who sat very still with her head lowered.

"*Nihau*, Lilly." Mary sat in a student chair facing Lilly. "I'm sorry if Julie gave you a difficult time today."

Lilly made an effort to smile. "Oh, no. It is fine, Miss Sibley. I don't mind."

Mary tipped her head. "I mind. I don't want girls to be mean or unkind to anyone, especially in class. Do you want to tell me about it? I thought you girls were going to be friends?"

Lilly pursed her lips. "Her parents don't want to go to church anymore."

"And why is that, Lilly?"

Lilly looked trapped, glancing side to side. Mary thought back to some encounters she had had with strong pro-China people in the past few years. Often these were successful businesspeople who supported the communists, trying, she supposed, to get the Canadian government to recognize Mao's Red China. Were Julie's parents like that?

Her father had often quoted the elder James Endicott, secretary of the Board of Foreign Missions, who'd said that it was "wise on the mission field for, say, the first twenty-five years, to keep eyes open and mouth shut."[13]

Perhaps the same was true for immigrants coming to Canada. They were finding out what the political climate was before jumping in, or perhaps, in Julie's parents' case, they'd felt welcomed at the Presbyterian church and then had second thoughts.

Lilly's family worked long hours to make a modest income, but they were happy to be living in a democracy and enthusiastic about church attendance.

"Never mind, Lilly. Don't let Julie trouble you. If she gives you any more bother, please speak to me." Mary smiled at the shy, humble girl. "Thank you for staying. I don't want Julie to cause you any trouble. If you wait for just a few moments, I'll walk you out to the street."

Mary wasn't sure that Julie might not be waiting around the corner, ready to belittle the girl again. Lilly demonstrated such a kind and thoughtful personality that Mary found it difficult to watch Julie browbeat her.

Thirty-Four

1970

KINGSTON

Mary dished out the rice while Claire grabbed the oven mitts and lifted the simmering vegetables and pork casserole off the stove element. They tried to share at least two dinners a week, but sometimes, with their busy teaching schedules, it was only once—and that, on Sundays. With only her father's youngest sister, Eunice, still living, Mary had few family obligations during holidays and weekends. She corresponded with her Aunt Beatrice and cousins on occasion, but she was free to attend concerts and help with the symphony and attend Chalmers United. She still had the strength to play badminton on occasion in good weather.

"Mmm, this smells delicious," Claire said. "I don't know how you get so creative, Mary."

"A little chili gets the appetite stimulated. Knowing how much and what combination of spices to use comes with training, and of course the need to be frugal. How is the new girls' athletic council working out?"

"Much more balanced, I think. The girls themselves are pushing for more equal use of the facilities. But they are meeting with resistance when it comes to individual girls travelling to tournaments." Claire removed the oven mitts and sat down across the table from Mary. "Would you do the honours?"

Mary bowed her head and prayed a heartfelt thanks for the many blessings God had bestowed upon them.

"Do you think we'll find enough to keep us busy when we retire next year?" Claire picked up her fork.

"I think we will be busier than we expect with renovations to the Wolfe Island cottage. Between the refurbishing of the exterior and overhauling the existing gardens, you'll be golfing, playing tennis, and skiing as often as you want. With my church and music involvement, I'll hardly have time to do all the reading I'd like. Don't you think you'll have enough?"

"Probably. It's just that I've put my heart and soul into developing the department, and I'm not sure how they'll carry on without me." Claire laughed. "Listen to me. The foundation is strong enough; I'm sure it will expand. I am hoping to volunteer with the sophomore tennis students. The athletic council is somewhat supportive. You could help too. Didn't you play tennis at university?"

Mary nodded, her mouth full. She wiped her lips with a linen serviette. "Yes, but that was decades ago. I'd need tutoring myself. And really, girls have so much more encouragement to get involved than ever before, so the girls' athletic department can do nothing but grow."

"Oh, I meant to tell you—my sister Catherine is coming to visit next weekend. She misses our brother Alex terribly, so I thought a change of scenery would do her good. Just don't let her talk about us getting a television."

Mary hid a smile. She had been thinking it would be a nice retirement gift for herself. "With company coming, I better get busy deadheading the tulips this week and make the gardens presentable. The daffodils and lilacs are coming along. This spring air reminds me of the summer holidays we spent at Camp Quentin on Mount Omi when I was young. There's a particular freshness, but here there is the added fragrance of blooming flowers. In China, it was such a relief to get into the higher elevation among the trees."

"You didn't tell me much about your visit to the Chinese church in Toronto last month. How did that go?"

"Surprisingly well. I did wear a hat and pulled down my veil so I wouldn't appear conspicuous among the congregation members, who were nearly all of Chinese descent. The message was in Mandarin, of course, and the minister not long out of China. It gave me a great sense that there were many Christians of strong faith, despite the persecutions, and his message was full of hope."

"Any updates that we wouldn't hear in the news?"

"I spoke with the minister after the service for quite some time and believe the number of converts is slowly rising. They have contact with a few who attend the Three-Self regulated churches. It's challenging to find copies of the Bible, though. Reverend Chung intimated that he's often trying to send over unregulated copies, but it's risky and many refuse to take the chance."

Claire shrugged. "Getting resources to where they are most needed is the world's biggest problem today. Isn't it hard getting any written material into or out of China these days?"

"That's why on their return home the Chinese nationals try smuggling in Bibles, but they must be in Chinese, or the people can't read them. Western literature is confiscated if found, as are reel-to-reel tapes."

Claire scooped up the last morsel of food and glanced toward the counter, no doubt hoping for more. Mary pointed to the fridge while continuing to eat, chewing every bite carefully.

Claire stood. "That's true here too, if a person doesn't have retirement savings. Older people like the Misses Wilder must work until they're on their deathbed."

"Things will change, I hope, as the old age pension is implemented. We'll be fine with that and our school pensions. Unfortunately, it's coming too late for our parents' generation."

"Pudding, Mary?"

"Just a small dish, please."

Claire brought over two dishes of pudding and set them on the table. "True, but it seems we're living longer now, so we do have to plan for the future. I'm really hoping to spend time in retirement building up the confidence of the women in the Kingston chapter of Zonta. Service and advocacy. Planning and confidence. That's what they need when they face the disparaging remarks of the men in other businesses and from council. All women need to exercise their freedom to have their own bank accounts and savings."

Mary dug a spoon into her pudding. "I agree. Could Zonta give more support to the United Way? And what about scholarships?"

"I'm working on it. Our budget is always tight, but I believe we'll be able to give a scholarship to a Queen's female athlete this year. After all, the club began in 1943, so we could have established a more prominent place in Kingston by now."

"Perhaps more women should get into politics. We do need to make changes, but we still have so many advantages over women in other countries."

Claire propped an elbow on the table and supported her chin with a hand. "Do you think there is a difference if the country has Christian values?"

"Absolutely. The British can be blamed for many things, but their law and court system have mirrored Christian values of justice for the most part. We're so fortunate in this country."

Claire glanced at her watch. "Okay. I'll clean up here and be off to the gym."

Mary finished her drink of water and was placing her dishes on the counter when the phone rang. She lifted the receiver to her ear. "Mary Sibley speaking. How many I help you?"

"You Julie teach in kitchen?"

"Yes," she replied. The woman's English was strongly accented, so Mary switched to Mandarin. "I can speak Chinese if you like."

She pulled the receiver away from her ear as the woman on the other end of the line broke into a barrage of Mandarin.

"Please speak more slowly," Mary replied, able to at least figure out that the woman was Julie's mother, demanding that Mary apologize to the girl for speaking to her rudely. "Mrs. Wong, Julie was being unkind to another classmate. I need all my students to be cooperative for the class to learn well. Would you like to visit our class someday?"

Mrs. Wong refused the invitation and returned to her broken English. "You born in China, but you white woman. You no understand Chinese. Mao no good for important Chinese business in Shanghai. Peasant revolution bad for intelligent businesspeople."

"We treat all people equally in the classroom… in *my* classroom." Mary wanted to be specific, as not all people in Canada were treated equally. New immigrants had to work especially hard to find their place in society.

"This one not equal. She from Szechwan, small town, farmer."

Mary explained that she herself had been born in Chengtu, Szechwan and had friends there, many of whom were very intelligent, hard-working, and kind.

She hadn't finished trying to win over Mrs. Wong before the line was broken and a dial tone rang in Mary's ear.

Did Julie's mother know that, in Chiang's attempt to end Mao's People's Democratic United Front and get rid of the Russian advisors in 1927, hundreds of thousands of Chinese lives had been lost? The Nationalists had done their share of damage. She would never convince this woman of the equality of all humans. It was clear that being free to make lots of money in a democracy like Canada was more important to her than the value of human life.

"Wow," Claire remarked after the call ended. "That was a bombardment. A parent?"

Mary's shoulders dropped. "Yes, and a very challenging one. Politics should *not* have to enter into a domestic science classroom, especially foreign politics. People seem to need to find someone to blame for everything."

Claire nodded in agreement as she dried the last dish and closed the cupboard door. "Sorry. I can't help you with that one."

Mary met Claire's gaze. "We'll never fix the world, will we?"

"Say, why don't you come down to the gymnasium this evening to watch the tennis doubles match? It'll take your mind off school."

"Well, I was thinking of baking this evening for the arrival of your sister…"

"Oh, that would be wasted on her. I, on the other hand, would very much appreciate it. Perhaps the tennis match wouldn't be so interesting for you. Were you thinking of chocolate cake or date squares or oatmeal cookies? Or maybe all of them?"

Mary was laughing by now at Claire's eagerness for her to bake. Although Mary ate very few desserts herself, she did like to bake, and Claire took advantage of it.

"I don't know how you stay so slim and eat so many sweets," Mary said.

"Exercise!" Claire flicked an elastic around her thick hair to make a ponytail, grabbed her purse, and headed toward the door. "There's a tournament you should come to next week, Mary. There will be strong competition in that one."

"Enjoy your evening," Mary said as she tied on an apron.

Thirty-Five

1971

KINGSTON

Mary shuffled through the files, preparing to burn as much as she could. There was no point in taking it all with her across to Wolfe Island on the St. Lawrence River, where she and Claire would be moving to at the end of June.

Retirement. Will I find enough to do? Once Claire had asked the question, Mary began to wonder, but she had so many books to read. All her favourites were packed and ready to make the move. Every one of Pearl S. Buck's novels were carefully wrapped in a layer of tissue. The still well-known author had been her favourite in the 1930s when she could read about the China she knew and loved, without the stinging heartache of earlier years.

She paused, sitting with an unopened file on her lap, thinking of the decade in which she and Claire had owned this house. Though shared, it was an investment and had given her stability and a sense of peace she hadn't considered necessary prior to that. She thought of the garden she'd tended with interest and care, planting exotic plants to bring colour to the yard in every season. Even the deep orange Chinese lanterns had popped colourfully up out of the snow during the winter when the subdivision could look grey and bleak. Through to the final melt in spring, those filmy seedpods always gave her a lift.

Now she had to get busy. There was a concert tonight, and she needed to arrive early to man the box office.

The file of old news cuttings on her lap bulged. She'd tackle it first.

The 1954 death notice of James Endicott Senior was shorter than the July 15, 1952 article in *Maclean's* entitled "How Dr. James Gareth Endicott Fronts for the Reds" about his son.[14] James Senior and his wife had been missionaries in China since 1894, and their five children had all been born there. Her own father had often reported to him from the mission field, when Endicott was the Foreign Missions Board general secretary. Having urged efforts to merge into the United Church of Canada, Reverend Endicott had then become the second moderator in 1926.

His son, Dr. Jim Endicott, had followed in his footsteps only so far; he became notorious for his Communist Party connections. Young Jim had worked as an interpreter for Mao Zedong, been friends with Zhou Enlai, and worked for the Communist Party in Canada, ill thought of during the Cold War. Mary understood why Jim might be tempted to believe that communism would be most beneficial to the majority of the hundreds of millions of Chinese. If—and it didn't appear to have happened—the equality of resources was spread throughout the country as Mao claimed it would, the poor would benefit. The rich? They seemed to have left China.

Mary unfolded the recent article about Dr. Norman Bethune and his training of dozens of "barefoot" doctors and nurses for emergency medical work high in Jinlin Province, among the mountains of China bordering Russia and North Korea. All those fighting wounded were treated by the well-known Dr. Bethune.

The article ended with the assertion that it was "time to set aside Dr. Bethune's Canadian clashes and bring him home a hero."[15]

So many missionaries strived to convey the spiritual healing of Christ to the people, while healing their illnesses, feeding the starving, and trying to help them toward a better life. Christians persecuted during the Great Leap Forward had been ordered to do manual labour and reform their thinking against "spiritual opium," as Mao described it.

Mary shook her head and tossed the articles onto the burn pile.

A letter dated December 1966 came from her friend Ruby Chang, who was now living in Bejing, the new capital.

> Most of the ancient city wall has been destroyed or removed for the bricks. Just this year the fourth and last remaining city gate, Chongwen, has been torn apart for the new subway lines. The city is now totally modern, housing millions of workers and government officials.

So many things were changing. And Canada had just announced its recognition of the Chinese Communist Party, saying that the government was a *friend of China.* Hadn't they always been a friend of China?

Mary sifted through other obituaries, news items about Asian missions, and articles pertaining to people who had been friends with her parents.

And here was Judge Coatsworth's death notice. His passing had received remarkable coverage after an illustrious career. Vida had explained the limitations in central China during the 1930s, but he hadn't seemed to grasp the distance, isolation, and sacrifices missionaries made.

"He didn't understand China," Mary said aloud. "Even with his own daughter's efforts to educate him…"

"Mary? Do you have someone with you?" Claire called to her from the hall.

"Claire… you're home." Mary grinned at her friend, who poked her head around the corner of the doorway. "You caught me talking to myself. I'm trying to get through this pile of papers before the concert tonight. I have yet to decide about the larger items. I hate clutter, as you know."

Claire tipped her chin toward a small pile of boxes, decorative items, and pictures. "Is that the giveaway pile?"

"No, that's my keep pile. I'm trying very hard to get rid of anything that doesn't mean a lot or have some practical use." Mary pointed to a much larger pile. "That's the giveaway pile, and I'm hoping the church rummage sale can make use of it."

"Are you sure? The Wolfe Island place isn't that small. You could bring more with you."

"And have you or someone else, when I'm too old to care, be forced to get rid of it? No. I want to keep life simple in retirement and not worry about *things*."

"You've always sparsely furnished every room. Except the kitchen, of course. I don't know how to use half the gadgets you've got in there."

Mary laughed. "I've offered to show you how."

"Humph. We know how well that worked. I better get busy and find more things to get rid of. What time is your concert tonight?"

"It starts at eight, but I need to be there early to work at the ticket booth renewing symphony memberships."

"Dinner at six?"

"The pot's in the oven simmering until then."

Claire smiled. "You are so good."

"I've left you the cleanup."

"Of course you have."

As Claire spun around to head to her room, Mary smiled. Claire had always buoyed her spirits and made life fun. The years spent in this house had been as joyful as those spent in a university dormitory, but cleaner. Yes, much tidier, more organized, and cleaner. But the laughter and comradery had been the same, with frequent visitors, teas, and dinner guests.

Mary broke out of her reminiscing to open a small, leatherbound book by the Chinese poet Chen Mengjia. It had been a recent birthday gift from her old roommate Ruth at teachers college. She turned to the silk ribbon marking her favourite line: "I crushed my chest and pulled out a string of songs."[16] It was a shame the man had gotten to such a point of despair that he'd ended his own life in 1966. But wouldn't any sensitive artist be so disheartened under the strict rule of Mao's communism?

Placing the book on the keep pile, she sifted through the folder on her lap. She lifted out the first draft of a letter she had written in 1962 but never sent.

Dear Mrs. Buck,

Your stories have long held a fascination for me. After reading your mother's biography, *The Exile*, it is clear to me that she gave everything to stay in China as a missionary's wife. Her perseverance in seeking God, and loyalty in supporting her husband in order for him to be a disciple of Christ, cost her dearly. What more could a woman give up than the life of a child, or, in your mother's case, four children? Naming them makes the loss real to us.

Her physical suffering alone would have many men and women scurrying back to the safe and secure world they knew in North America or Europe.

In response to your delivery to the Presbyterian Women's League in New York City 1932, I would like to reply to your inferred question as to whether the missionary movement in China for the past ninety years has been worth it. I will attempt to defend my response of an unqualified *yes* in the following paragraphs.

Please understand, I know why you might ask the question, and I myself have asked it. Born in Chengtu, Szechwan, China in 1908 to missionary parents from Canada, I can empathize with you in watching the toll it took on my parents and, indeed, every missionary who worked in China.

As one who was left in Canada at boarding school from the age of fourteen on, as one who lost her mother to an angry Chinese man in the street with a broadsword, as one who might have had a brother had he been born alive, and as one who watched a father grow gaunt and fretful about the country he served in for decades, I can clearly see the angle from which you view this question.

I myself have met several Chinese Christians who have returned to the land of their birth (and I know there are many more) to minister to their fellow countrymen and women. They have come to Canada and the United States and trained as preachers, nurses, and doctors and returned to carry on the work of foreign missionaries among their own people. They go beyond caring for family members, to all who need help. They reach out as Christ taught. Even from prison, Watchman Nee continues to preach and teach Christ. He has suffered beatings, poor food, no food, unclean conditions, and yet we hear that the guards are regularly switched because he converts them to Christianity.

When one counts the number of Chinese-speaking churches in North America, one is overwhelmed with the spreading of the Gospel in the manner Christ commanded: to go and make disciples of all nations. The Chinese have not always been free to follow Christianity in their own country, but thousands have come to ours and continued as followers of Jesus. I am sure many in China continue to practice their Christian faith, even to the point of death.

In this country, we are indebted to the early priests and ministers, and the laypeople who have contributed to the building of churches and Christian communities. Sunday schools full of boisterous children, youth groups who work in the community, women's organizations who have reached out to isolated farmer's wives, those who are still serving in the mission field, and those who provide services in hospitals and prisons are giving people the hope of Christ. We owe them our continued support. Perhaps one day we will be in need of the services of these nations where we sent and supported missionaries and missions.

At the moment, China appears to be a closed country, but I have no doubt the spirit of Christianity can survive. It will survive and thrive through the lives that have been touched by missionaries.

And so, I would encourage you not to be disheartened by what has not been accomplished, but to be heartened by those who have been reached. In places where the church has been eradicated, we can pray new life will appear and people will carry on loving their neighbours as themselves.

It ended there. Mary folded the letter and hesitated before setting it on the burn pile. Perhaps she should have sent it, but Mrs. Buck had had other Christian projects to work on, and at the time Mary had lacked the courage to approach someone so famous.

Who will care now? she asked herself. *Will others appreciate the great, wide effort made in evangelizing China?*

With all her heart, Mary fervently hoped so.

ENDNOTES

1 Matthew 19:14, KJV.

2 "The Missionary Gang: Toronto to China," *Acta Victoriana*. February 1907, 291–297 (https://library.vicu.utoronto.ca/exhibitions/vic_in_china/sections/missionaries_and_mission_stations/attachments/missionary_gang_acta_30_5_feb1907_291.pdf).

3 Chester Holcombe, "The Missionary Enterprise in China," *The Atlantic*. September 1906, 348–354 (https://cdn.theatlantic.com/media/archives/1906/09/98-3/129536112.pdf).

4 "The Missionary Gang: Toronto to China," *Acta Victoriana*. February 1907, 291–297 (https://library.vicu.utoronto.ca/exhibitions/vic_in_china/sections/missionaries_and_mission_stations/attachments/missionary_gang_acta_30_5_feb1907_291.pdf).

5 Arthur E. Moule, B.D., "The Responsibility of the Church as Regards the Opium Traffic with China," *Anglican History*. December 15, 1881 (http://anglicanhistory.org/asia/china/moule_opium1881.html).

6 Mark 16:15, KJV.

7 "Victoria College and the Student Volunteer Movement," *Victoria University*. Date of access: September 19, 2023 (https://library.vicu.utoronto.ca/exhibitions/vic_in_china/sections/vics_commitment_to_west_china_missions/victoria_college_the_student_volunteer_movement.html).

8 Pearl S. Buck, *The Exile* (New York, NY: P.F. Collier, 1936).

9 Arthur Campbell Ainger, "God Is Working His Purpose Out," 1894.

10 Rev. V.C. Hart, "The Printing-Press in China," *Acta Victoriana*. 1901, 75–79 (https://library.vicu.utoronto.ca/exhibitions/vic_in_china/sections/missionaries_and_mission_stations/attachments/acta25_2_1901_hartpress_1.pdf).

11 Adrienne Clarkson, *Extraordinary Canadians: Norman Bethune* (Toronto, ON: Penguin Canada, 2009), location 167.

12 "Canadian Woman, Wife of Missionary, Slain by Chinese." *The Toronto Globe*, June 10, 1926, 1.

13 "1920s James Gareth and Mary Endicott and Family," *Victoria University*. Date of access: September 20, 2023 (https://library.vicu.utoronto.ca/exhibitions/vic_in_china/sections/missionaries_and_mission_stations/1920s_james_gareth_mary_endicott_and_family.html).

14 "How Dr. James Gareth Endicott Fronts for the Reds," *Maclean's*. July 15, 1952 (https://www.vintagemagazines.com/product/16030/Mcleans-Canaas-National-Magazine-15-July-1952).

15 J. Deslauriers and D. Goulet, "The Medical Life of Henry Norman Bethune." *Canadian Respiratory Journal 22(6)*, November–December 2015.

16 Peter Hessler, *Oracle Bones* (Toronto, CA: Harper Collins Canada, 2007), 244.